TO

SEE

GOD

BRUCE J. BERGER

Black Rose Writing | Texas

ISBN: 978-1-68513-157-9
PUBLISHED BY BLACK ROSE WRITING
www.blackrosewriting.com

Printed in the United States of America
Suggested Retail Price (SRP) $22.95

To See God is printed in Calluna

*As a planet-friendly publisher, Black Rose Writing does its best to eliminate unnecessary waste to reduce paper usage and energy costs, while never compromising the reading experience. As a result, the final word count vs. page count may not meet common expectations.

Readers of Bruce J. Berger's two previous novels will be rewarded with this closing volume of a trilogy: . . . the story of Jewish siblings separated by time, continents, and religious traditions but joined by complex histories. *To See God* enters unexpected territory when Kal Covo - who, in *The Flight of the Veil*, had disappeared many years earlier and taken the veil at a Greek convent as the nun Theodora - visits her brother Nicky and his family in America. Berger moves deftly among matters of faith and spirituality, miracles, mental illness, and the scars of war. The crisp dialogues virtually spring off the page as his complex characters wrestle with demons both sacred and profane.

–Roberta Rubenstein, Author of *Literary Half-Lives: Doris Lessing, Clancy Sigal, and Roman à Clef.*

ALSO BY BRUCE J. BERGER
THE FLIGHT OF THE VEIL

Winner—Illumination Bronze Award in General Fiction
"A well-crafted tale about trauma and miracles."
-Kirkus Reviews

"In the intelligent historical novel *The Flight of the Veil*, a psychiatrist returns to places that were treacherous in his childhood, reconciling internal contradictions."
-Clarion Reviews

"Berger has created a compelling Everyman, who must wrest with grand theological questions: in times of great calamity, why does God save only some?"
-Stephanie Grant, author of
Map of Ireland and *The Passion of Alice*

"The text skirts between fantastic realism, real realism, and a protagonist who has not taught himself how to go entirely insane ..."
-Carolivia Herron, author of *Thereafter Johnnie*

"Provocative character discussions span a variety of topics, including religion, mental health, and family and love, achieving an enlightening balance between logic and emotion ... Illustrative language is used to render the Greek landscape in gorgeous terms. An intelligent historical novel."
-Foreword Reviews

"With deft, vivid prose, Bruce J. Berger's *The Flight of the Veil* takes the reader on the searing and inspiring journey of Nicky Covo, a man who thinks he has buried his World War II memories, only to have them demand his attention again with news of a possible modern-day miracle."
-IndieReader Reviews

ALSO BY BRUCE J. BERGER
THE MUSIC STALKER

"What drives the characters of *The Music Stalker* to their highs and lows, their togetherness and their times apart, is also what artfully holds them locked in patterns of an intricate harmony. The heliotropic center of this novel is desire: desire for the Other; desire for talent; desire to be seen; desire to be held; desire for safety and peace of mind; even the desire to be left alone. Bruce Berger exhibits a sensational knack for imagining lives, real lives lived with triumph and weakness, mental illness and ordered reason, as well as daily flubs and foibles. His skills make for a page turner ..."
–David Keplinger, author of *The World To Come*

"Although Berger's work is replete with depictions of life with mental illness, it's never reductive or one-dimensional. Instead, it immerses readers in the lives and perceptions of those with psychological differences. It's also about the power of family members to pull loved ones back from isolation and distress, even when they're suffering themselves. ... A tale that shines a light on the redemptive power of religion and relationships."
–*Kirkus Reviews*

"Bruce Berger's THE MUSIC STALKER is a thoughtful, enjoyable story and an interesting study of mental illness, spirituality, and artistic genius—and the possible relationship between them. ... [He] writes with warmth and attention to detail, bringing the Covo family's experience to life. His exploration of mental illness makes Adel a fully-fledged character, a woman aware of her brain's misfirings and yet helpless against them in many ways. And if Kayla's own mental imbalance is obviously telegraphed, his exploration of its connection to her rapturous, effortless musical genius is fascinating."
***IndieReader* Reviews**

ALSO BY BRUCE J. BERGER
RETURN TO SENDER:
224 UNANSWERED LETTERS TO THE WHITE HOUSE
(NON-FICTION)

"Well Worth It! Well written. Eloquent. Unanswered. A perfect chronicle of [Trump's] presidency. Bruce says what the majority of the country was thinking at the time."
–Carol Little (on Amazon Reviews)

"I love Bruce's wit and eloquence. A damn shame he writes to someone unable (or unwilling) to read.
–Janet (on Amazon Reviews)

For Cole and Neely

"Like cold water to a weary soul is good news from a distant land."
–Proverbs 25:25

"He who strives in the Torah to know the Holy One, blessed be He, and His mysteries is 'the son of the Holy One blessed be He,' and in all the heavenly hosts, there is none that will stop him from entering his Father's presence at any time he needs to. Happy is his portion throughout the worlds."
–Zohar, Behar v. 81

"By night on my bed,
I sought him whom my soul loves.
I sought him, but I didn't find him.
I will get up now, and go about the city; in the streets and in the squares I will seek him whom my soul loves.
I sought him, but I didn't find him."
–Song of Songs, 3:1-2

"Take ye heed, watch and pray: for ye know not when the time is. For the Son of Man is as a man taking a far journey, who left his house, and gave authority to his servants, and to every man his work, and commanded the porter to watch. Watch ye therefore: for ye know not when the master of the house cometh, at even, or at midnight, or at the cockcrowing, or in the morning: Lest coming suddenly he find you sleeping."
–Mark 13:33-36

TO
SEE
GOD

THE BONES

"To see God."

Sister Theodora's words, uttered in little more than a whisper, lingered on the cool air as she looked out across the vineyards sloping down the hillside toward the dark purple mountains. It answered the question posed by Abbess Fevronia, who was gently holding Theodora's arm, trying to steady herself after what was becoming an ever more difficult climb from the monastery's church to its winery. As she tried to put away the slight twinge of pain in her chest, Fevronia followed Theodora's gaze. Theodora had spoken with the conviction she would imminently see Jesus Himself, that He was waiting that very minute to reveal Himself again to humanity in the forests of northern Greece. But of course Fevronia could see nothing more than what she usually saw: the healthy grape vines carrying their burden of newly formed grapes, the fruit that brought the Holy Monastery of St. Vlassios most of its revenue.

"And do you see God now?" asked Fevronia, straining to keep doubt from her voice.

Theodora did not respond, but turned, looked into Fevronia's eyes, and smiled warmly. Fevronia wasn't surprised. For decades, Theodora had spoken to no one, and her voice could be heard only during prayer, only then in the softest of tones, so soft that a listener—and Fevronia listened frequently—might have imagined hearing Theodora's thoughts alone.

Recently, Theodora had more to say out loud to Fevronia, not in prayer, but in reminiscing. A Talmudic story about Rav Huna, which Theodora had heard as a Jewish girl at her father's side, had struck its way back into her heart. Fevronia's attempts to question her about the story, to learn more of what the story's miracle meant for Rav Huna, had been futile. All Theodora would say in response to the inquiries was: "I pray to the Lord Jesus Christ to forgive me, a sinner."

Theodora took Fevronia's hand; they walked to the last stone bench at the top of the path, close to the winery. Theodora intended that the two of them, as tired as they were, should sit to pray, and so they did, heads bowed. Fevronia, eyes closed, heard Theodora breathlessly recite the Jesus Prayer. Although Fevronia tried to match the emotion of Theodora's prayer, her mind soon wandered. The hired men's voices—there had been cursing about a stuck valve at the winery—intruded into her thoughts. Fevronia felt the uncanny warmth emanating from Theodora, a warmth that made the hot day feel even hotter. She was impatient to head back down the hill and into the monastery's much cooler stone buildings.

Her mind drifted once again to Rav Huna's wine. Theodora must have left something out in the story's retelling. The monastery's library had no copy of the Talmud. She wasn't even positive the Talmud had been translated into modern Greek. It occurred to Fevronia that she could write to Sister Theodora's brother, Dr. Covo, and ask him if he knew of a translation. Perhaps Dr. Covo could even tell her over the phone the entire story, with the details Theodora must have omitted. Surely that was possible. Then the mental image of that tall, dark, Greek American psychiatrist who'd visited months earlier, discovering his sister still lived and had not been gassed at Auschwitz, drew her to reflect upon the three letters he'd sent to Theodora since his visit. They remained unopened, under Theodora's cot. She knew they were unopened, because she'd searched through Theodora's cell.

Why had Theodora not opened them? Curious what the letters might contain, Fevronia wondered whether she should have urged Theodora to read them. Did they contain another appeal for Theodora to abandon the monastery and join her brother permanently in America? Did they contain memories of their lives together as older brother and younger sister? Did they contain news that Dr. Covo and his girlfriend, Helen, were planning a wedding?

Fevronia's thoughts turned to Helen, who'd been with Dr. Covo when he visited. Helen was a religious Jew, in sharp contrast to Dr. Covo. Fevronia could see Helen served as a stabilizing force for him, a guide, a safety net, a solid and mature companion, the kind of person he had needed when he realized Theodora would not return to America with him, notwithstanding his begging.

Fevronia finally noticed that she could no longer hear Theodora's prayer. Minutes might well have passed since she'd last heard Theodora's voice. Fevronia turned to see that Theodora, looking across the vineyards again, was crying.

"What is it, my precious daughter in Christ?"

Theodora stood unsteadily as she swiped at tears with the sleeve of her black cassock. She pointed at the distant hills; the dark purple had now brightened to vibrant indigo as the sun climbed.

"What are you seeing?" Fevronia asked, alarmed. She now stood herself and clutched at Theodora with the vague idea Theodora was ready to fly off toward the horizon in her search for God. Theodora had once flown across Greece with the Mother of God, the Theotokos. Would she now be able to take off on her own in search of God? And, if she flew away, would she ever return?

"There are the bones. I've seen them. Oh dear Lord Jesus Christ. Forgive me, a sinner. It is I who killed them."

With that, Theodora collapsed.

SHABBAT DELIGHT

Nicky Covo and Helen Blanco woke on a Saturday morning, in Nicky's Manhattan apartment. It was not the first time they'd spent the night there, but it was the first Friday night. Nicky had cooked *Shabbat* dinner as best he could: a tossed salad with lettuce, scallions, and cucumbers; Empire chicken and green beans with slivered almonds prepared on a new set of kosher cookware, an OU pareve dessert, and tea. Helen had politely complimented him on his efforts.

Helen began the slow trek into consciousness before Nicky. She'd been dreaming about participating in a service at her synagogue, *Aish Ahaim*, in which nothing had gone right. Helen had found herself on the wrong side of the *mechitza*, among the men, and knew she shouldn't have been there. But she wanted to pray among them, not next to them, not separated by a physical barrier as if she were unclean and unholy, as if she were a distraction best ignored. As she tried to pray, though, the words kept getting lost. She couldn't remember the prayers she'd wanted to say, and as she flipped through the *siddur* looking for the right spot, at which the men were now reciting the nineteen daily benedictions, the pages kept flipping of their own accord back to page one. Finally, she understood that the supposedly knowledgeable men around her were themselves reciting the wrong prayers. It was *Shabbat*, a day for special prayers, not the usual weekday routine.

Then she woke, and it took her a couple of seconds to remember where she was. A wave of guilt swept over her. Putting aside her recent trip with Nicky to Greece, this had been the first *Shabbat* in many years she'd not prepared a meal for her family to enjoy in the familiar and comfortable confines of her suburban New Jersey home. Her three children and eight grandchildren had celebrated the incoming *Shabbat* without her, because she'd let Nicky convince her to stay with him. Just one time, he'd promised, one time to see if it could be done well.

Well, it had been done well, but to what end? She wanted to return immediately to New Jersey, to see her family, but she couldn't travel in a car until *Shabbat* was over. Since it was June, *Shabbat* wouldn't be over until half-past nine in the evening, and then it would be too late to see anyone. She'd might as well stay with Nicky another night. And, because it was *Shabbat*, she couldn't even call her family to say how sorry she felt to have abandoned their weekly ritual.

"Helen, you awake?" Nicky asked softly.

Helen opened her eyes and leaned over to kiss Nicky fully on the mouth. She had no idea how long he'd been watching her. "Mmm, I guess so. *Shabbat Shalom*."

"*Shabbat Shalom*." He reached to caress her. "Up for a little *Shabbat* delight?"

She could see Nicky was up, no doubt imagining what they might do together. She felt a deep inner glow of happiness, a glow that came so suddenly after her guilty ruminations that she couldn't recall what had bothered her moments earlier.

"Just let me brush my teeth first. And, you too."

CAPTIVITY BY THE RIVER

Fevronia and Sister Zoe managed to revive Theodora and get her to stand, unsteadily. Despite Theodora's shakiness, Fevronia felt she looked well enough not to need medical attention. She directed one of the workers to drive Theodora down to the cell house in a motorized cart. That night, Fevronia and Zoe looked in on Theodora, always finding her asleep. They let her be, thinking they could delay any questioning about why she'd fainted.

Theodora had no recollection of how she'd gotten to her cell. She remembered trudging up the hill toward the winery with Abbess Fevronia and praying. Then something had grabbed her physically and yanked her to her feet, something unpleasant and unspeakable, yet so strong it would have been futile to resist. Her head had been held in a vicelike grip, forcibly turned to where the June sun would set, and she'd been compelled to stare. Through her eyes, she'd seen nothing. In her mind, she'd seen copious amounts of blood, pooling and flowing on the ground.

And her memory faded there. Lying on her cot, surrounded by darkness, she struggled to gain a greater sense of what had driven into her. She barely recalled the sensation of falling, as if from a great height, as if she had almost seen God but then been batted away. It must have been Fevronia who caught her. Then, oblivion.

She sat up warily on her cot, hearing from the distant hills a chorus of angels singing. They sang from a whirlwind, no discernible melody, but in an agony of yearning at the feet of the crucified Lord. They were trying to take His pain into themselves, but there was too much pain. Were they singing words? She thought she could make out a message intended for her, but the voices were too faint in comparison to the thunder of the vortex. From her prayer corner arose the devilish scent of cinnamon mixed oddly with the holy scent of roses. She felt the terrible heat of a raging fire, fueling itself to grow ever larger.

She pulled on her cassock, lit the solitary candle of her *lampada*, kneeled before her icons, and grabbed her prayer beads with her left hand. The Jesus Prayer bubbled out of her, for a moment blocking the angelic whispers. She closed her eyes tightly and saw flashes of lightning envelop the amber patterns that played on the back of her eyelids. Suddenly, in place of the terrible heat, she felt intense cold, even as the fire of devotion spread through her. Her body shook with chills.

She stood and walked to the cardboard box in the corner of her cell opposite the *lampada* and withdrew from its bottom the winter jacket she wouldn't have expected to need until October. The jacket did nothing to dispel the cold. She sat on the edge of her cot and waited and listened again. She soon heard the angelic voices articulating more clearly what they had been trying to tell her before. Αιχμαλωσίας επί του ποταμού. (*Echmalosias, epi tou potamou.*)

The journey with Fevronia to the top of the hill—she'd prayed to see God, could remember that clearly, but it had been a foolish, dangerous prayer. How could she have presumed? No one could see God, the Father, a lesson engraved in her learning, and yet that's what she'd wanted. And how could she have confessed such a childish desire to Fevronia? Surely Fevronia would want to punish her for forsaking her oath of humility. She'd behaved in a way antithetical to her life as a devoted nun.

And yet, Theodora could not stop listening to the angels. They kept up their refrain, now even louder and clearer, as if answering her wish. The blazing fire surrounding the voices had extinguished itself, the lightning had stopped, and the wind no longer blew as in a tornado. The words were clearer than ever. She covered her ears but couldn't block the sound.

"Captivity by the river."

Words found in Prophets, but where? She felt she should have remembered, and yet, after much praying, after thumbing through her worn copy of the Bible, she didn't find the passage or discern why the angels persisted on conveying it or why their message resonated so strongly in her heart.

IN THE TRASH?

While Helen showered, Nicky sat at his desk computer and opened the file containing copies in English of his letters to his sister. He'd worked hard to get the exact right tone. He'd rewritten both letters many times before transcribing them into careful Greek printing on plain but high-quality white stationery. He'd taken them to the post office to assure he had the right postage for Greece. Now, he reread his first letter, in which he had placed so much hope. As he had done for months, he wondered again why Kal never responded.

> *My Dearest Sister,*
>
> *It is so hard to believe we've seen and held each other again, that we've talked and had time to remember Mama and Papa and Ada and all that befell us during the war, all that changed our lives. It's amazing how different our lives are, as we were pushed into separate paths by fate or the will of God, as the Holocaust ripped us apart. And yet, I must believe, because I was able to hug you and hear your voice again, a voice I could never forget. I wasn't even sure it was you until you spoke. I must believe because I looked into your eyes and saw everything good in the world.*
>
> *Truthfully, it didn't surprise me you couldn't accept my invitation to come back to America with Helen and me. I had already seen it in your humility, in your gestures, in the peaceful surroundings of the mountains where you know a kind of serenity I*

cannot imagine for myself. I could hear it as you spoke, your devotion to a way of life nothing could ever displace.

If only I'd been as focused on healing my patients as you've been in your prayer and devotion. If only my counseling and medications had been as helpful for my patients as confessing to you has been for the villagers of Inousa. How did we both happen to choose lives whose main purpose is to bring comfort to others? Isn't this because our beloved Papa was a doctor, too, because he gave generously of his expertise to those who were sick, whenever they sought it, and for free, when they couldn't afford to pay?

I feel so close to you now, even though we're thousands of miles apart. I feel I can confess to you again, even from here, and yes there's more to confess. There was this man I fought with during the war. He and others called me Chrisma. His war name was Churchill. He met up with me again in Athens a week before I came to the monastery, and he followed me around Greece—followed Helen and me, I should say—and now he's followed me to the United States. What I need to confess is that I've unforgivably lied to Helen about this. Helen thinks this Churchill was just a figment of my imagination, and I've humored her and told her she's right and that I'm confident I won't see him again. But he's everywhere. Sometimes he seems as real as the computer at which I type a draft of this letter. But he's elusive. He disappears as quickly as he appears, and so I'm left to wonder.

There's nothing you can do about this, I know. You can't make this man disappear. If you could once again fly with the Theotokos, you still couldn't enter my mind and wipe him away. And if he's real, well, he's here, and you're there.

I'm thinking about you, Kal, day and night. I hope you will always let me call you Kal. I hope you'll write back to me quickly and tell me how you are. You don't need to write a long letter. Just a few words.

Your loving brother, Nicky

He must have offended her, even though that was the last thing he'd wanted to do. He'd called her Kal, not Sister Theodora, and by doing so he'd ignored who she was. Or she'd been repelled by his admission he'd been lying to Helen, the one person in the world with whom he should've been completely honest. And he must have offended her by suggesting there were limitations to what her Theotokos could accomplish.

One possibility was much worse, one he feared more than the others combined: that she'd never read the letters at all, that he meant so little to her now, that she'd have no curiosity about what he might say, no desire to stay in touch. That his letters had been thrown in the trash.

AGONIZING LEAPS

Max walked into Jackie's room as he was practicing the clarinet. In
the corner, a music stand held a bound copy of Higgins Beginner
Clarinet Exercises, and Jackie, sitting on a folding chair, attempted
leaps from middle C to a high G. The going was tough, it seemed to
Max, with screeching the main sound and fumbling the main
physical activity. He watched silently for minutes, trying to gauge
Jackie's resolve. Despite his difficulties, Jackie kept trying; he
adjusted posture and hand position, rested only for a second or two,
took deep breaths, and continued to practice. Perhaps he was
progressing, Max couldn't be sure, but if so the progress was slow
and painful.

It was late, and the practice had to be brought to an end. Kayla
had warned Max she might be delayed at the *Chabad* this evening,
there was a talk to be given by a famous rebbe whose name Max had
forgotten the instant Kayla mentioned it, and Max had volunteered
to make sure Jackie got to bed on time. Now, five minutes past nine,
it was his job to get Jackie to bed.

"No, Uncle Max. I'm not going to bed now. I'm practicing."

Max could sympathize with Jackie's desire to improve; he had
been the same way at seven and had resisted his parents' efforts to
separate him from the piano at bedtime. And of course Kayla had
been fanatic about practicing, would practice silently in the middle
of the night whenever she could. But that was then, and Jackie was

no Kayla Covo. Of greater importance to Max was that he had had a very stressful day in the office—he was preparing for a major role in a fast-approaching trial—and needed to get to bed himself. He needed to be dressed and on his way to the train station by five in the morning.

"Now listen, Jackie," he said harshly. "Hand me your clarinet, get to the bathroom to brush your teeth, and call it an evening."

That should have done it, but Jackie acted as if he hadn't heard the command and continued to screech his clarinet. Max reached to yank the instrument from Jackie, who surprised him by turning abruptly and digging his elbow into Max's groin. Whether the blow had been meant to smash Max's testicles or merely to push Max away, the effect was the same. Max doubled over in agony and fell to the floor, fighting the urge to cry in front of his nephew.

"Well, you little shit," he managed to say through clenched teeth as Jackie, horrified at what his elbow had wrought, stood and backed away from his crumpled uncle.

"I'm sorry, I'm sorry."

"You're not as sorry as you will be, you puking piece of shit, as soon as I get my hands on you."

Jackie dropped his clarinet on the carpeted floor and bolted past Max, who—struggling to stand—had made it onto his hands and knees. Max grabbed at him in vain. Jackie bounded down the steps and Max heard the front door slam just as he got to his feet. His anger was as intense as the lingering pain. He tried to walk but could barely move. Now what? Limp out of the house looking for his nephew? It was getting dark. And where the fuck was Kayla? It took Max another fifteen seconds to make it down the stairs to the open front door, where he watched Jackie disappearing from sight, still running down Knudsen Drive.

Max stood in the doorway for a few minutes, trying to clear his head, when he saw Kayla's blue Dodge returning up the way Jackie had come. Had she seen him? Still intensely angry, still wanting to strike out in punishment, Max yet hoped Kayla had intercepted his nephew. Indeed, he realized as Kayla pulled the car into the driveway she'd done exactly that. Jackie sat in the front passenger seat. Almost before the car stopped, Jackie pushed open his door and ran, crying, up to his room.

Kayla rushed up to him with the expected concerned look on her face.

"What was that all about?"

"What did he say?"

"Nothing. He just cried. Uncontrollably. He could hardly breathe for the crying. Good thing I saw him and he stopped when I beeped. *Baruch Hashem*. So, tell me please. What's he upset about? And what—*Baruch Hashem*—happened to you? You look green, as bad as Jackie."

Max was tempted to tell Kayla that her fucking son had slammed him in the balls for no good reason, but thought better of it. It would have sounded as if he was claiming no responsibility for taking care of his nephew, to whom he stood in the posture of ersatz father. And it was not the language Kayla cared to hear.

Max walked slowly inside to the living room sofa, sat gingerly, waiting until Kayla had seated herself on the other end. "I was trying to say lights out and he wanted to keep practicing. Maybe I grabbed at his clarinet ... well, I did grab, foolishly, but he body-slammed me in ... a sensitive area. Your son has a very sharp elbow. And he ran away. Escaped before I could catch up."

"You were going to strike him?"

"I don't think I would've."

"You know Dr. Evans has warned us about any kind of physical punishment. You *know*, don't you? And you were in therapy with us ..."

"Yes, of course, Kayla. I wouldn't dream of disobeying the shrink, but I wasn't acting rationally. When you're punched in the balls—sorry for the language—your brain doesn't operate in its normal, calm, thoughtful, and generous way. At least mine doesn't."

Kayla reached into her bag, withdrew a small plastic case, opened it, took out a smooth stone, and nervously fingered it. It had come from beside her mother's grave, in compliance with Rabbi Beck's advice. "Let me talk to him, calm him down a bit, and then I think you might try to apologize to each other. I'll remind him he must listen to you, obey you, particularly when I'm not home, and even when it involves having to put down his clarinet. Even though I love that he wants to practice so much."

"I have to apologize?" He saw anger and disbelief pass over Kayla's face with his question. "Yes, will do. As soon as you're done talking to him."

Max thought it would only be a minute or two before Kayla came down to tell him it was his turn with Jackie, but the minutes piled onto each other, and almost three-quarters of an hour passed before Kayla returned. She seemed in shock.

"You talked to him?"

"We've g-g-got bigger p-problems than I thought." She picked up her stone from the end table on which she'd left it.

"What do you mean?"

"Jackie won't t-t-talk at all."

"He's embarrassed about what he did, right?"

"He won't talk," she said slowly and carefully. With difficultly, she brought her nervous stuttering under control. "Literally will not utter a syllable. He won't say goodnight, or hello, or how he's feeling, or if he loves me." She shook her head, and a couple of tears slithered down her face. "I tried everything, Max, everything I know to coax a kid into talking. My kid. Tried to make jokes. Picked up and read from one of the *Harry Potter* books. Tickled him. He squirmed away. He cried, but didn't talk. He wouldn't even tell me to leave him alone. Then he just pushed the pillow away and pulled the sheet up over his head, like a shroud."

"Should I talk to him? Maybe he needs to get things right with me first?"

She clutched her stone and sighed. "Go ahead and try, but I don't think it will change anything."

It didn't take long for Max to discover that his efforts would meet the same failure. Jackie had climbed out from under his sheet and lay on his bed, staring at the ceiling. In one arm, he clutched a brown plush teddy bear he'd owned for ages. When Max apologized to him, Jackie was listening, at least Max thought so, but, if listening, either not comprehending or not caring to comprehend. Aliyah, the cat Jackie's grandfather had given him, sat on Jackie's desk and watched impassively. Max felt he was making a fool of himself trying to get a six-year-old to speak when the child had no intention of doing so. No interest in addressing Daryll Strawberry's homerun binge. No interest in talking about the Mets' fight for the pennant. No interest chatting about music generally or the clarinet in particular or Artie Shaw.

"Okay, Jackie. I got it. You won't talk to me or your mom. You're going to be stubborn. You're punishing us for what you imagine are the injustices we've done to you. You're punishing us for how unfair you think we are. I appreciate the willpower it takes not to talk. Still, I'm sorry I scared you. I said so before and I'll say it again. I'm sorry I grabbed at you and threatened you. I was hurt, but I know you didn't mean to hurt me. Can we make up? Can we forgive each other?"

Nothing. Nothing but Jackie squeezing his bear tighter, so tight Max thought its seams might burst.

Max reported to Kayla how he too had failed and to suggest they give up the mission for the night. Sleep would do all of them a world of good.

He hoped.

BREAD AND CHEESE

As Fevronia expected, Theodora did not join the rest of the nuns for the morning prayers. Following *Orthros*, Fevronia knocked softly on the door to Theodora's cell. She carried with her a small paper bag with a chunk of *horiatiko psomi* and a piece of *graviera*. Fevronia heard no response, but hadn't expected to. Theodora would most likely be praying in her corner—at least that's what Fevronia hoped—and so focused on prayer that only a small explosion might dislodge her. As she'd done countless times after knocking and hearing nothing, Fevronia entered. She knew she'd be welcomed in due course.

Fevronia smelled the smoke from Theodora's *lampada*, but the candle had gone out, how long before was anyone's guess. Theodora did not seem to have noticed, remaining bowed in front of her icons until Fevronia loudly cleared her throat. Then Theodora rose unsteadily from her knees. She smiled at Fevronia and motioned for her to sit next to her on her cot.

"Are you quite all right, Theodora? You scared us so yesterday."

Theodora smiled again and nodded. She looked around at her extinguished *lampada* as if in wonderment she should be in a cell without a burning candle, retrieved a new candle from under her cot, and lit it. Then Theodora kneeled before it again and resumed her prayer. Had Theodora not been speaking recently, Fevronia would have thought nothing of the silent greeting and the willful way in which Theodora ignored her. She would have left her in peace. But the last time they'd been together, Theodora had been confiding in Fevronia, and the subject of that confidence couldn't have been more important. It seemed now that Theodora had again decided that speaking was too dangerous and the only safety was immersion in prayer. Nonetheless, Fevronia needed to find out what she could.

"Maybe you don't want to discuss this, but just before you fainted, it was as if you were transfixed, as if you had seen something." Theodora slightly raised her head. "So, can you please tell me, in the name of Our Lord Jesus Christ, what happened? Do you know?"

Theodora slowly rose and turned, but would not look into Fevronia's eyes. Rather, she dropped her head onto her chest; her right hand reached out to hold her small dresser. Fevronia knew she would have to wait as long as it took to get an answer. Time crawled through the cell like a worm. Fevronia spent the time praying herself, standing upright, shoulders back, to be as close to God as she could. It might have been over ten minutes before Theodora lifted her head, opened her eyes, and looked at Fevronia.

"What did I say, Mother? I remember vaguely I spoke before everything went dark."

Fevronia breathed deeply. She knew she must answer honestly, yet greatly feared to do so. "You said, my beloved, you saw bones and that you had killed them. And, as always, that you were a sinner, but that last part, that you were a sinner, wasn't said within the Jesus Prayer."

"Yes. I can hear myself now saying these things. I don't know what they mean but ... I was trying to confess, wasn't I?"

"You never killed anyone. How could you confess a sin for which you weren't responsible?"

"I so wanted to see God, though. I remember. My desire—and I still feel it deep within—all the more proves I'm a sinner."

"God forgives all if you repent in sincerity. But that desire, to be with Our Lord, is certainly no sin. We long for such communion with Our Lord in the afterlife. And, to stare out there as you did, doesn't that echo the Psalm? Θα σηκώσω, μέχρι τα μάτια μου στους λόφους. (*Tha sikoso, mechri ta matia mou stous lyofous.*) I will lift up mine eyes to the hills.'"

"And the bones? What could I have meant? The prophet Ezekiel's valley of dry bones? I haven't thought about that for quite some time."

"If I hazard a guess, you're imagining you saw the monks' graves. You're imagining you saw exactly where the Nazis led them to slaughter. But it's too much now to hope, to think, that's what you really saw. Too much to believe my brother's body and the bodies of his fellow monks might still be found, after so many decades." Fevronia sighed deeply and paused. "Too much to think anything remains."

"It's so important to you. To me as well, now."

Fevronia considered for a moment what had changed, that Theodora should now share her desire to find the graves. She was tempted to ask outright but decided to simply express her concern for Theodora's wellbeing. "Please," she said. "Don't be fixated on an impossibility. Don't let my obsession become yours. What's lost to us has been lost, but they are still with Our Lord Jesus Christ."

Theodora frowned. Then, seeming to resolve to herself that she had to go forward rather than backward, she leaned closer to Fevronia. "It's not impossible, Mother. I feel I can help you now. As we sit here, as we talk, I feel my eyes being opened by the hand of the Holy Mother. I feel Her presence. Can you not feel Her here with us?"

Fevronia couldn't help but to glance quickly about her to confirm the two were alone in Theodora's cell. "How can that be?" she asked.

"It must be Her, yes?"

"I cannot know what you feel."

"Let us go into the vineyard, Mother, and look again. With the guidance of the Holy Mother, perhaps you shall be successful this time."

TO THE CREEK

They made their way through the vineyard, heading slightly downhill to the creek that formed the boundary of the monastery's property. As they walked, Fevronia played over in her mind the history of that vineyard section.

Farthest from the church, it was the last of the land to be replanted. She and the other nuns had been there for two years when, in '55, they began to recultivate. Properly growing grape vines should have yielded good fruit by '58 or '59, but their growth had been abnormal. At first, vines came in too quickly, spreading wildly and unevenly. Then plants began setting fruit too early, and the grapes did not do well. Andros, the villager and friend who'd first taken her through the then-ruined church and abandoned vineyard, suggested that the grape leaves were too large, creating too much shade and not allowing enough airflow. He explained that, without enough sunlight and air, the plants could not properly form sugars. It didn't take an expert to understand that the grapes were not sweet enough for winemaking.

Still learning about viticulture, Fevronia directed the workers to trim the leaves regularly. That, too, was a losing battle. The workers could never spend enough time at that corner of the vineyard. Once trimmed, the leaves grew back faster and larger. Soon enough, Fevronia told the workers not to waste their time. Yet, hoping against hope, Fevronia tested the grapes produced there. Through the late 50s and early 60s, they were rejected for all uses.

In '62, repeated bouts of Botrytis infected these very peculiar vines. Fevronia had all the vines near the creek—two acres—dug out and burned.

Andros was perplexed why these vines behaved so poorly and—before they were destroyed—begged Fevronia to consult with a real expert, someone, anyone more knowledgeable. His suggestion had been sensible, but Fevronia decided otherwise, wanting to be done with the problem of those two acres forever. She complained she was pulled in too many directions, and other matters relating to the monastery were of greater importance. The truth had been otherwise.

Through her reading, Fevronia concluded that the soil nitrogen levels must have been too high. The only sensible explanation was that the vines were planted near the mass grave and that only badly decomposing bodies could produce so much nitrogen. Even though soil tests showed up negative for excess nitrogen, Fevronia adhered to her opinion: the tests were wrong. That one mass grave couldn't possibly raise nitrogen levels throughout two acres didn't matter to her.

But no mass grave could be found. She'd repeatedly tried and failed. They had brought in cadaver dogs, which were allowed to prowl through the entire monastery grounds, but particularly were brought to the creek. At times, the dogs responded as if they smelled decomposition, but the results were never consistent. They ran in ever-widening circles shortly after they began to get the scent.

They'd tried ground-penetrating radar, experimenting with multiple frequencies, to no avail. The experts who operated the equipment at the monastery—more than once, as technology evolved—explained why they might not find a grave. The soils were always too wet, always inexplicably retaining moisture. Or, they often suggested, there was no mass grave at all.

Fevronia ultimately learned the obvious: the best way to locate hidden graves was through eyewitnesses. Perhaps, in any particular case, the only way. If there had been witnesses to the massacre, all they needed to do was point. But the obvious was no help. Who could be a witness? The German unit responsible for terrorizing Inousa had been withdrawn to fight in the Third Reich's futile battle against the advancing Soviet army and had been wiped out.

Fevronia did try to trace the remnants of that unit, if there were any, with little assistance. The massacre at the Holy Monastery of St. Vlassios, as horrific as it was, paled in comparison to many other massacres in Greece during the war. Ten monks were nothing compared to the more than 400 civilians mowed down by German machine-guns at Kalavyrta or the more than 200 civilians slaughtered by the Waffen-SS at Distomo. Many German military records had been destroyed, she learned, and others were archived in the United States. Perhaps, if she'd found someone willing to spend the time searching through archives, she might have identified the German soldiers occupying the Inousa district, and maybe some might still be alive. But then what? Ask a seventy-year-old ex-soldier if he'd participated in the murder of ten holy men? Invite all the surviving members of the platoon to the monastery for forgiveness, tea, and grave-finding? After years of fruitless inquiries, Fevronia gave up the idea of locating a witness. She accepted that the remains of her brother and his fellow monks would never receive proper last rites. Accepted it, that is, until Theodora's outburst and collapse.

It took Theodora and Fevronia—who found it difficult to walk even with the *glitsa* she invariably used—about twenty minutes to traverse the vineyard and emerge into the largely barren area of the creek. The villagers called the creek *Microdervis*, the small dervish, a vestige of the centuries of Muslim rule of this part of Greece. Clumps of grasses and sage broke up the ground. The sun was high, she felt its force on the exposed skin of her hands, yet the air was chillier close to the creek.

"Can you sense where the graves are, my child?" Fevronia asked Theodora, hardly able to restrain herself from even more emphatic questioning.

Theodora patiently scanned the edges of the creek, barely four meters across at its widest. Then she walked slowly up the slight grade to the northeast, stopping every few steps to look around. Occasionally she inclined her head, leaning her right ear closer to the ground, as if trying to listen to some faint noise, perhaps the dying groans of the monks.

Theodora searched in this manner for twenty minutes, then turned to Fevronia and shook her head sorrowfully.

"I'm so sorry, Mother," she said. "I see nothing. I no longer feel the presence of the Holy Mother. If the monks' bones are here, they are well hidden."

A HEAVY BURDEN

Fevronia was angry with herself and greatly disappointed. As much as her rational mind continued to tell her that the grave would remain hidden and the mystery never solved, she still yearned to provide proper burial rites for her brother and his fellow monks; she briefly allowed herself to believe that, after decades, Theodora had acquired from God a vision of the exact location of the grave.

The Church taught that God shares at least a portion of His consciousness with His people, with all human beings who are receptive. Surely God knew what occurred in the world He had written, knew the curves in every letter of every word, knew where every last atom lay, and thus knew where the monks met their end. God could have shared that consciousness had He wanted. Would it have been such a diversion from His plan to grant Fevronia—through Theodora's eyes—her unending prayer?

When Theodora said with regret at the edge of the *Microdermis* that she could see nothing, a wave of nausea welled in Fevronia and she felt a squeezing in her chest. She turned from Theodora, stumbled a few steps toward the creek, and kneeled to vomit, the bitter taste of defeat in her mouth. Theodora looked away.

Now, once again foiled, Fevronia knew it had been wrong and unfeeling to place such a heavy burden on Theodora. Fevronia looked upon Theodora as a saint-to-be. She could not have considered Theodora otherwise, once she'd realized that the

Theotokos had saved the little Jewish girl from certain death based upon the strength that girl's prayer, once she understood how that girl, together with the Theotokos, miraculously shielded her brother, Nicky, from a grenade blast that should have blown off his head. Fevronia had wanted to believe that Theodora could see with uncanny vision what others could not.

Fevronia felt a great need to confess her sin of arrogance. Who but the arrogant could believe that a personal obsession might be so important as to require God to alter His plans? Fevronia habitually confessed to the local priest to obtain the sacrament of Christ's body and blood, but those confessions were minimal. For many years, she had saved her deeper and more complex sins to confess to Theodora herself.

A confession regarding how she'd tried to use Theodora—was still trying—was one she'd need to take elsewhere.

ARTIE SHAW

Nicky received the call from a distraught Kayla early the next morning, a Friday, and spoke to her from his bedroom telephone as Helen dressed nearby, then sat next to him on the bed to listen more closely. When he finally put down the phone, he turned to Helen with a puzzled expression.

"What was that all about?" Helen asked. "Something's wrong with Jackie?"

"He's shut down. Won't talk. Won't utter a sound. Kayla wants to know if we'll come this evening for *Shabbat*."

"We're supposed to have *Shabbat* with my family, Nicky. You know that. And we missed last week with my family too."

It irritated Nicky that Helen did not immediately see the need for changing their plans. But she'd not heard how anxious Kayla sounded and wasn't focusing on how bizarre it was for a six-year-old to suddenly give up talking to those who most loved him.

"This is serious, Helen. Very serious." He was at a loss to explain more fully. How could he explain, when he himself didn't know what was going on? There had apparently been some unpleasantness between Max and Jackie that triggered—but didn't really illuminate—the event. "I have to go there after work. If you still want to make *Shabbat* at your house, I'll drop you there and then head back up to West Orange. Or, of course, you can come with me and tell your family they're on their own tonight. I know they'll understand and find a way to manage."

As soon as he spoke, the look on Helen's face made him regret his tone and choice of words. Helen marched out of the room without comment, and he soon heard her slamming shut a cupboard in the kitchen.

Nicky finished dressing by putting on the gray tie that had once been a favorite of Helen's father. She'd given it to Nicky for his birthday only a week earlier. He joined Helen in the kitchen and could still see dismay on her face. When was he going to learn, he wondered, to be more diplomatic in the way he spoke to her? More sensitive to her concerns?

"Helen, I'm ..."

"All right, Nicky. I see you're upset. I'll call Naomi and beg her to do dinner for the family again tonight. I'm sure she will. But I don't know quite what to tell her when she asks why."

"At this point, just say that there's a family problem I need to deal with, you can even say crisis, and you're going to graciously and lovingly be by my side. You can say it has to do with Jackie. Something emotional. She'll understand."

"So be it. Now, tell me exactly what happened, exactly what Kayla said to you."

He relayed as much as he could remember, editorializing along the way. Max could be a pain in the ass, sure. Six-year-olds could be weird occasionally, and Jackie was undoubtedly still affected in some way by Kayla's rough treatment of him when she was off her meds. No, he couldn't remember a case quite like this, but Jackie's refusal to speak would probably pass quickly. At least, that was his professional opinion on the basis of little evidence. Nicky shared an idea, but it could work only if they could get to West Orange early, well before *Shabbat* kicked in, when they would be prohibited from playing music.

"Artie Shaw? He's going to talk again if he hears your favorite CD? That's a stretch, Nicky."

"Well, that's my hope. He loves Artie Shaw too. Even more than Jimmy Hamilton. Have you got better ideas? Anything in social work research that tells you how to deal with this?"

"No."

"Then what time does the sun set?"

She pulled a small calendar out of her purse. "Eight twenty-three. Candle lighting then at eight-oh-three. We should have plenty of time."

OPEN WOUND

Not long after her failed attempt at grave-finding, Theodora realized that something was not quite right about her prayers either. She couldn't say exactly what was wrong.

For years, her routine hadn't changed. Prayer consumed virtually every waking moment that was not spent either in hearing confessions or in eating. On a typical evening, an hour or so before midnight, she would rise from her kneeling posture to lie on her cot and sleep for five hours before the cycle began again the next morning. It was usually easy to fall asleep, as exhausted as she was. True prayer was physically difficult. She'd learned that when locked in the closet in which she would have died were it not for the intervention of the Theotokos.

Often, Theodora would briefly emerge from sleep, finding herself immersed in prayer—"to forgive me a sinner" or "to bless you, O Theotokos, ever-blessed and most pure, and the Mother of our God, more honorable than the Cherubim ..."—as if she had never stopped praying. Then, just as suddenly, sleep would return until Theodora woke herself to begin the new day by lighting the candle under her icons.

For as long as she could remember, Theodora's prayers when most effective would dissolve away her own personality, just as if Theodora was a pinch of salt dropped into the sea. She would lose consciousness of her existence as Theodora, the name given her by the Holy God Bearer, and would enter a realm of purer consciousness, aware solely of God as the force encompassing and going beyond the universe of His creation, aware solely of the Lord Jesus Christ at the center of the Father's realm. She was no longer a human being but an incorporeal thought, a striving to be more perfect, a nothingness that could yet feel—had no choice but to feel—intense love for her Creator. It was as if the Creator entered and filled her being.

But it was impossible to obtain this highest level of prayer on a daily basis. Occasionally, stray thoughts intruded, or the concerns of her body—hunger, thirst, aching muscles, even memories—interfered with concentration. Yet, through arduous practice and with Fevronia's loving guidance, Theodora might pray at this highest level for a succession of four or five days.

And then things began to change with the shock of her brother's arrival at the monastery, a brother she'd not thought about for more than four decades. When he'd found her, when she recognized him with amazement and acknowledged who he was, he'd further shocked her by begging her to leave the monastery. Leaving the holy place that sustained and nourished her soul was something she could never have imagined doing, and yet his entreaty—which she firmly rejected—tugged at her endlessly. A longing to once again be united with her family arose, and, despite her efforts, she could not fully repress that longing.

She was tormented by memories of Nicky's visit. How could she not have been? It was as if he'd ripped open a long-forgotten wound, a wound so scabbed over she knew nothing of its existence until his arrival. While her loving brother was there, she'd become Kal Covo again for a short time. This conjunction of her true Theodora self and the little girl Kal she'd once been was a collision of polar opposites, as if two repelling magnets were forced together against all rules of nature.

Since Nicky's visit, it had become harder for her to achieve that wonderful, mysterious elation of prayer. She would pray to the

Theotokos, but a vision of a grenade blast—no, these were more than visions, and the actual outrageous percussion of the blast deafened her for minutes—would ply its way into her head. She'd lie on her cot to control her breathing and heartbeat; she'd have to calm herself and wait until the sensation faded. Or, if not the grenade, a picture formed in her mind of the deaths Nicky caused during the war and confessed to her. As did her brother, she herself now saw that innocent young girl in a yellow smock, torn by bullets from Nicky's gun, fired in haste and in fear for his own life; she could see, hear, smell, and feel the warm blood gurgling out of the *koritsaki*. She'd heard thousands of confessions over the years, but nothing like this had ever happened to her before; there'd never been a time when she became so engrossed in a confessor's sins that they interfered with her prayer.

Other, more ghastly visions newly tormented her. When she did come close to achieving her desired union with God during prayer, she might see—as if in a cinema—images of the massacre. She became an unwilling eyewitness. She could hear the monks' final prayers, could sense with amazement that they met their end rejoicing in the knowledge of imminently joining the Lord Jesus Christ at God's feet. It was beautiful and yet horrible, horrible and yet beautiful, and the sounds of the rifle fire and the German soldiers urging each other on resonated painfully. When this scene first played before her eyes—a message she knew was sent by God—Theodora came very close to telling Fevronia about it. Indeed, she had begun to walk toward Fevronia's cell, only to retreat when she realized she wouldn't be able to explain adequately. To proclaim simply that she believed the images came from God—that she miraculously obtained powers of sight beyond any other mortal—would have been to exalt herself without sufficient proof. She hoped at times that such visions would disappear forever and that she would forget ever having them.

But they continued and in the past weeks increased in frequency, further confirmation that God planted them in her mind for His holy purposes. But what purpose? The only purpose she could conceive of was to allow her to direct Fevronia to the graves. Maybe then the visions would mercifully stop. But she had tried and failed, unable to pinpoint any location. If she'd involuntarily become an eyewitness, she was yet an eyewitness whose powers of recall and accuracy were limited.

Between sessions of prayer, Theodora continued to deliberate with herself whether she should talk to Fevronia about everything: about how prayer had become increasingly difficult, about the visions lingering from Nicky's confession, about the massacre playing out inside her eyelids as a movie seen through a cloud of smoke, about how these visions were a direct message from God. But she feared, not only that Fevronia would not understand, but that Fevronia might also withdraw her blessing to Theodora to continue hearing confessions. It was an aspect of her life she cherished, her gift of giving comfort to those who needed it.

Theodora could not risk this difficult conversation with Fevronia before she was sure she needed to.

CALL ME KAL

Troubled as she was, Theodora prayed to the Theotokos, the Holy Virgin, for guidance. She prayed for the strength to talk to Fevronia, share with her what she could, and listen closely to Fevronia's counsel. She prayed for a clearer picture of the massacre, so that she would find the graves once and for all and be relieved of an awful burden. She prayed to be spared the horrible visions of Nicky's sins. None of these prayers had been answered. And yet she remained steadfast in her belief that God is One Who Hears Prayer. She could feel her father's soft and loving voice in the faraway distance reminding her God hears our prayers. *Hu shomeya tifilah.* It was the only Hebrew she remembered.

Early one morning, as Theodora awoke to prepare herself for prayer, there was the form of an answer; she heard herself talking, indeed, in the middle of a sentence, the only fragment of which she could recall was "under my cot." So, after washing, she pulled out the first of Nicky's letters and carefully tore open the envelope. It took her a few minutes to read the letter; then she reread it, hanging on every word.

"Pushed into separate paths by fate or by the will of God."

The way he chose to express this made her sad. She'd given him incontrovertible proof that God Himself, not callous fate, had been intimately involved in saving their lives. She'd made it absolutely clear that God Himself had done so through the holy offices of the

Theotokos, and yet here was Nicky still clinging to the fantasy that an unknown, unfeeling mystery of circumstances governed their existence. She saw him as disabled, bent into a stubborn reluctance to accept God as the real power behind his survival. The pain he'd endured had pulled a veil over his eyes that their bittersweet reunion had not yet removed.

Yet, reading his letter reminded Theodora that she loved Nicky dearly. That he'd written to her, no doubt sincerely, made her long for his presence again, kindled a hope that he'd come back to the monastery and stay longer. Perhaps he might succumb to the beauty of the mountains and the voice of God that could be heard in their birdsong and in the chanting of the nuns and in the bells calling the faithful to prayer.

"The peaceful surroundings of the mountains."

Yes, of course, he could sense it himself. He would embrace God again if he didn't so adamantly fight against God's presence. The prayer bells, when they rang, touched every fiber of one's body. Yes, the mountains were beautiful. Every aspect of God's creation was beautiful. He could return, seclude himself in the monastery for as long as it took for him to remember the faith he once had. For Theodora herself, as beautiful as were its surroundings, the monastery could just as well have been set into the heart of Thessaloniki as on the outskirts of the Greek mountains, as far as her prayer was concerned. It was the solitude of her cell, the closet in which she unburdened her being, that enabled her to reach the pinnacles of prayer.

"And now he's followed me to the United States."

For some reason Theodora could not fathom, this was the phrase in Nicky's letter that most intrigued and frightened her. She felt great sympathy for Nicky because his friend, Helen, would not believe the reality of the person pursuing him. Why wouldn't a former comrade chase around the world to torment Nicky? How terrible for him to see that the woman he loved—they clearly loved each other—would not countenance the possibility that evil lurked everywhere, in America as well as in Greece. Nicky could well be in danger; this person who'd called him Chrisma could try to finish what a German grenade had not. This man, this comrade—ghost or real made no difference—could go anywhere in God's world and perpetrate evil. God might not want Nicky to die just now but would not stay this man's hand if it was ready to strike Nicky down.

"Make the man disappear"?

Of course she couldn't do that. She hadn't put the man there in the first place. She was but a simple nun, never formally educated, a poor girl who'd once flown across the skies of northern Greece with the Theotokos forty-six years before and tried to live in the memory and joy of Her glow ever since.

"Permitted always to call you Kal"?

She would always be Theodora. She was no more Kal than Nicky had been Chrisma. The name Kal had been a mere waystation on the way to her real life of devotion to the Savior and His Holy Mother, a placeholder for the name Theodora. When the Mother of God bestows upon you a holy name, it is your name forever, your link to the Eternal, not to be squandered or disregarded or superseded. The Theotokos had saved Nicky, not because of his faith but because of hers, Theodora's.

But should that mean Nicky must call her Theodora? How could she deny Nicky this simple request, to be Kal for him? He'd crossed the world to find her again. He'd put himself through hell to renew contact with her, to hold her once more, to hold her as when she was but a toddler and he was her big brother.

If she ever wrote to him, she would say "Yes, you may always call me Kal." But she didn't think she would write; she didn't think she could. Her writing skills were minimal. Although she'd begun to write simple Greek while still in her family's home, she'd never found a reason to write more than a few notes to herself while at the monastery, usually thoughts about what she'd read that particularly resonated with her. She kept these notes—it was years since she last created one—in a small box in her cell. The box also contained an extra set of prayer beads and her candles and matches.

If she ever communicated with Nicky again, she imagined it would have to be in person.

VICTIM IN WAITING

The whole world was a cold dark cloud surrounding him, shutting out, not only the sunlight, but the very air he needed to breathe.

If Jackie could have expressed himself, say perhaps in a journal, he would have written that you couldn't trust anyone, particularly those who were closest to you. That the love and support he'd grown up expecting to be his due turned out to be masks hiding the truth, the violence and unpredictability of *Ima* and his uncle. That it was up to him, Jackie, alone to find a way to protect himself and survive.

He had but the dimmest memory of the terrible thing that had happened, a memory pushing against the borders of consciousness whenever he touched his neck. It was *Ima* who was somehow responsible and who, seeking his forgiveness, sought always to make it up to him with more cuddles and treats. But he couldn't be sure what he was supposed to forgive. They never spoke of the incident directly. The therapist they'd visited weekly for months seemed interested only in having them play games and talk to each other while playing. And so he'd learned checkers and backgammon and gin rummy. They'd talked about *Ima*'s piano career and his own clarinet lessons, about Chopin—which Jackie had never liked—and Artie Shaw and Jimmy Hamilton and jazz.

But what had *Ima* done? It had hurt him, scared him, but he couldn't recall. If only he could remember, then he might understand. Perhaps then he wouldn't need to be so afraid. He couldn't find a way to ask.

Uncle Max made him nervous, too, another person he couldn't fathom. Why was Uncle Max there, helping *Ima* take care of him, and not Jackie's real father? When it dawned on Jackie that Uncle Max couldn't have been his real father, when he recognized in his first moment of racial awareness that his real father had to have been a black man, he'd begun to ask questions any child would ask. The answers had never been satisfactory. All he could gather was his real father—August Sorel—was a famous violinist required to travel constantly and therefore a man who could not participate in Jackie's life. As far as he knew, Jackie had never even met this August Sorel.

Although largely true, the story about his missing father brought him little comfort and only gave rise to additional questions. From his friends, some of whom enjoyed relationships with real fathers, he'd heard that real fathers gave big hugs and expressed words of love. Uncle Max was sparse in his hugs and physical contact generally and had never mentioned loving Jackie. If he'd been able to express such thoughts, Jackie would have said that Uncle Max tolerated him, that it was expedient for Uncle Max to do so because Uncle Max's first priority was to take care of *Ima*, that Uncle Max needed to be close to her, and that he, Jackie, came along as part of the bargain.

When Jackie realized that his physical safety in his own home was not guaranteed, that his home was a place where anything bad could happen at any instant, he'd subconsciously built additional defenses. He could not trust himself to feel love, either for *Ima* or for Uncle Max, because they could abuse that trust arbitrarily. They knew everything and he knew nothing. They were big and he was small. They posed mortal danger to him; he was a victim in waiting.

The idea of running away frequently played in his mind. But to whom could he flee? And how would he get there? And if, by great fortune, he'd been able to tell Grandpa and his nice friend Helen how scared he was and even made it to Grandpa's apartment in the big city or to Helen's house, which was somewhere in the other direction, what then? Grandpa and Helen would take him back to *Ima* and he'd be in even more danger.

Jackie had wanted to say these things to the therapist, but there was never a chance to do so alone. *Ima* was always there at his side and often Uncle Max as well. They called it family therapy.

Jackie pretended to be happy, pretended to feel safe, doing what everyone wanted him to do, saying what everyone wanted him to say. The times in which he most wanted to feel in control were his hours with the clarinet, but there too he found frustration at every turn.

He remembered a discussion about *Ima*'s meds, the pills she had to take every day. She would keep taking them, she promised to the therapist. Her promises had to do with Jackie in a way he couldn't explain.

The therapy sessions ended.

BEGIN THE BEGUINE

Jackie sat disconsolately at his desk. The snappy Artie Shaw version of "Begin the Beguine" jaunted from Jackie's CD player. The big band harmonies and bouncy rhythm and Artie's high riffs had done nothing to make Jackie feel better. Nor had "Stardust" or "Moonglow" or the three melodies preceding them.

Although Jackie loved the music, and although the songs made him sorely hope that he could someday play the clarinet with the same bravado, the music didn't make him want to talk. It only emphasized one of the many things Jackie felt would never be his. How could he ever play like Artie Shaw? You had to feel safe if you wanted to practice well and see improvement. You had to feel safe if you wanted to concentrate. Whenever he placed the mouthpiece below his lips, he heard Uncle Max's harsh, demanding voice in his mind and couldn't blow a pure tone to save his life.

As "Smoke Gets In Your Eyes" began, Grandpa reached over from where he sat on Jackie's bed and shut off the CD player. "Will you talk to me now, Jackie?"

He had a strong urge to respond, because he loved Grandpa, but he feared the consequences. Grandpa could never believe that he was in danger or that the grownups who were supposed to take care of him—Grandpa's own children—had instead become the threat. Rather than be disbelieved and mocked for childish fears, he would keep his mouth shut. He could do it. He could be stubborn. Everyone always said that *Ima* could be stubborn; well, he could be just as stubborn. He would take after her. He said nothing.

Nicky waited a full minute. When it was clear to him that nothing positive would happen, he changed tactics. If music wasn't the answer, the answer had to lie elsewhere. If Jackie were his own patient and they were in Nicky's office, what would he do to get the patient to talk? He looked carefully around Jackie's room for props he might use.

His eyes rested on the framed photograph of Jackie Robinson that Jackie's grandmother—Nicky's deceased wife Adel—had given to Jackie on his first birthday. The photo hung on the wall to the side of Jackie's bed. That particular photograph was a peculiar choice, Nicky thought. Although there were many photos of Jackie with a smile on his face or photos of the great Brooklyn Dodgers slugger swinging a bat or stealing home—two such photos hung in Nicky's apartment—Adel had selected a photo of Jackie sitting by himself, looking sternly at a baseball in his hand. It was as if the great Jackie Robinson thought that, by staring at baseballs, he could better learn how to make them fly out of Ebbets Field. You couldn't tell for sure, but it looked like he was in the Dodgers' dugout. The camera had been close to him, so no other players were visible, no clue as to the year the photo was taken.

Nicky had not been in America for very long before Helen's dad, Elie Saltiel, took him, as well as Helen and her husband David, to an early April game. Jackie had just broken the color barrier in major league baseball, and the stands that day were filled with black fans. Nicky thought he remembered a bit about the game. He seemed to recall a lot of excitement when the Dodgers came from far behind to beat the crosstown rival Giants. He thought he remembered Jackie making a spiffy play on a difficult foul pop off the first base line and turning a double play as well. And was that the first time Jackie stole home, something Jackie seemed to do all the time? Or did he just score from first on a double?

Nicky gently urged his own Jackie out of the desk chair in which he'd been sitting and guided him to sit alongside him on the bed. He took the photograph from the wall and put into his grandson's hands.

"Okay, I get it. You're not ready to talk to me yet. Or to anyone. So let me talk. Let me tell you about this great ballplayer you're named after." He could see Jackie looking intently at the picture, almost as if praying that the long-gone hero could magically appear in his bedroom and help him put away his fears. "This man was given every reason to quit. Thousands of white people came to stadiums to call him bad names. Ugly names that I hope you never hear. He got threatening letters. Bad people said they wanted to kill him. You've heard this before, right?"

Jackie looked up at Nicky with tears in his eyes. It was a look that seemed to ask Nicky why he needed to be tortured with this information. It was a look that pleaded with Nicky not to torment him.

"This man did not give up, Jackie. And I don't want you to give up either. And neither does your mom and neither does Uncle Max. What's bothering you can be fixed, but you need to be able to talk to us. If Jackie Robinson were here, he'd tell you the same thing. You remember Grandma, right?"

Jackie nodded, a bit uncertain. He'd been only three when Adel died, and his memories of her were foggy.

"Well, Jackie Robinson met your Grandma once and told her the same thing. Don't give up." In truth, it wasn't quite the story Adel told, but close enough. "And she didn't. And that's why Grandma and I had your mom and Uncle Max. And that's why you're here now. So what I'm saying is: Don't give up. When you want to talk to me, pick up the phone and call me."

Nicky removed one of his business cards from his wallet, jotted down his home phone number, and handed it to Jackie, taking back the photograph and rehanging it on the wall.

"You know how to use the phone."

As he left, Nicky added, "And when you're ready to talk to your mom, she'll listen to you with all of her heart. She loves you very much."

The door closed, Jackie waited a few seconds, then calmly tore Nicky's card into four pieces, stuffed them into his mouth, and chewed.

NEW ORLEANS OR MEMPHIS?

Shabbat dinner was a disaster as far as Kayla was concerned. Jackie showed little appetite, even for his favorite mac-and-cheese. He drank barely half of his cup of grape juice, ate one slice of Kayla's delicious *challah*, and left the table without being excused, returning directly to his room.

Fighting to hold back tears, Kayla led the four adults in *Birkat Ha-Mazon*. Instead of the celebratory prayers they were supposed to be, they had the ring of a dirge in Kayla's mind. Not conscious of what she was doing, Kayla had transposed the traditional major key melodies into minor keys. At the end, they closed their prayer books, then looked at each other expectantly.

"I guess it's time for a family council," Nicky began. "The boy is troubled."

"It has to be my fault," said Max glumly. "He was good until I forced him to stop practicing and then grabbed him."

"That's nothing, Max. If anyone's at fault, it's me." Kayla paused to wipe her eyes. "I'm the one who almost killed him. He's reliving that. The therapist warned there would be times like this. Jackie will never get over that."

"If you'll allow me to comment as a non-family observer ..." Helen started.

"You're family, Helen. You and Dad are practically married." Kayla tried with difficulty to smile.

"Thank you, Kayla. No, we're hardly married. But that's off point. What occurs to me is that you and Max not try to allocate blame. It's not useful."

"But if I hadn't gone off my meds ..." Kayla let her sentence drift, knowing everyone understood.

"Kayla ..." continued Helen. "You love Jackie and you didn't want to hurt him. You're dealing with an illness that is not your fault. It's the nature of the beast, regrettably, that sometimes, too often, its victims go off their meds. You're trying hard now to be good about them. Max is staying after you, as I understand ..."

"Yes, I am."

"And so the root cause of Jackie's struggles, it would appear, is under control. Although he might not realize that."

"No, he wouldn't," Nicky added.

"So, secondly, putting all blame aside, I wonder if a change of environment wouldn't be in his best interest."

"What do you mean?" asked Kayla, suddenly alarmed.

"Take Jackie on a trip somewhere. Or, have him live with one of his friends, for a week or two." As Helen laid out her suggestions, she sensed the amazement in Nicky's mind, the immediate agreement in Max's, and what could only be described as the horror in Kayla's. Kayla was the first to speak.

"Helen, you can't be serious about having Jackie live elsewhere. That would confirm his fears are grounded, that we're not to be trusted to take care of him properly."

"Don't dismiss the idea out of hand, though, Kayla," said Max, glancing at his father. "Dad, are there data to support the therapeutic value of a brief vacation from one's home?"

"I can look into it. Helen, do you know of any studies?"

"No. It's just my intuition and experience as a social worker. But let's not forget I presented two completely different ideas. Kayla, what about a trip? Maybe your dad and I—if he wants to have a short vacation from his practice—can take Jackie someplace he'd greatly enjoy? He's into jazz, maybe New Orleans or Memphis?"

"You're trying to get him away from me? It's so obvious." Kayla felt that Helen's suggestion was the first small step in separating her from Jackie forever. Well, why shouldn't they be separated? She was an unfit mother who didn't deserve to have a child of her own. And she would lose Jackie to her schizophrenia, just as she'd lost her musical career.

"It might seem like that to you," Helen continued, "but that's not the intent. We want what you want, to figure out how to rip away this blanket of silence Jackie's thrown over himself."

Kayla thought. The idea of Jackie staying for a couple of weeks with a friend's family seemed ludicrous, primarily because such an arrangement would require their finding out about the abuse Jackie had suffered and thus about her illness. It was something she tried to hide from the people in her *shul* and from her neighbors. She consistently explained to outsiders, when pressed, that she'd given up performing to concentrate on composing. The only idea that might work would be sending Jackie off with her father and Helen. Kayla knew they'd take good care of him but doubted such a trip would improve the situation. At the trip's end, Jackie would return home to her and Max, and everyone would be back where they started.

"Look. I'll do research over the weekend. At least Jackie's eating something. Maybe you can get him to practice the clarinet again, Max. Maybe if you ask him to show you how it's done. He could break out of this silence suddenly. He's almost seven. He can't possibly be stubborn enough to keep this up forever." Nicky tried to speak with authority, but he realized he sounded more like someone grasping at straws.

"I don't think so, Dad," said Max. "I hardly see myself as being able to pretend I want to play the clarinet. It would be an obvious ruse. The kid is smart."

"The kid? Fine, then. Kayla, please think about Helen's idea of a short trip. I'm willing to cancel a week of patients if I have to. Shit.

I'd give up my practice entirely if Jackie needed me to." To his surprise, the idea of no longer practicing psychiatry appealed greatly.

Kayla studied everyone's faces. They all seemed to sincerely want to help, even Max, although Max had rejected her father's suggestion about the clarinet. Well, Kayla could pretend to want to learn too, if it came to that. She could say she was thinking of writing a sonata for clarinet and piano. And maybe a trip would in fact do the job of getting Jackie back into the sociable and talkative boy he'd always been.

"All right, Dad. I'll think about it."

BLACK JESUS

Despite reservations about her lack of writing ability, Theodora continued to mull the idea of responding, at least minimally, to Nicky's letter. Maybe she would suggest his visiting her again the following spring. If she were going to write, she would not only have to seek Fevronia's blessing, but would need to be given sheets of paper, first to practice her printing and then for the note itself. Fevronia would ask what was now motivating Theodora to write so long after Nicky's first letter, and Theodora wasn't sure how she'd answer such a perfectly logical question.

What had changed was nothing less than the onslaught of occasional memories of Theodora's life as Kal Covo: the loving family, its immersion in Judaism, and—although she could not remember the languages—Papa's patiently teaching her Hebrew and Aramaic as they sat before the Talmud. Each memory came unbidden, often at the most inopportune times, just when Theodora, in the midst of deep prayer, felt she was on the verge of a new awakening to the Lord Jesus Christ and His Father. The memories would pull her back from the brink of religious ecstasy she so devotedly sought. It was almost as if something in her upbringing was cautioning her against going too far along her chosen route of salvation.

Theodora didn't resist these memories, nor did she dwell on them. These diversions into memory typically lasted only seconds, and when Theodora concentrated on getting back to her prayer, the memories faded. She knew though, in part because the visions of her prior life had begun to creep into her dreams, they could be reached whenever needed. She began to pay more attention to her dreams, heedless of many warnings she'd heard over the years that dreams are often instilled in one's mind by the Devil.

The dream that changed Theodora's life forever took place on the night after she first considered seeking Fevronia's blessing to write to Nicky. In her dream, she was Kal, unmistakably inside her family's house in Salonika. The weather was stormy, with occasional flashes of lightning and rumbles of thunder. She felt uneasy, almost trembling with nervousness, and in part it was the weather, but it was something else as well, exactly what she was unsure. Only Nicky and she herself—grown to adulthood—were home. She knew with overwhelming grief that Mama and Papa and Ada had perished in the gas chambers; she yearned for a way to make them return, even as she understood the impossibility of bringing them back from their scattered ashes.

Nicky and Kal had stood together in the family kitchen, facing each other, each waiting for the other to speak. How had they gotten there, long after the war? From where? Why? It made no sense.

Everything was so familiar, though. She felt as if she'd been away for only a day. Then she began to prepare their evening meal of chard, lentils, onion, and raisins. She felt her stomach yearning to be filled, she smelled and almost tasted their food, even as she cooked it over a slow fire. She sweated; her hands trembled. Then the feeling of nervousness returned even more strongly, a sensation of being on the brink of something amazing but impossible. Her anticipation grew to the point where she could hardly move.

As she was readying to serve dinner, a young, tall, thin black man in his early twenties, a man whose blackness was tempered to sepia, entered their kitchen, passing through a closed door, and Kal's nervousness immediately turned to joy; she felt the overwhelming urge to cry in happiness. He had come in from the rain and was wet;

drops of water puddled around his feet. Kal noticed that the man wore sandals. She studied his face carefully, noting how his eyes were a brilliant hazel. His appearance was unexpected, but yet in a way she felt she had been waiting for His entrance for the entirety of her life. Jesus was much taller and darker than she'd imagined. As He moved closer to her and Nicky, smiling to them both, she smelled the unmistakable but complex scent of roses in bloom.

Jesus wasn't a stranger to her, nor was He a stranger to Nicky. Kal recognized the black man immediately as Nicky's grandson, and he was Jesus, too, come home finally to rejoin the family.

She wondered for an instant where He had been hiding. Then Nicky and this man—both Jackie Covo and Jesus Christ, Her Savior—embraced. The black man with hazel eyes, Jesus, turned to her next and reached out to her in the fullness of unimaginable love. He was about to hug her too, and she knew she would finally feel herself the physical embrace of her God, but before He could touch her, she awoke.

The first few moments of waking left Theodora scared. She didn't recognize her own cell in the darkness. Her heart beat rapidly, she sweated profusely, and her lungs felt as if they were in a vise. She sat abruptly, disoriented, almost ready to scream, dreading something so amazing it was awful. Slowly though, as she forced herself to breathe—shallowly at first—she drew aware of where she was, and the reality of her cloistered life came flooding back into her consciousness. But the dream lingered as well in her mind, and the visage of Jesus remained with her full force. She dwelled on that image—of her Lord Jesus Christ and of a grown-up Jackie Covo—for many minutes.

Finally, she resumed praying. She directed her prayer to the Theotokos. "What is happening to me, Sainted God Bearer?"

LOUIS ARMSTRONG

With Kayla's consent, Nicky and Helen broached to Jackie the possibility of an adventure, a "music-loving trip to the jazz capital of the world." They would fly to New Orleans and attend the annual summer Jazzfest. They would seek out the best clarinetists and listen as much as Jackie wanted. If possible, they would try to meet the clarinetists Jackie liked best. And Jackie could bring his clarinet along to practice, but wouldn't be forced to do so.

Nicky and Helen calmly presented the prospect of the trip to Jackie in his bedroom, while offering him ricotta-stuffed blintzes, one of his favorite foods. Helen did most of the talking, showing Jackie brochures of New Orleans she'd picked up at a travel agency. Nicky added his own comments, remarking how he'd heard about incredible crepe restaurants in New Orleans, but they would be sure to keep kosher, as Helen was very observant, and crepes were just another name for blintzes.

Jackie knew that this trip was being offered to him because he'd refused to talk. He felt a stab of guilt at the concern that he had caused his family, but the guilt wasn't sufficient to countervail his desire for the exciting excursion being offered. He could think of nothing that he'd like more than to be away from his mother and uncle for a few days or a week.

"I won't have to talk to anyone if I don't want to, will I?" he asked, innocently breaking his vow of silence.

Nicky and Helen barely concealed their smiles.

"No, Jackie. You don't have to talk to anyone you don't want to talk to. Even to Grandpa or me, but if you want to talk or you need something, of course, we'll gladly listen."

"I don't have to talk to *Ima* or Uncle Max now, if I don't want to?"

"No, Jackie," Helen continued. "They would love it if you did talk to them, but you don't have to. No one will force you. Only when you're ready. Before our adventure, if you like, or after, or not at all. We'll leave that completely up to you."

Jackie arose from his bed and walked to his music stand, where the last exercises he'd been practicing still sat open. He picked up the soft-bound volume, flipped a few pages as if looking for something, then replaced the book as it had been.

"Have you ever been to New Orleans, Grandpa?" Now that he knew he was really going, that Helen and Grandpa would certainly keep their promise, a slight chill went through him. What would it be like to be in a strange place, far away from his home? What would it be like to fly on a real airplane, not just a make-believe plane?

"No, Jackie, and neither has Helen, but we're good travelers. We found our way around Greece, even in the mountains of Greece, and that's a whole different country. New Orleans is in the United States, and we'll be able to get around and have a great time with you. We'll get all the maps we need."

Jackie took one of the brochures from his bed. It showed on its cover a painting of three black musicians. One, on a chair, wore a red long-sleeved shirt and held a clarinet to his mouth. Another, on a second chair, wore a yellow shirt and blue bowler and held a bass saxophone to his mouth. The third, wearing a red shirt and blue long-sleeved undershirt, stood behind them playing a trumpet. He could almost hear the music.

"What are they playing?" Jackie handed the brochure to Helen.

"You can read as well for yourself. It says 'New Orleans Summer Jazzfest' and 'Louis Armstrong.' They must obviously be playing New Orleans jazz." She gave the brochure back to Jackie, as Nicky nodded in agreement.

"When are we going, Grandpa?"

MY BROTHER'S GRANDSON

Theodora knocked hesitantly on the door of Fevronia's cell. When the abbess was praying, almost no one dared to intrude. Only months before, Theodora had come close to disturbing Fevronia at night, a week before her brother visited, Theodora recalled, but she hadn't known he was coming. She hadn't even been aware that she had a brother.

Theodora thought perhaps she'd been troubled by something. Or maybe she'd thought that Fevronia was troubled and needed her. On that night, Theodora had not been able to knock. Instead, she quietly kneeled outside Fevronia's cell for hours, unseen, praying directly to the Virgin, immersing herself in prayer: "είθε να είναι η θέλησή σου να φέρεις θεραπεία, θεραπεία του σώματος και της ψυχής, στις καλόγριες που ζουν εδώ, όλες τις κόρες της Αγίας Θεοτόκου." ("May it be your will to send healing of the soul and body to the nuns who live here, all daughters of The Most Holy Theotokos.") As she prayed, she felt suffused with the holy orange glow of the Theotokos, Her warmth at an intensity she hadn't experienced in a long time. Only when the warmth suddenly disappeared, as if a cold draft had blown in from the closed windows, did she regain her feet and retreat to her own cell.

When there was no response to her hesitant knock, Theodora had to knock with greater fervor. Finally, she heard Fevronia stirring. Fevronia opened her door and wordlessly invited Theodora in. They sat on Fevronia's cot. Fevronia had the urge to admit to Theodora her fear that she'd been abusing the younger nun, but understood that Theodora, who'd come to her, needed to start the conversation. God in His Holiness would direct their meeting.

Theodora's calm question shocked Fevronia.

"Did you know Jesus is black?"

Fevronia stared at Theodora, wondering if she'd heard correctly. Then Theodora repeated the question, more insistently.

"Did you know Jesus is black?"

Two seconds passed before Fevronia responded. "I don't know any such thing. Our Lord Jesus Christ is not a color that we can truly see, as we see the skin color of mere humans, any more than we can see God's countenance itself."

Theodora grasped Fevronia's hands before continuing. "No, Mother. You must forgive me for saying so, but you are wrong. Jesus was and is a human being, and I did see him just now in a dream—a vision from God Himself directly—and Jesus was most decidedly black."

"How ..."

"Why didn't you tell me? Why do we have icons of only a white Jesus?"

Fevronia removed her hands from Theodora's, reached behind her with her left hand for the prayer beads she'd dropped on her cot, and began fingering them. She prayed fervently for the wisdom to fashion a compelling and true answer.

Theodora waited, hopeful, yet not confident—despite her great love for Fevronia—that the abbess could guide her correctly. It took a full minute before Fevronia responded.

"In my dreams, when I have seen Christ, Our Lord, he does appear white, as he appears in our icons. Look at my Icon of Iveron." Fevronia leaned over to turn on a small lamp on her night table, then lifted the lamp and held it closer to the corner of the room where her icons were mounted. But in examining the holy image, she saw that the Theotokos and Her Child did not look exactly white. They appeared to be of a Caucasian race, but olive-skinned, more Mediterranean than anything else, identical in skin color to Theodora.

Theodora kneeled before the icon, kissed it, crossed herself, and turned toward Fevronia. "Did the human painters of the holy icon actually see Jesus? Is that what you're telling me?"

"No. The painters did not envision Jesus as other than they themselves were. It is natural to represent God in our image, if you will, because the Holy Scriptures tell us that human beings were formed in God's image. .. εἰκόνα Θεοῦ." (*eichona Theo*)

"Our image, you say. But Jesus is black, and I saw Him in my dream. Jesus is also my brother's grandson. Such is the vision that God has seen fit to send me."

It occurred to Fevronia that the great pressure she'd been putting on Theodora had dangerously unsettled her mind, to an extent now jeopardizing Theodora's sanity. Fevronia had caused a crack to appear, much as an earthquake might sunder a valley into separate pieces of land, and the crack had allowed the Devil to infiltrate. She recalled a mention of Dr. Covo's grandson during his visit to the monastery, but nothing about the boy's race. She would have remembered such a detail. But to think of Dr. Covo's grandson as Jesus! It would have been laughably absurd, if it hadn't been so dangerous. Nor would laughter have been a proper reaction when the vulnerable Theodora was in her cell, urgently begging to be believed.

"We often like to think that dreams come from God, Theodora, but sometimes they come from His nemesis. They can be planted in the minds of human beings who are, for the moment, susceptible. Whatever you saw must be such a case. Do you not sense that the Devil is nearby?"

"No." Theodora paused briefly, thinking how best to explain herself. "I know, Mother, that the Devil can infect our dreams, but if this dream came from the Devil, I would have sensed that immediately, of that I'm sure."

"You can't be sure."

"You see what this means, don't you?"

"No," Fevronia answered almost before Theodora's question had been completed. "I see only that something of great moment disturbs you. I feel I must be to blame."

Theodora shut her eyes and prayed, determined to remain for hours inside Fevronia's cell until she developed the courage to speak again. But even as the Jesus Prayer sped through her, bathing her soul, the part of her mind that stood apart from prayer asked how Fevronia could be blamed for anything and why indeed this was a situation where blame had to be considered. And why did Fevronia believe Theodora was disturbed? As she sat there, she felt, not disturbed, but exhilarated with her message from God and the great discovery God had led her to. Jesus was here again, and Theodora knew where He was and how to find Him.

Ultimately, Theodora breathed deeply and continued, "I understand that we might like to see Jesus looking exactly as we do. Honestly, until my dream, I thought He was as white as the whitest skin in the icons we have. Most of our icons show Him and the Theotokos much whiter than in the Icon of Iveron."

"Yes, but ..."

"Please let me finish." She sat again on the cot, wondering what to say next. "But Jesus was a real man and had one skin color, not an array of colors depending upon who looked at Him. There's no reason he couldn't have been black."

"But he was Semitic. The Semites aren't black. But there's the ..."

"Mother, please. I know if you could show me a photograph of Jesus as He appeared at the time of His birth and during His first life, you would have done so long ago. There is no such photograph, I know, so there's no way to prove me wrong. And ..."

"And?"

"I seek your forgiveness for saying so to you. But just as I know in the depths of my soul the Theotokos lifted me in Her veil and brought me here, I know that the young man I saw, Nicky's grandson, is Jesus. As I have said, the dream is a vision from God Himself, I cannot say it more clearly, and that is something I will always know in my heart to be true."

There was no point arguing with her, Fevronia concluded. Obviously, she couldn't prove Jesus's race with a photograph. "So what would you like me to do, then, my angel, my precious one?"

"Tell me, Mother, what it means. Please tell me what I must do."

MY SON?

Nicky sprang for first-class seats, with Jackie sitting next to Nicky, at the window, and Helen across the aisle. After repeatedly changing his mind, Jackie elected to take his clarinet with him, and it rested snugly in its case in the overhead luggage bin.

Jackie spoke little on the trip, content to read. He'd brought two books. Nicky looked over occasionally to help Jackie with the words. Jackie had brought *Little Grunt and the Big Egg*, in which a young boy improbably becomes close friends with the dinosaur whose hatching is the climax of the story and *Pretend You're a Cat*, in which the reader must make a variety of animal sounds. It was good that Jackie had found a way to keep entertained, but Nicky would have preferred that they talked more. Nicky took the opportunity, as Jackie read the latter book, to ask how Aliyah had been doing and whether she was still sleeping with him.

Nicky had made reservations at the Tremé Hotel, which had the main—perhaps only—advantage of being the closest to the Fair Grounds where the Summer JazzFest took place. Helen would not get in a cab or a trolley on Shabbat; for the long weekend, they would need to stay within walking distance. Nicky estimated that, with Jackie along, it would still take them a good half-hour to make the trip up Esplanade Avenue. The Fodor's Guide to New Orleans warned, though, that the Tremé had the disadvantage of being much less elegant than the hotels nearer the French Quarter. It was a small sacrifice to make for Helen. Although Jackie, not nearly the age of *mitzvot*, was allowed by Kayla to ride with his uncle on *Shabbat* when she deemed it necessary, she was happy to know that her son, too, would be walking.

Tired from the trip, Nicky and Helen agreed that they would forgo the JazzFest on Friday afternoon. They rested at the hotel, then walked around the local neighborhood for a few blocks before supper. It was too far for them to walk to the nearest synagogue, which Helen might have wanted to do if left to her own devices. This was the other advantage to the Tremé, thought Nicky. He wouldn't have to pretend to pray.

Saturday brought brilliant early summer sunshine to New Orleans and a large, boisterous crowd to the Fair Grounds. Nicky and Helen had all they could do not to lose Jackie, who absolutely refused to hold anyone's hand. But they found good seats on the lawn before one of the stages and quickly were all engrossed in the music of B.B. King. Following him, the crowd was treated to the perky voices of The Dixie Cups. After a lunch of corn-on-the-cob and lemonade, they heard the Kenny Neal Blues Band and his rendition of "Bloodline." Jackie seemed enthralled, and Helen, paying close attention to the lyrics, wondered how far Jackie's apple had fallen from the various trees on which he'd grown.

Nicky found it hard to relax. He had noted with some concern that the program for the weekend didn't feature any clarinetists as soloists. He thought of letting Jackie know, but decided to remain silent. Surprisingly, Jackie hadn't asked about clarinetists. His own clarinet still rested in its case in their hotel room, unused so far on the trip.

On Sunday morning, they weren't sure where to turn until Nicky heard a bouncing rendition of "Humoresque" at a nearby stage. Checking his program, he saw that a group called the Stuff Cooper Quartet was there. Nicky and Helen gently guided Jackie in the direction of the sound. They soon saw that the head of the quartet was a dark-skinned violinist with close-cropped black hair, wearing a dark suit with wide pinstripes. Was he black? It was hard to say, but his coloring was not greatly different from Jackie's. Stuff Cooper, smiling and dancing as he played the violin, was accompanied by two white guitarists, also in suits. Behind them, a blonde woman in a black dress worked the strings of a double bass.

Nicky, Helen, and Jackie happily sat down to listen to Stuff Cooper, but the next group to take the stage was even more exciting, at least to the crowd that had been waiting for it. The Billy Bang Quintet, with Billy Bang leading on the violin, played a more abstract jazz style than Cooper, one that Nicky himself couldn't get into. The violin part wandered aimlessly, at times screeching, or so it sounded to Nicky. He was about to stand up from the blanket that he and Helen had spread out, when he felt a hand on his shoulder pulling him around.

"Dr. Covo, of all people."

He stood then, face to face with a tall, very dark black man wearing a large diamond earring in his left ear. The goatee that Nicky remembered was gone, and Sorel appeared taller than Nicky by about three inches instead of two, the indisputable result of the gradual compression of Nicky's spine with age. In other respects, August Sorel looked the same as he had seven years earlier.

Nicky inadvertently looked down at Helen and Jackie; she had turned toward him questioningly and lightly touched Jackie's shoulder, but he was intent on the music and not conscious of the visitor. Sorel followed Nicky's glance and was about to say something when Nicky put up his hand toward the visitor, and said, softly, "Let's step back so we don't bother anyone."

When they had walked to a place where a conversation was much less likely to disturb the ardent jazz fans, Sorel demanded to know what he obviously suspected.

"Is that young lad who I think it is? Is that my son?"

IMAGE-NOT-MADE-BY-HAND

"What you must do first, my dear one, is listen to me." Fevronia spoke firmly, if not sharply, trying to convey as much love for Theodora as would a natural doting mother.

"I am sorry for interrupting. I pray to the Lord Jesus Christ to forgive me, a sinner." Theodora felt her face redden as she looked down at her feet.

"Now, then. There are many venerated icons of Jesus in which He does indeed appear Negroid or of one of the darker races, even though He had to be born Semitic. I have seen them, although we don't have any here."

Theodora waited a long second as Fevronia breathed deeply, a pained expression on her face. "Tell me more, please."

"The one I remember best, the one best known in all Orthodoxy, is the Image-Not-Made-By-Hand. It comes directly from our Savior's face, as tradition goes, and I have no reason to doubt it. Maybe it's as close to a photograph as we have. Our Lord is very dark there, certainly the antithesis of Caucasian. And this is an icon linked with innumerable miracles. So, if you've concluded that Jesus is black, if you want to call Him so, our tradition allows that view— that appearance—as well as other views of Jesus."

"Of course. Now I remember. The Third Feast of the Savior in August. And it seems like I have seen that venerated icon somewhere, although I don't remember when or where."

"It may be that you saw it in a book once, or in the church of the priest with whom you hid as a child."

"Father Theodore."

"Yes. But what troubles me about your dream, or shall I say your interpretation of your dream, is that you posit Our Lord Jesus Christ existing, today, as your brother's grandson. That would make Him, not only present in our world, but your grandnephew."

"You are troubled?" Theodora quite unconsciously brought a fist up to her mouth. "Have I sinned by saying this, that Jesus has returned? Or that He is my grandnephew?"

Fevronia thought carefully before venturing an answer. "You have not sinned, as such, but you're in error. What you say is contrary to the teachings of the Church, and again I worry that the Devil is stealing into your thoughts."

"I don't see how."

"His ways are devious."

"How can I be myself if I must doubt that which I firmly believe? How can I disavow what I've seen, what God has granted me to see?"

"When Christ has risen, He appears in all places. Our scriptures make that clear. And yet you feel you alone can recognize Him? That God has given only you that power? To see Our Lord's face?"

"That's what we strive for every day, Mother, is it not?"

Fevronia fought not to snicker. Even as she spoke, it was hard for her to believe she was having this conversation. Everything she thought she knew about her church was called into question. "Look, Theodora. Your brother told me about your family history. If your ... let's call it a vision ... if your vision reflected truth, then Our Lord, in His present appearance on earth, is descended from the Great Rabbi of Salonika."

"Something you choose not to accept? Our Jesus is descended from King David, but yet you cannot accept that he's also descended from a Great Rabbi?" Utter dismay crossed Theodora's face; she was ready to cry.

"I would accept it, if it were true. But it can't be true. The Second Coming hasn't arrived."

"And you know that how, Mother?" asked Theodora, as she tried to suppress the anger and disappointment growing within her.

"Because you and I are here talking to each other."

BLEEDING FROM THE EAR

"What are you doing here, August? Following us?" Of course, it was impossible that August Sorel had followed them. Churchill, maybe, because Churchill knew where Nicky was all the time, but not Sorel.

"You're as crazy as your son, who by the way I owe a punch in the face. That boy there is Jackie, isn't he? What the fuck are you doing here with my son?"

"My girlfriend and I have taken him to the JazzFest for the weekend, obviously. He plays the clarinet. We thought it would be good for him." Nicky immediately regretted having said too much. Sorel hadn't ever been involved in Jackie's life. He hadn't sent money to Kayla in many years. He had no right to know anything.

"Good for him? Where's his mom? Why isn't she taking care of him? I'm going to ask Jackie himself." Sorel started to march back into the crowd toward where Helen and Jackie sat, but Nicky grabbed his arm and spun him around.

"No. You're not going anywhere near my grandson."

"Let go of me you fucking kike."

Nicky swung with his right hand for all he was worth, his hand still closing into a fist as it smashed into the side of Sorel's head. Good luck or bad, depending upon one's point of view, had guided Nicky's hand into the diamond stud, which gashed Nicky's middle finger. The blow stunned Sorel, but only for a moment. He lunged at Nicky, who'd instinctively brought his bleeding finger to his mouth and was unprepared to defend himself. The taller and stronger Sorel knocked Nicky down, then tried to knee drop onto Nicky's chest. It was a move worthy of World-Wide Wrestling, but Sorel managed mostly to knock the wind out of himself.

In seconds, two New Orleans police officers, one white and one black, pulled them apart. The black officer who'd grabbed Sorel, as it happened, was a sergeant and took charge. Nicky unbelievingly heard Sorel accuse him of being a kidnapper. Sorel pointed toward the front of the crowd, where he said the officers would find his son "with an old woman who's helping this turd."

"That's nuts, officers. I'm Dr. Nicholas Covo, a psychiatrist, and I'm here from New York with my grandson, Jackie, for the weekend. His mother is my daughter, Kayla Covo, and you can call her right now to verify." He gave Kayla's phone number, and the white officer, smirking, jotted it down in a small notebook. "This creep—August Sorel's his name—has had nothing to do with his son for years and years."

"And where is this Jackie right now?"

Nicky wrapped a handkerchief around his bleeding finger, then pointed in the direction Sorel had already pointed. "With my girlfriend, Helen Blanco, who is not an old woman."

"Yeah, yeah, right. So let's find them." He turned to his colleague. "Bobby Joe, radio that number into the station and have them check it out." Then the sergeant grabbed the combatants by the arm and ordered them to show him specifically where the boy and old woman sat. "But don't say a word when we get there. I do all the talking."

The set had just ended as they approached Helen and Jackie. The crowd of jazz fans—Helen and Jackie along with the rest—was standing and applauding. The sergeant pulled Sorel and Nicky in front of Helen. Helen immediately grabbed Jackie and held him close to her, their blanket on the ground before them.

"Miss ...?"

"Mrs. Blanco, officer. What's going on?"

"Young man," he said, kneeling down before Jackie so that they were at eye level. "Do you know either of these two men?"

The boy said nothing.

The sergeant waited a few seconds before trying again. In his second attempt, he obviously wanted to make his voice kinder. "I should have said hi first and introduced myself. I'm Sergeant Anthony." He extended his hand toward the young boy. "And you, I believe, are Jackie, is that right?"

The boy said nothing.

"What's his last name?" Anthony directed the question to Helen.

"Covo. What's going on?"

"He doesn't seem to want to talk."

Helen glanced at Nicky, and Anthony followed the glance. Nicky tried to keep his voice neutral and matter-of-fact. "He hasn't been talking much lately, as it turns out."

"Can't you see he's scared of them, officer?" pleaded Sorel.

"Jackie, is this your father?" He pointed to Sorel.

He shook his head. Definitely not.

"And is this ... white guy ... Grandpa?"

Jackie nodded uncertainly. Certainly it was his Grandpa, but he was confused by the racial adjective. Why was it important that Grandpa was a white guy?

"Jackie, I *am* your father. Your mom is Kayla. She's a concert pianist. We performed together. We're ..."

"That's enough, Sorel. Wait, let me get this ..." His radio had started to squawk. Nicky couldn't hear clearly, but it was obviously the precinct calling to bring Anthony up to date on the effort to call Kayla. "Got it. Okay, thanks." He carefully put his radio back into his utility belt. "Okay, shitheads. Excuse my language, son. By rights, I should bring you both in for disorderly conduct, but I have to keep an eye on this crowd, so I'll just warn you. I have your names and numbers and I will run—excuse me, Mrs.—a tire iron up your fat butts if you don't settle down and stay the hell away from each other." To Nicky, he continued, "His mom confirms your story, Mr. Covo .."

"That's Dr. Covo, please."

"Yeah, whatever. His mom says get him away from Sorel and call her as soon as you can. Good advice, although I'm not sure which one of you got the worst of it. Better get stitches in that finger, *Dr. Covo.*"

"I'm not going to let this end here, Covo," snarled Sorel.

Anthony turned to Sorel and snarled back at him. "You got a grievance, asshole, bring it to a judge." With that, Anthony left, pulling Sorel along with him. "Come with me to the medical tent, Fuckface. Looks like you're bleeding heavily from the ear."

THE MOUNT OF OLIVES IS INTACT

"No, Mother. With great respect for your learning, for everything that you have given me for so many years, I feel otherwise. That we're here talking to each other while Our Lord Jesus Christ has returned is ... a Divine mystery. We must accept it as such."

"But Scripture clearly says that the Mt. of Olives will be split in two at His coming. That hasn't happened. We would have heard about it."

"I know well the verses in Zechariah to which you refer. Nor are the nations obviously aligned against Jerusalem, nor has Jesus come down to us as He was when He ascended to heaven, but that tells me only that we might not have understood these verses correctly. Nor are other things happening that the Scripture promises will happen, but ..."

"Our glorious Church has interpreted these verses in the same way since it was created. We will know for sure when our Lord returns. It will not be a mystery, Divine or otherwise. And it is completely against our tradition to think of Jesus returning as a child. *Eleusitai on tropon.* He will return exactly in the manner in which He departed. He must."

Theodora knew that the dream had been sent to her by God Himself. She felt called to announce to the abbess—if not to the whole world—that Christ had returned. If God wanted Jesus to return as a child, God's will would be done, and yet, inevitably,

Fevronia's emphatic rejection of her vision did give her pause. If she failed to convince her Mother in Christ, the person to whom she was closest in the entire world, how could she convince anyone else? She did not to want to be castigated as a fraud or as sadly unbalanced. And yet, to know of Christ's return and say nothing? That was unthinkable as well. But the time was obviously not right.

"Fine, Mother. I hear you. Perhaps I have not understood my dream clearly enough. I will pray for more guidance. I will say nothing to anyone else of what I have seen, the message I feel God has sent to me, at least until we can confer further. I pray to the Lord Jesus Christ to forgive me, a sinner."

With that, Theodora quickly returned to her cell. She dropped to her knees at the side of her cot, put her head down on the thin mattress, and cried, ending her prayer tired, upset, and confused.

WHY ARE YOU CRYING?

Nicky found a phone booth and asked Helen to take Jackie off for a snack at a nearby corn-on-the-cob stand while he tried to reach his daughter. Kayla picked up even before the first ring ended. He explained briefly what had happened, at first leaving out the fight, but upon Kayla's close questioning, he explained again in more detail and more honesty.

"I don't believe it. I mean, I have to believe it, Dad, but shit."

"The damnedest thing. How could anyone have predicted Sorel would be here too and run into us and ..."

"And be such a prick."

"Well, that I could have predicted. He called me a kike, too, would you believe it? A great guy you ended up ..."

"Stop it, Dad. Can I talk to Jackie? How's he taking this?"

Nicky signaled for Helen to bring Jackie over to the phone and handed the receiver to the boy. "It's *Ima*, Jackie. Say something to her."

At first, Jackie held the phone as if it might explode and didn't put it to his head. Nicky took the phone from his hand and guided it to where it needed to be.

"Hello? *Ima*?" Nicky couldn't hear Kayla's side of the conversation, but didn't need to hear to understand what she would be saying. "I'm alright," said Jackie after listening for a few seconds. Then he listened more, shook his head briefly, and handed the phone back to Nicky. Jackie turned to Helen and wrapped his arms tightly around her torso. Helen kissed the top of Jackie's head.

"What did you tell him, Kayla?" asked Nicky. "He seemed shaken when he gave me back the phone."

"Tell him? That I loved him, I wanted him to stay very close to you and Helen, and you needed to bring him back immediately."

"Here we are, helping Jackie get his bearings, and of all things. I hope this doesn't reverse his progress. He's talking a bit, but now could keep seeing himself grilled by the cop, keep seeing two angry bleeding men glaring at each other. I'm supposed to be making things better, not worse."

"Look, Dad. Get home as quickly as you can. We'll talk then. And make sure you get someone to look at your finger. Don't be that fool of a doctor who's his own patient."

"It will be okay."

He hung up and saw Helen and Jackie still hugging. He joined them in a three-way. Helen's eyes were teared up.

"Why are you crying?"

"I don't know."

"Let's get to the hotel, call the airlines, and beat it out of New Orleans. And, let's keep our eyes open for Sorel. Nothing he did now would surprise me."

They each took one of Jackie's hands and made their way toward the Fair Grounds exit. Jackie's walk was too sluggish for Nicky, however. Within a minute, he picked up his grandson and carried him, putting him down only when they reached Esplanade.

VULNERABLE

She tried futilely to pray to the Theotokos. When she closed her eyes as she repeated the Jesus Prayer, she could see only that remnant of her dream. She could picture the black man she knew to be Jesus; she could still smell the essence of rose emanating from His holy presence. She could still picture the warm embrace He had shared with her brother. She could still feel her overwhelming excitement and joy as He approached her. As she dwelled upon these memories, they seemed as fresh in her mind as they did when she'd awoken.

Fevronia, her Mother in Christ, had warned her the Devil can place dreams in one's mind and pointed out what she considered logical flaws in Theodora's belief that Jesus had returned in the form of Nicky's grandson. True, the Scriptures did very clearly say that the world as we know it would transform when Jesus Christ comes again, and, yes, such a transformation hadn't happened. If this was the Second Coming, why not? Would there now need to be a Third Coming?

Just the same, Theodora knew the Devil could place false logic in anyone's mind, including the mind of an abbess, including the mind of Abbess Fevronia. And why wouldn't the Devil want to discourage the belief that Jesus had returned in human form after His two millennia absence? Theodora had no less reason to distrust Fevronia's logic than she had to distrust her own beliefs. Indeed, there was more reason to distrust Fevronia's logic—no matter how well-intentioned—because Theodora had seen Whom she had seen and knew Him. If she was not prepared to believe when her Lord returned to her presence, then why had she spent her life praying for His return? She would never give up that belief.

But why Nicky's grandson? Why the biological great-great-grandson of a famous rabbi? That was a question neither logic nor Christian doctrine could answer.

Theodora got up slowly from her kneeling position to sit on her cot. The thought occurred to her to read from the writings of St. Basil the Great. As she recalled, he had written extensively on the concealed nature of divinity, once concluding that God was ultimately unknowable. If so, she thought, who could prove her wrong when she believed she'd seen God return, in the form of a black Jesus? She reached under her cot for her volume of *On the Holy Spirit.* As she picked it up, the three letters from Nicky, which she'd tucked inside the back cover, fell to the floor. One was opened; the letter had been read. The other two envelopes were still sealed. She pushed St. Basil's book aside, opened the most recently-arrived envelope, and read its letter. If she didn't respond, she worried, he'd never write again.

"My Dearest Sister, My Dearest Kal,

My heart grieves for my not having heard from you. Perhaps it's too hard for you to write or it goes against the rules of your monastery. Perhaps you no longer remember who you are, or were, the Jewish girl who was born and lived the first six years of her life in Salonika. Perhaps you no longer remember even that I came to visit. If you knew how painful that trip was for me, at least until I saw you again, maybe you'd ... maybe what? What difference would it make if you knew?

Still, I have to assume you are reading these letters, that you do remember and care, and that our communication—even limited as it is now—will be meaningful to you. I have to believe you want to hear from me, that my words are reaching a sympathetic ear.

I won't make this long. The family news isn't good, and I don't want to belabor it. Jackie, my grandson, is having a very rough time. As I mentioned briefly during our visit, Jackie's mother, my daughter Kayla, suffers from a serious mental illness, and, I'm ashamed to say, once almost killed Jackie when she'd gone off her medications. The genetic cause for this, if there is one, relates to Kayla's mother, my deceased wife Adel, who suffered from the same malady. It doesn't seem to be coming from our side of the family.

Jackie's been in therapy—Kayla has been good about staying on her medications now, of course—but a recent episode with my son, the main father figure in Jackie's life, has set him back. They got into a scuffle, nothing that doesn't happen occasionally in every household, but Jackie's a particularly vulnerable child. Now, he won't talk to anyone, won't utter a sound. The therapist was useless. Helen and I decided we're going to take him for a long weekend to New Orleans—a city in the United States known for jazz music—and see if that helps to get him talking again. Our idea is to get him out of the house, into motion, so to speak. Find him some fancy clarinetists to watch, inspire him to practice more, although he needs little inspiration. He loves his clarinet.

Why am I telling you all this? The situation with Jackie has been pressing on my mind. I know you were voluntarily mute yourself, for decades. I imagine the muteness became so much a part of your nature that you quite forgot how to speak. Although I'm not seeking the kind of advice one might seek from a fellow sufferer, I still feel you might understand Jackie, that you have at least that much in common, the stubbornness to remain silent in a world of speakers. I hope you will write back and share your thoughts.

May this letter find you in continued good health and spirits. May it be the letter that prompts you to write back. If you don't want to write, have Abbess Fevronia place a collect person-to-person call to me and put you on the line. Beg her, if you have to.

All my love,
Your brother, Nicky"

Theodora consulted the dictionary in the monastery's small library and read the letter three times before she thought she understood it all. She'd not heard about the problems of Nicky's daughter, only that he felt he'd not been a good enough father. She'd not realized there were problems with Jackie.

It troubled her that she hadn't read the letter sooner. Upon their arrival, Nicky's letters had been an intrusion. Now, she began to see what might have been lost by her shunting them aside.

Where was she when Jesus needed her? The world was attacking Jesus all over again, and no one but her knew He was there.

TWO HARD RAPS

The flights out of New Orleans that evening were all booked, and, although the three of them could have waited stand-by, Nicky decided it would be best to get on the first open flight back to Newark, leaving at 11 am the next morning. Scared to venture out, even for a meal, they ordered room service and set Jackie up in front of the television watching *Jetsons: The Movie*. It was a double treat for Jackie, who was rarely allowed to watch television and rarely taken to the movies.

Sometime in the middle of the night—Nicky later thought about two in the morning, but Helen insisted it was directly at midnight—the loud banging of a police baton startled them awake. Two hard raps, followed by a man's voice, were loud enough to wake everyone on the floor.

"Nicky Covo. This is the New Orleans police. These papers have been issued by a judge of the Orleans Parish Civil District Court. You are to bring Jackie Covo before the court on Monday at 10 am." Indeed, papers were pushed under the door, even as Nicky was jumping up, ready to take a swing with his bandaged hand at whoever was creating the disturbance. This had to be Sorel's doing, but the voice didn't sound like Sorel's, and the sheer arrogance in the command did point to a police officer as its owner. Nicky looked through the spyhole and saw nothing. Then he cautiously opened the door to see someone in what might have been a police officer's uniform walking away down the hall.

"Hey! Come back here!"

The figure turned and stared at Nicky; in the darkness, Nicky couldn't tell whether the police officer, if that's what he really was, was black or white. Then the man said "Monday morning. And don't try to leave the state with him. We'll be watching." The man turned once more, walked a few steps, and entered the elevator.

Nicky closed the hotel room door to see Helen, in her bathrobe, sitting on Jackie's bed with her arms around him.

"What in *Hashem's* world is going on, Nicky?"

"I wish I knew."

But it didn't take long to figure out from the court papers, which looked official enough. Nicky read and explained in a voice he kept calm, although with difficulty. Sorel had filed a child custody action against Nicky and Kayla. Helen wasn't named. The complaint described Sorel as Jackie Covo's biological father, whose "visitation rights had been undermined by the concerted efforts of the Respondents" and that, Jackie having been found fortuitously in New Orleans, "the court had jurisdiction to determine an appropriate custody arrangement." Because of the likelihood they would leave Louisiana, an emergency hearing at the first available slot on Monday morning was sought and duly granted *ex parte*.

"You're kidding, right? Sorel can do this? Keep us in New Orleans? Have a judge ..." Helen was about to say "have a judge take Jackie away from us" when she followed Nicky's glance at the boy and caught herself. Of course, she could say no such thing, with Jackie listening closely. She held him all the more tightly and could feel him shivering, no doubt from fear, even as her own heart was beating wildly.

"Helen. Let's pack. We'll leave within the hour."

They sent Jackie into the bathroom to pee, wash, and brush his teeth. While he was there, Helen and Nicky planned their escape from New Orleans. They concluded that the best way to leave would be to take a taxi out of the city, rent a car in a suburb, and drive back to New Jersey. They could share the driving and make it, if they didn't stop to sleep or eat, in less than twenty-four hours. Nicky pulled a well-worn telephone directory from a drawer in his night table, found a place in Metarie that rented cars at any hour of the day, and made arrangements.

"How do we get out of here in a cab if the police are really watching?" asked Helen, frowning.

"We sure don't call the front desk. They obviously told our room number to the cop or whoever pretended to be a cop. So it looks like Sorel has a lot of connections in town. We just call the cab company, tell them to come around to the service entry, wait until we see it, and hop in. If the cops are going to follow us, they still have no reason to stop us until we're heading out of state."

"Well, we are."

"We're just going to Metarie to rent a car."

"With our suitcases."

"Well, yes, but ..."

"And they don't need a valid reason to stop us."

"No, I don't suppose they do, but it's our only ..."

With that, Jackie came out of the bathroom, saw Helen throwing clothes into a suitcase, and asked, reasonably, "Why are we leaving now? It's nighttime. Is it because of that bad man who woke us up?"

Nicky and Helen looked at each other, unsure for a moment who would explain. Then Helen ventured an answer. "Yes, Jackie."

"And this is because of the man at the JazzFest who said he was my father, isn't it?"

"Well, yes."

"I don't like him."

"Neither do we," said Nicky. "Now, let's get going."

THEN HE SCREAMED

At first, Theodora hoped she might see again in her dreams the vision of Jesus's return, and she hoped she might somehow see Him as well during her daily prayer. When a few days passed without further visions, she decided Jesus—now back on earth—might come to find her, but that He would do so only if she found an even more holy place than her cell or the church in which to pray. He might find her if she was completely alone, so that no one else would see Him until He was ready to reveal Himself. So Theodora resumed what had been her habit as a young girl, the habit of taking long walks in the hills, at times straying as far as five kilometers from the church. She knew every ridge, every copse of trees, every shadow as it played across her path.

It was mid-June, and her walks began again during a stretch of early summer weather splendid for the purpose. The warming afternoon sun commanded the sky, with few clouds, and humidity was low. Without telling anyone where she was going, Theodora hiked well beyond the monastery's boundaries, always watching carefully in case she should catch a glimpse of Him. She listened to hear His voice behind the high sweet whistling of warblers, the peeping of the red-backed shrike, the occasional screech of an eagle, and the rustling of wind in the trees. His voice would guide her to where He was waiting to be discovered.

During these walks, she said the Jesus Prayer, fingering her prayer rope, and often felt closer to Jesus, even though she knew Jackie—now only six or seven years old, she couldn't recall—was certainly in America with her brother's family. The seeming conflict between that reality and the expectation she would meet the older Jesus of her dream didn't in the least trouble her. Jesus could be in as many places at the same time as He wanted. He was God, after all.

Walking back to the monastery at the end of each pilgrimage, disappointed that Jesus had not made Himself known to her again, but resolved to continue searching for Him, or be found by Him, she circled around to the *Microdermis* and worked her way to the general area where the monks had to have been buried. Invariably, she tried to sense the exact location of their grave, but without success.

A week passed in this way since Theodora's last conversation with Fevronia about Jesus and the possibility that the Devil had planted a false vision of Him into her dream. During the week, as the energy and length of her walks increased, the urgency Theodora felt about needing to tell the world of Jesus's return decreased. Then, one night in late June, just as Theodora began thinking about discontinuing the walks—it was starting to get uncomfortably hot in the afternoons and she had begun to despair whether the walks were the right way to see Him—she dreamt again.

Theodora was in a large city somewhere, in a room looking out over tall buildings, with Nicky, Jackie, and an older, frail woman she didn't recognize., a woman she sensed was meaningful to her in a way she couldn't quite understand. The woman was worried, afraid, trying to explain a life-threatening situation. Then the woman inexplicably became the Theotokos herself, taking on Her otherworldly orange glow. The Theotokos addressed Theodora, asking her for some incredibly important action, but Theodora couldn't hear well enough to make out the words, could not understand what she was being asked. Even without comprehending the specific words, Theodora gradually realized that the Theotokos was extremely anxious about Jackie's wellbeing, the wellbeing of Her son, Jesus.

The Jackie in this dream wasn't the tall young man of Theodora's earlier dream; He hadn't grown up yet. Nor was He fully Jesus yet, but she knew His complete transformation to Jesus would occur in due course. Sensing His holiness, she dropped to her knees in front of Him, bowed low to touch her forehead to the floor, and knew that Christ the Lord had come back to save humanity.

Then she lifted her head, still kneeling, and saw that the Theotokos had vanished. The boy approached her. Once again, as in her earlier dream, she caught the fragrance of roses, which strengthened the nearer He got. She thought: Will He smile at me? Will He give me His blessing? But how could He, when he wasn't fully Jesus? He was but a child. She sensed that He was uncertain about his own role in her dream, uncertain about her in particular, and perhaps even a bit scared by her presence. Yet, he stepped toward her, first smiling and then not smiling. The look on Jesus's face—no, really Jackie's face—betrayed an awful pain.

He opened his mouth, and His tongue fell out on the floor in front of her. Then He screamed.

AN UNCOMFORTABLE SECOND

Kayla thought first she might lose her mind, then realized ruefully that many would say she'd lost her mind years before when she'd been diagnosed with schizophrenia. How does one lose again what had been lost before? But losing one's mind was a cliché, a way to speak for those who didn't understand extreme emotional upset or severe mental illness. It was a way to pretend that the lost mind might still be found hiding somewhere and returned, no more the worse for wear, to its owner. It was the response sane people had to those whose actions and thoughts were grossly out of place.

She strode purposefully along on her daily morning hike, mulling over the situation, tormenting herself with doubts and self-recrimination. Breathing heavily, she sweated inside the long grey workout pants and long-sleeved sweatshirt she favored for exercise. She had made up her mind years before: the more she sweated the fewer pounds she'd gain. The exchange was well worth it.

It had been an almost fatal mistake letting Jackie go to New Orleans with Dad and Helen. Jackie might well have been kidnapped. Indeed, if Dad were to be caught, if custody had to be handed over to a court, it would amount to a kidnapping just the same, a kidnapping with the imprimatur of the legal system. Of course, she would have flown down immediately to fight such an action, even though she loathed the thought of once again getting onto a plane. But as things stood there was nothing she could do to help, nothing to do but wait until the next time they called. Nothing to do but pray.

The idea of Jackie being taken from her made her more than ill, as if the ground beneath her had fallen away. Jackie was her life. Without him, she'd have no reason to go on living. It was for Jackie and Jackie alone that she tried to make a home, investing so much energy in her composing, tolerating the sometimes bizarre behavior of her brother, who'd lovingly invited Jackie and her into his house.

And to lose Jackie to August would be the greatest injury and insult she could imagine. Clearly, August wanted to spite her, but why? She'd given her virginity and love to him. She'd given him every ounce of her performing genius, had taught him so much that he didn't understand about music despite his advantages in years and experience.

And to think that Dad and August had now come to blows. Dad was too old to be fighting anyone, let alone someone less than half his age.

Finishing her walk, she made her way to the shower. As she toweled herself off, she stepped on the bathroom scale to see with dismay that she'd gained a pound since she'd last weighed herself. Her annoyance at what her medications did to her body momentarily took her mind off the problem with Jackie, but when she encountered Max in the hallway on the way back to her bedroom she was reminded immediately of what—or who—had caused this calamity.

He stared at her for an uncomfortable second, looking as if he wanted to say something, then walked past her silently.

WHAT'S RACE?

For the first few hours of their trip, Jackie managed a fitful sleep in the back seat of the rental car driven by his grandfather. His head lay on Helen's lap. To help him relax, she'd gently rubbed his back. Now, her arm rested on his hip. Then he woke, needing badly to pee. Nicky got off the interstate in Meridian, found an open gas station at the Texaco Food Mart, and took Jackie into the bathroom. When they got back to the car, Helen had already bought two black coffees for herself and Nicky and a chocolate shake for Jackie and taken Nicky's place behind the wheel. Nicky sat in the front passenger seat, and Jackie sat behind him. They made sure his seatbelt was fastened properly before starting out again. It was just past five a.m.

"Why does this town give me the creeps, Helen?"

"You've heard of the Meridian race riots? Eighteen-seventies, I believe. So I had a client whose great-grandfather was killed here. Scores of black men, freedmen, people no longer slaves were murdered. It was ..." She stopped when Nicky gestured toward the back of the car, where Jackie appeared alert.

"I shouldn't have asked."

They both hoped Jackie hadn't been listening or, if he had, hadn't heard enough to become concerned, but their hopes vanished in the next second.

"What's a race riot, Grandpa?"

Nicky was of two minds about answering. The events of the past day were troubling enough, particularly for Jackie, such that he didn't want to add fear by explaining. He could have easily put Jackie off, told him to try to sleep again—the sky had not yet lightened with the approaching day—and ended the discussion. On the other hand, legitimate questions, even from children, needed honest if simple answers, and getting Jackie to talk was a positive end in itself, the very reason they'd made the trip to New Orleans. He glanced at Helen, who, while keeping her eyes on the road, nodded at him encouragingly. Of course. Helen believed keeping the bad things in life hidden made them much more powerful. He decided to answer as best he could.

"Sometimes people of different skin, some white, and some black, for example ..." What was it exactly he needed to say? He knew he'd started out poorly, avoiding the issue.

"What Grandpa means is this," Helen said. "In a race riot, bad white people attacked innocent black people and killed some of them."

"What's race?"

Having gotten Jackie's attention and piqued his curiosity, she continued. "It's a word people use to explain why some ... some people have one color skin and other people have a different color."

"Like *Ima* and Grandpa and you are white, and I'm black, and my father is black, right?"

"That sums it up. Many would say that your grandpa and Mr. Sorel, the man we saw, who is your father, are different races."

"What's murder?"

"Let me get this one, Helen," Nicky said, turning to face Jackie. "It's killing someone on purpose, just to be bad. It's killing someone, sometimes just for the sake of killing. It's what the Germans did to the Jews in the *Shoah*."

"Would someone murder my father because he's black?"

Helen and Nicky sighed simultaneously, neither sure who should attempt an answer or what honest answer they could give.

The conversation was helping them put more miles behind them, though. Nicky thought it was just like an inquisitive six-year-old to ask impossible questions. But he had to answer.

"Jackie, very probably not."

"But you punched my father, didn't you?"

"We did get into a fight, but sometimes people with different skin color get into fights and it has nothing to do with their color. And sometimes people with the same skin color get into fights."

There was a long pause. Helen leaned forward to catch a glimpse of Jackie in the rear-view mirror. He was quietly watching the guardrails of I-20 speed by. She wondered whether he was also contemplating how much of the truth he'd learned, and whether he should ask yet another question.

"I don't want any more of my milkshake, Grandpa. It's freezing my tongue. It's like my tongue is going to fall off!"

ON ONE CONDITION

Fevronia had always had misgivings about her obsession with Theodora, starting from the moment she felt Theodora's unnaturally warm touch on her skin, as they met for the first time and Theodora washed Fevronia's feet. The young girl who lived alone at the ruined monastery, the *koritsaki* waif who incessantly repeated the Jesus Prayer, carried about her the essence of something entirely holy, ethereal, and otherworldly.

Thinking about that encounter, as she often did, Fevronia saw unmistakably that she had been enthralled, had succumbed immediately into loving Theodora as if she were her own biological daughter. Fevronia became Theodora's mother, not only in the sense of a guiding abbess, but also as a mother needing to nourish and protect her child from all of life's possible misfortunes. Try as she might, Fevronia could not stop herself from feeling closer to Theodora—a nun only because of Fevronia's blessing—than to any of the others, who'd become nuns only after years of careful training and observation.

And yet, despite this unnatural closeness, or perhaps because of it, Fevronia had embarked upon a mission to learn Theodora's origins, a mission leading to her discovery of Dr. Covo and her virtually forcing him to visit the monastery. Yes, it was mostly because Fevronia wanted to satisfy her curiosity and to learn what Theodora had meant when she'd told her that the Theotokos brought her there with Her light and Her veil. But even as Dr. Covo was on his way to the monastery, just as Fevronia had hoped, she worried she'd made a great mistake, that only ruin could come from Theodora's reuniting with her brother.

The meeting of these siblings, who'd grown up together until the Nazis began to deport the Jews of Salonika to the death camps, had gone reasonably well, or so she'd thought at the time. Fevronia had learned what she wanted to learn: the Theotokos had indeed miraculously saved Theodora (whose name had been Kal) and her brother from certain death. Dr. Covo confirmed these events in a sworn affidavit as well, which she shared with the Metropolitan and others in the church hierarchy. They had been duly impressed, praising Fevronia for nurturing Theodora and making her a nun. Although Fevronia would very unlikely live to see the day when the Church made Theodora a saint—she shuddered at the thought that Theodora might die before her—she hoped in due course such would happen.

In the weeks after Dr. Covo's visit, there had been slight changes in Theodora that Fevronia felt were good. Theodora began to talk more and, in doing so, rediscovered part of her Jewish roots. She'd remembered a song her family had sung at Pentecost, what Theodora called *Shavuot*. And she'd remembered that story of Rav Huna, who had been saved from ruin by a miracle when he'd repented of his sins. The new Theodora, if that was an appropriate term, seemed even more energetic in her pursuit of God.

But on the morning Theodora collapsed when she tried to see where the monks' bodies lay buried, at the instant Theodora crazily envisioned herself as their murderer, Fevronia knew that the reunion with Dr. Covo had been a mistake. This realization was painful for Fevronia; the Theotokos, who visited Fevronia one night in her cell before Dr. Covo's visit, had counseled Fevronia otherwise, assuring her that she had been doing God's will. In light of later events, Fevronia knew it couldn't have been so.

It was not that Fevronia thought the Theotokos had deceived her. The Theotokos had been sincere, and perhaps it had in fact been God's will at the time. But God had changed His mind, Fevronia surmised, or the Devil had gotten in the way of God's will. Perhaps the Devil had used Dr. Covo as his agent. However it had occurred, they were now on a downward course. Theodora's conviction that Jesus had returned to this world as Dr. Covo's grandson was just the next element of an impending disaster. It was exactly the kind of delusion the Devil would spread.

Fevronia was sorrowfully pondering the situation at the conclusion of *Orthros* when Theodora put her hand gently on Fevronia's arm, indicating the abbess should follow her. Fevronia did so as if she knew exactly what was going to happen. Outside, Theodora led Fevronia to the first bench on the path that ascended to the winery. They sat and watched the early morning mist rise silently into the air over the vineyard. Fevronia waited, sure Theodora would speak when she was ready. The summer sun was not yet high enough to reach them over the nearby cluster of pines. They might have sat for ten or fifteen minutes; as the silence stretched, Fevronia bowed her head in prayer. "Help me, O Lord, to be strong. Beloved Christ, be merciful to me and to my charges and to my dearest Theodora."

Finally, Theodora did speak, almost breathlessly. "Mother, I came to ask you for a blessing, a most urgent blessing."

"Please then ask, my child."

"I want your blessing to go to America and see Jesus."

It was an extraordinary request and yet, once Fevronia heard it, she knew it was what she'd feared most and what she'd known all along would happen. A blessing to return to her brother. Dr. Covo had certainly done all he could to urge Theodora to return with him and his girlfriend when they visited. Theodora had shown no interest then in going, but the seed had been planted. Now the seed had sprouted, and Theodora's memories of her childhood had watered and cultivated the seedling. True, the request was couched in terms of wanting to see Jesus, whom Theodora imagined was Dr. Covo's grandson, but that was just a ruse. Perhaps the whole story of the dream was part of the ruse, a way that Theodora could argue that going to America was in fact a service to their Orthodox faith.

"What you mean, dear child, is that you want to return to your brother." Fevronia tried to sound sympathetic and understanding, but worried her words would be interpreted otherwise. "Which I fully understand," she added after a moment. "But his grandson isn't Jesus."

"He is. I know it."

"When Jesus returns to us, there will be an unmistakable flash of lighting, from east to west, as it states in Matthew. ἡ ἀστραπὴ ἐξέρχεται ἀπὸ ἀνατολῶν." (*Hé astrapé exerchetai apó anatolón*)

"I have seen that lightning in the message from God."

"There has been no such lightning in our world."

So there they sat, fundamentally at odds over what should have been obvious to both if it was true. Fevronia had tried to explain that, upon Jesus's return, the entire world would know, that His return wouldn't be perceived by just one person, albeit a devout nun in a monastery, one who'd shared in a miracle with the Theotokos. But Theodora was adamant. Fevronia saw that Theodora believed fully in her vision, as much as she believed anything. It had been wrong of Fevronia to think Theodora was lying. Her distrust of Theodora's sincerity would be another sin for Fevronia to confess.

"Theodora, if I grant you this blessing, you will go to America and never return to the monastery. You might deny it now, but I feel it strongly, that the Holy Monastery of St. Vlassios will suffer a grievous loss. The Devil will use all his power to convince you that life in America would be better for you. He will trick you with all the material things that America and your brother can offer."

It horrified Theodora to realize Fevronia had so little faith in her. Had she not devoted her entire life to prayer, as the Theotokos had asked her to, so that she might be saved? She turned in shock to look into Fevronia's eyes. Was this her true mother, this old woman blind to her daughter's needs and sincerity? Who doubted her daughter's vision? She felt great disappointment, sensing she wouldn't receive the blessing she'd asked for and without which she would never leave. She imagined herself in the years to come, struggling to continue her devotion while knowing that Fevronia had not given her the chance for an even greater experience, to be eyewitness to Jesus's return. And then the woman she looked at, into whose grey-blue eyes she stared, became her beloved true mother once again.

"And yet .."

"What, Mother?"

"You have my blessing, Theodora, on one important condition."

"And that is?"

"I shall go with you, to be able to look after you and, once you have done what you've set out to do, to make sure you return here."

"Then it is settled, Mother."

MISCALCULATIONS

Fevronia had not carefully thought through the condition she'd set—accompanying Theodora to America—and she immediately regretted her lapse of judgment. She could easily have denied the blessing. But when she'd given Theodora her blessing, subject to that one major condition, her action had made sense.

Theodora vanishing in America would be as bad as losing a real child to a deadly disease. If Theodora disappeared back into her brother's family, she would be rejecting her calling and her promise to the Theotokos. And it would be the worst imaginable betrayal of Fevronia herself. It would mean that the decades Fevronia had looked after Theodora and nurtured her in their faith would have been for naught. It would mean that Fevronia had grievously erred when she pronounced Theodora a nun at their first meeting. And so it had seemed that the best way to prevent this calamity was to offer the blessing in exchange for the promise that Fevronia be at Theodora's side every step of the way.

Fevronia kicked herself mentally for her miscalculations, her foolish assumption that Theodora would reject the condition. Fevronia had told Theodora squarely and without reservation that she couldn't have seen Jesus, that Jesus couldn't possibly be embodied in Dr. Covo's grandson or anyone else. With that rejection, Fevronia was sure Theodora would be unable to tolerate Fevronia's presence on her proposed pilgrimage. Fevronia castigated herself now for not seeing what she should have seen, that her offer gave Theodora the opportunity to prove to Fevronia that Theodora had been correct all along, that Jesus was now indeed living among other human beings again. Now, Fevronia realized she'd committed herself to becoming a witness either for or against Theodora's vision.

The only hope was for Fevronia to convince Theodora in America, face to face with Jackie, that she'd been wrong.

PERSON-TO-PERSON COLLECT

It had been as unpleasant a night as Nicky and Helen had ever spent together in one bed. They'd wanted to sleep immediately upon their arrival at about 1 am on that Tuesday morning, bedraggled, hungry, confused, but they'd been kept up for another two hours, first by helping Kayla and Max get Jackie fed, bathed, and to bed, and second by explaining to Kayla and Max over and over again all that had transpired since they'd taken Jackie to New Orleans. They handed the court papers back and forth, arguing about what power a Louisiana court might have in New Jersey, whom Kayla should call for legal advice, and whether Jackie was recovering from his difficulties. Every discussion led to irritation and disagreement, which they struggled to contain in low voices lest Jackie be woken up and scared all the more.

When Nicky and Helen had finally made it to the spare bedroom, the one they regularly used when visiting from New York, Nicky tried to be affectionate with Helen in a way that often led to sex. She pushed him away. It seemed to Nicky that everyone was against him, even his lover. A more patient and perhaps more understanding person than Nicky might have laughed it off, but Nicky felt little like laughter. Rather, he muttered "damn it all" under his breath, but not so much under his breath that Helen couldn't hear, and she took offense. She sat abruptly and turned on her lamp, unwilling to let the matter rest.

"Listen. I won't stand for that kind of behavior, not from you and not from anyone. If I'm not in the mood—and *Hashem* knows I've never been so tired—I'm not in the mood. Grow up."

Now Nicky himself sat and turned on his lamp, seething. His fatigue had almost overwhelmed his self-restraint. He counted silently to ten, then twenty, then thirty, before he spoke. "I just thought ... You know, we're both so tense, it would help us ..."

"That's the worst excuse I've ever heard. That's not what lovemaking is supposed to be about. If you want that kind of release, just use the bathroom and do it yourself. I need to sleep. And don't ever mutter to me like that again." She shut off her light, got out of bed, and for a second Nicky feared she'd find another place to sleep, but she left only to use the hallway bathroom and returned. In the darkened room, he lay facing away from her and started to list in his mind all the ways he'd been tormented in the last two days. Sleep wasn't possible for hours.

When they were both awake much later that morning, he tried to apologize, but Helen acted at first as if she hadn't heard him. He'd been forced to repeat, carefully and directly to her face, "I'm sorry, Helen. I was in the wrong," before she would hug him again. They had just finished getting dressed, and Nicky thought for an instant that it was still early enough to undress again when they heard Kayla's excited voice yelling from downstairs. A long-distance operator was on the phone from Greece—how had they not heard the phone ring?—asking for Dr. Covo.

He rushed down, grabbed the phone from his startled daughter, and announced himself. Yes, he would accept the charges. In a few seconds, his party was on the line.

"Dr. Covo, this is Abbess Fevronia ..." She spoke in her solid English, even though she knew well that her Greek would be equally understandable.

"Is Kal ... is Sister Theodora all right?"

"That's why I'm calling. There's nothing physically wrong with her. But she urgently wants to visit you and your family in America ..."

"What?"

"And I'm calling to see if we can make arrangements. But I'm also calling to say that I'm not sure it's a very good idea." She waited for his response, certain she'd confused him.

"Whatever are you talking about? We would love to see her. Coming here! I never thought ..."

"How is your grandson, Dr. Covo? This trip has everything to do about him. His name is Jackie?"

So Kal had read his letters after all, he thought. "Jackie, yes. He's had some problems recently, as I've written to my sister, but surely you know that already. I think he's ..." He paused, uncertain how much he should reveal. Was it anyone else's business outside the family that Sorel had threatened, had actually attempted, to wrest custody of Jackie from Kayla? He thought not. Yet, shouldn't Kal herself know? He'd told her a bit about Jackie's issues. Whatever he told Kal he assumed would eventually be known by the abbess, if not the other nuns at the monastery.

"Yes?" A hint of impatience colored the abbess's voice.

"We've had a rough couple of days recently, but I think he'll be all right. Why do you say that this trip concerns Jackie? Kal ... Sister Theodora has never met him."

"That is something I feel Sister Theodora should explain to you. I'm at a loss myself to explain it."

"Is she there? Can you put her on?"

"Please to hold."

He overheard some background discussion in Greek, but couldn't make out the words. In a few seconds, however, he heard his sister's voice clearly, if frail and uncertain, in Greek.

"Nicky ... Are you with Jackie? How is he?"

"Well, beyond what I told you in my letter, Jackie's been riding in a car for almost twenty-four hours, with Helen and me, trying to get away from his father. His father who wants to kidnap him." It wasn't accurate from a legal point of view, although it was certainly accurate emotionally. Nicky had just felt the need to explain why

Jackie had suffered a rough couple of days and immediately felt he'd chosen the wrong words when he heard Kal's gasp.

"Kidnap! That can't be!"

"We've dodged the threat for now. But, Kal, I know I wrote to you about him, the difficulty with muteness, but that was long ago. Why now your sudden concern? If that's what you are concerned about? Is this why you now want to visit? Of course, you're ..."

"I saw Jackie as an adult, Nicky."

"You saw?"

"A vision from God."

Of course, Nicky thought, how could it have been otherwise? "And in this vision ...?"

"I know you're going to reject what I'm telling you, Nicky, but please listen. Please believe me. I'm serious. Our Lord Jesus Christ has come back to our world. He's your grandson."

MISSING THE FOREST

"Is that the most incredible thing you ever heard?" Nicky asked.

Nicky had just finished recounting the conversation after checking that Jackie was still asleep. The news that Kayla's Aunt Kal would actually leave the monastery and visit them in New Jersey was astounding enough in itself. From the moment that Kayla heard that she had an aunt who'd survived the Holocaust and lived as a nun in a Greek monastery, she'd hoped someday to meet this incredible woman she was named after. It was only a matter of finding the right time to visit Greece and assure herself she could maintain absolute *kashrut* as well as her strict observance of *Shabbat*. She would have felt the same even if this Sister Theodora, as Aunt Kal was now known, had not been saved by the Virgin Mary.

But as Nicky briefly explained Theodora's plan to visit, accompanied by the monastery's abbess no less—and she'd overheard him say to the abbess in English that he would happily pay both their expenses—Kayla now saw this first meeting in a different light. She supposed that she'd have to be the hostess and felt a pang of anxiety as to how she could accommodate the two women, deal with an aunt who spoke only Greek, and continue to manage her life with the interruptions their visit would inevitably bring.

As Nicky explained further, though, her anxiety immediately grew into utter confusion, dismay, and horror. The object of Theodora's trip was meeting Jackie, who clearly had enough trouble in his life. And it wasn't just because Jackie was a blood relative she'd never laid eyes on; that also applied to Max and Kayla herself. It was because Theodora believed that Jackie was Jesus, the Messiah, the Son of God.

"It's more than incredible, Dad. It's downright scary. How could Aunt Kal possibly think that?" Kayla had wanted to accuse her aunt of being downright crazy, but caught herself. She closed her eyes and thought for seconds. "I mean, is that really possible in the Orthodox Christian religion?"

"I have no idea, and I wish I had someone I was close to, someone knowledgeable, I could talk to about this. But, whether it's kosher under Christianity or not, Kal sounds convinced beyond any doubt. She told me just now it was her dream. Στο όνειρό μου. (*Eto oneiro mou.*) In my dream, she said, από τον ίδιο τον Θεό (*apo ton idio ton Theo*), from God Himself. She believes God planted this vision in her. For some unknown purpose that she will discover if she comes."

The four sat for a long moment, each lost in their own thoughts.

The Kayla broke the silence. "But, Dad, you invited them here. You think they should stay in my house? Hasn't Jackie had enough t-t-trouble without some ..." Kayla stumbled, unable to complete her question. Even as she spoke, she knew that she was the last person who should denigrate anyone suffering from a mental illness—and it seemed likely that's what was happening to Aunt Kal—nor could she with justice object to religious fervor, even when such fervor seemed aberrant. That's what many Jews felt of the *Chassidim*.

Nicky stared at his daughter. "I haven't figured out yet where they should stay, Kayla. I just got off the phone. This is way unexpected for me too."

Helen said "Look, Kayla, this house has only one extra bedroom anyway. Unless the abbess and Kal want to sleep in the same bedroom, I'm sure this house isn't where they'll stay and it shouldn't be where they'll stay. We'll find a short-term rental apartment, if we need to, but why for *Hashem*'s sake wouldn't they stay in your apartment, Nicky? You have the two extra bedrooms."

"Well ..."

"And, for that matter, they could stay with me. I have the whole house in which David and I raised three children. Plenty of room. And that makes actually more sense than Manhattan, if it's Jackie your sister really wants to see. My house is a lot closer to West Orange than your apartment."

"But then if you were taking care of them, Helen, you wouldn't be in the city with me, so maybe we shouldn't rush into any plans just yet. We need more time to think."

"Dad, please," Kayla interjected. "You're entirely missing the forest. They're coming because they think Jackie is Jesus. How can we possible even let them meet him, if that's what they think? Golly. Talk about a messed up kid."

Kayla had the sensation that everything important to her life was being ripped away again. There was nothing more important to her than Jackie's welfare, and the people who should've seen that immediately, the people she was talking to in a state of shock, were ignoring what could happen to Jackie.

"Abbess Fevronia doesn't think that at all, that Jackie's Jesus. She's appalled. Only Sister Theodora—Kal—believes that. Fevronia thinks that Theodora has lost touch with reality, from what I gather, but she believes that meeting Jackie will help set Theodora straight."

"Wonderful. And that's who you want to bring into contact with Jackie. Jesus H. Christ." The words sprang from Kayla's lips before she could think to repress them.

Jackie had quietly gotten up and crept downstairs to listen to the adults.

"Who's Jesus?" he asked.

WHICH MISTAKE?

They looked at each other guiltily, as if the young boy had caught them misbehaving. Then Kayla and Nicky started to talk at the same time, stopped in deference to each other, again spoke simultaneously, and immediately fell silent.

"He's ..." This was Nicky, starting an explanation without knowing exactly where he wanted to go with it.

"Jackie ..." And this was Kayla, intending to divert the question, but unsure whether she could.

Helen stepped into the breach. "May I ...?" No one stopped her, so she continued, first reaching out to Jackie, hugging him tightly, then pulling him up on the sofa next to her. "Well, it's like this, Jackie. Jesus was a man who lived very long ago in Israel. He was Jewish, but Christians believe that Jesus was God. There are many Christian families on your street, right?"

"The ones who put up Christmas lights every year? They're very pretty. Uncle Max and *Ima* and I go for a walk in the night to watch the lights. And I really like the big Santa balloon that's all lit up from inside." Jackie smiled at his recollection of the many houses—unlike his own—that sported bright, glowing, multi-colored ornaments.

"Yes. Exactly that. Your Christian neighbors—Christians all over the world—believe Jesus was God or, as some say, the son of God."

"Rabbi Beck teaches us that there is only one God. *Sh'ma Yisrael, Adoshem Elokenu, Adoshem Echad.*"

"Quite so. That's what Jewish people like your family and I believe."

Jackie thought for a few seconds, then turned to Kayla. "But, *Ima*. You said someone thinks I'm Jesus. I heard you. Someone who's coming to visit?"

Kayla drew in a big breath, glared at Nicky as if, by her looks, she could reverse what he'd set in motion. "Well. Let's not get ahead of ourselves. First thing is: We know you're Jackie. We're all certain you're Jackie Covo, and most importantly you know who you are. Right?"

"Jackie Covo."

"Good. So, it seems your relative, Grandpa's sister who lives in Greece, has made a mistake. We all make mistakes. She will come with a friend of hers, and when they're here, they will see obviously you're Jackie Covo, and not Jesus, and they'll all be very sorry they made a mistake, but we'll enjoy their visit just the same. Do you think you can help us tell them nicely they made a mistake?" Kayla glanced back at Nicky, this time without the scowl, to catch him nodding ever so slightly in agreement.

"Which mistake?"

"What do you mean?"

"Shouldn't Rabbi Beck tell them there's only one God? That God isn't a person? Rabbi Beck teaches us God can't be seen, doesn't he? And don't you always teach me that too?"

Kayla had a difficult moment at first in suppressing a laugh of pure joy. In the midst of all the family troubles revolving around him, most of which the almost-seven-year-old Jackie couldn't appreciate, here he was demonstrating much greater intelligence than she imagined he had. She'd always felt he was very smart, but his response to the disclosure that someone thought he was Jesus proved to her once again, as if more proof were needed, that she'd still underestimated him. And it wasn't only his intelligence that made her smile broadly but his profound allegiance to the central doctrine of Judaism. She moved to where Jackie still sat next to Helen and embraced him in a mammoth hug.

"You're so right, Jackie. But—listen—this is what Christian people believe, and it's not our job to try to tell them they're wrong."

"But why not?"

Nicky picked up the thread of the conversation after a moment of silence. "It's like this, Jackie. Whom do you believe was a greater clarinetist? Artie Shaw or Benny Goodman?"

"I like them both."

"But if you had to pick ..."

"Artie Shaw."

"Yet someone else," Nicky continued, "Uncle Max, for example, might believe that Benny Goodman was greater, right?"

Jackie glanced at Max, who said nothing, whose face was unreadable. He wasn't going to weigh in. "Well, if Uncle Max said that, he's wrong and I'm right."

"Fine. So you believe, but many people do say Benny Goodman was greater. If I'm not mistaken, most people. Now, my point is that you can never prove one way or the other. It's not something like the science experiments we do. Everyone can have his own opinion. So, the same with God. Some people—we Jews for example—will say that God can't be a person and believe that strongly and will always believe that, no matter what. And others, they're equally sure God *was* a person at one time whose name was Jesus. We just have to accept that we have different beliefs."

"All right," said Jackie, without enthusiasm.

"So ... do you understand we're not going to prove to our visitors that the man Jesus was just a man and they 're not going to prove to us that he was God?"

He shrugged his shoulders.

"It's only important that they know *you* are not Jesus. Got it?"

Another shrug.

Jackie looked from Nicky, to Kayla, to Helen, and finally to Max. "Hey Uncle Max. Let's go listen to the Artie Shaw CD I got for

Hannukah, and then you can find one of your Benny Goodman CDs, and then we can decide for sure. But I'm going to prove that Artie Shaw was better."

He smiled broadly, like the old Jackie that everyone had yearned to bring back into the family. Nicky and Helen said their goodbyes and headed to Helen's house for the night.

TEMPTATION

It was with enormous relief that Max returned to Jackie's room with him and listened to Artie Shaw and Benny Goodman. They started with Shaw's greatest hits. As the clarinet solo to "Stardust" began, Jackie sat on his unmade bed, pushing his back against the wall, and closed his eyes to better enjoy the music. Max sat in Jackie's desk chair and watched his nephew carefully, mulling over their relationship.

He loved Jackie as if Jackie was his son. Indeed, as much as he loved his two own children, as much as he tried to keep in contact with them across the country, he knew in his heart that he loved Jackie more. No, it wasn't fair to Joseph and Rosina that his emotions were so tied up with his nephew that, occasionally, he might have forgotten to make his Sunday evening calls to Seattle. But the chief architects of unfairness were their mother, who'd taken them away, and the New Jersey Family Court judges, who had allowed that to happen. And yet, that terrible loss had led to something even better in Max's life.

When Cathy abruptly moved out one Sunday afternoon as he golfed, when she abandoned him for another man, taking his children with her, never giving him a chance to say a proper goodbye to them, she'd also opened a door. Two months later, Kayla and then four-year-old Jackie moved in. And what was originally intended to be temporary became permanent. Max and Jackie had always had a friendly relationship, but when Jackie came to live with him, they bonded even more tightly. All the love that Max might have given his own boy and girl now came Jackie's way. If only Jackie could understand how much Max loved him.

But it wasn't only Jackie. Through mutual necessity, living with Kayla had immeasurably brightened his world. He'd always tried to protect her, to be an understanding and reliable resource for her, and the ability to have her close—as close as the next bedroom— gave new meaning and purpose to what he otherwise felt would have been a dull existence.

He had loved Cathy, or thought he did, but the way she treated him left him devastated. There were no other women he was remotely interested in. There were a couple of female paralegals and young associates at the law firm he found attractive, but he had no interest in messing around where he worked and, in any event, they were too classy for him. When Cathy had walked out, he'd had absolutely no idea of seeing other women. He felt himself a failure at the game of male-female relationships. Thus, Kayla's arrival and the concurrent need for him to help look after Jackie didn't hamper other plans he might have had. His home would be Kayla's home for as long as she wanted to stay.

Max and Jackie were unable to agree who was the better clarinetist the first time through the CDs, so they started a second round. The Shaw CD hadn't concluded—Shaw was dancing through the opening riff of "Temptation"—when Jackie ejected the CD and said, "Let's switch to Benny Goodman." Max handed him the *Legends* CD again, and in seconds they were listening to "Lady Be Good." They continued to listen for another half-hour, going back and forth between the two artists, until Kayla poked her head in and told them both it was bedtime.

"But *Ima*, we haven't decided who's better!"

"Well, decide now." She looked at Max and gestured "out" with her thumb.

Max said, "You know what, Jackie? We can't decide now. We should sleep on it. And tomorrow we should listen to more. What do you think?"

Jackie jumped off his bed, stopped the Goodman CD, then rummaged around the other CDs on the back of his desk. Not finding what he wanted, he opened a drawer crammed with pencils, pens, and scraps of paper. At its back, he came up with what he was looking for, a Doreen Ketchens CD. They had listened to it together. Max knew that she was the first black female band leader in New Orleans and a virtuoso clarinetist.

"I wanted to see her on our trip," Jackie said wistfully.

"Did you tell Grandpa and Helen?" Kayla asked.

"No. I wasn't talking much then."

"Well, tomorrow, after a good night's sleep, let's listen to her first and then the others. After we rest, our ears will be healthy and strong for more music. Good?"

"Okay, Uncle Max."

They said their goodnights. Both Max and Kayla hugged Jackie as they tucked him in. As they exited, Jackie said, "I love you, *Ima*. I love you, Uncle Max."

CHASIDUT

Max and Kayla returned to the first floor of their house without discussion, both understanding they needed to talk. Now, with Jackie put to bed and the older generation likewise having retired, it was time. Max poured himself a Scotch and an amaretto for Kayla. Kayla softly intoned the appropriate blessing—*Baruch atah Hashem, Elokaynu Melech Ha-Olam, she Ha-Kol Niyeh Bidvaro*—to God, who had brought everything into being, and they sat again in their living room, Kayla on the upholstered rocking chair, Max on the sofa, near enough to each other to clink glasses and say "*l'chaim.*"

"You heard what he said as we left, didn't you?" asked Max.

"I did. He's always loved you, Max, even when you've had difficulties. You know very well he loves you."

"I'm a sorry excuse for a father stand-in."

"You're precisely what he needs in his life. If you weren't around, if you weren't close to him and to me, I'd be a single mom and terrible at it."

Max sipped his drink and looked at his sister. She was wearing a long-sleeved gray cotton blouse, the top two buttons of which were open, and a flowing black skirt that reached to just above her ankles. She wore no jewelry save for her gold Star of David necklace, her prized possession, more precious to her than even her Steinway. The star itself was often concealed under Kayla's clothes, but on this evening it was visible. Then Max looked away quickly when he realized he had been staring at Kayla's chest, and, as he turned his head, Kayla tucked the star inside her shirt and fastened an additional button.

"I'm glad Jackie seems more normal and is talking, but I'm worried," Max said. "There's so much going on. August popping up in New Orleans, fighting with Dad, and now trying to get custody. Making ridiculous allegations against you."

"And how did he find out about what I almost did to Jackie ... what I actually did?"

"Who knows? You're a great mother, Kayla, and most of his allegations are pure B.S."

"We're safe now, aren't we? Legally at least? In New Jersey?"

"Maybe? What I know of custody disputes as a lawyer, and having been involved in my own case, tells me there aren't guarantees."

"Great."

"And, maybe worse is that Aunt Kal is bringing with her the delusion that Jackie is Jesus Christ. How bizarre is that? I'm sure she's a lovely nun, this Sister Theodora, but my instinct is that she'd have been better off staying in her cell, and we'd all be better off too without a religious fanatic on her way to completely confuse our ... boy."

Kayla focused on the pause preceding the end of Max's sentence. He wouldn't have been far off if he had said "our son." He was indeed her chosen partner in helping to raise Jackie. Then her thoughts turned to Max's disparagement of Sister Theodora. "It's unfair to call her a religious fanatic. You don't know her, Max. Maybe what's bizarre to you, to us, admittedly, is what *Hashem* wants to happen." She knew he didn't believe in *Hashem*, but at least he always showed respect for her own beliefs. "Putting aside what Sister Theodora believes, we should want to meet her. She's Dad's sister, *Baruch Hashem*. Our Aunt Kal. That she survived *Ha Shoa* and was found again is a miracle, whether you believe or don't believe."

"It's true. I would like to meet her. She's certainly had an effect on Dad. He's different, in a way I can't quite put my finger on, since he and Helen returned from Greece. Happier, for sure."

"That's undoubtedly Helen's influence more than anything else, their relationship, but yes."

"And he's told us that he hoped we'd meet Theodora, but it was always with the idea we'd make a family trip to Greece. Which I didn't believe for a minute would happen, by the way."

"Well, that problem's put aside for now. We'll meet her here."

"She won't be the first in the family to ..." Max stopped short, realizing he was about to point out that their family had a history of mental illness and that his sister, the woman he loved as a brother should, was the prime example.

"Be nuts? Thanks."

"I didn't mean ..."

"It's okay. It's what Mom always called herself. Well, Sister Theodora might be, for all we know, but it offends me when you assume that anyone with deep religious feelings is unbalanced. You think my devotion to *Chabad*, to observant Judaism, is just another symptom of schizophrenia, right?"

"No. I don't think that, and you know it. I've always told you that *Chasidut* has been your lifesaver, Kayla."

"And thus Sister Theodora's religious ideas can be saving her life right now, too, can't they?"

"I suppose so."

"Will you pour me another small one?" He took the glass from her, happy to have something to do, happier still for a pause in their conversation about religious observance and mental illness.

As Max departed for the kitchen, Kayla felt once again a pang of guilt for the imposition that she made on her brother's life. In the wake of Cathy's sudden departure and demand for a divorce, it had been Max who first broached the idea that Kayla and Jackie move in with him. He couldn't bear the idea of staying by himself in the house, nor did he want to leave. But if Max had not suggested the arrangement, Kayla felt confident she would have done so herself before long.

Living in the house with her brother had been the perfect setup for Kayla, but she realized within months that the arrangement would sorely interfere with Max's ability to strike up a relationship with another woman. She also felt uncomfortable at times with the looks that Max gave her. He had been acutely cognizant of her body since she was a teenage prodigy, required to dress in what her managers felt were sexy performance gowns. He'd told her then that he hated her being marketed as a sexy young girl as opposed to merely a brilliant virtuoso pianist. And now, she felt, he still looked at her that way, despite her always modest attire. Perhaps Kayla needed to consider other living arrangements, but every time the idea crossed her mind, the difficulties of finding a suitable home near the *Chabad*, paying for it, and moving seemed overwhelming.

"Here." He handed her another glass of amaretto and waited patiently while she repeated the blessing. "Would you do me a big favor, Kayla?"

After a soothing sip, she smiled and tilted her head to the side in a gesture of warmth that Max loved. "Sure. What can I do to please you, big brother?"

"Play the D-Minor prelude."

It delighted her to perform for Max her own music, one of her first compositions, the short but complicated piece she'd given him on his fourteenth birthday. She loved to perform for him even though—and most likely because—she was unable to perform publicly. She knew the piece by heart, knew how much Max loved it.

As she moved to the Steinway, warmed up with a few scales, and gave her soul to the music, she felt his eyes constantly on her. But these were not lecherous eyes, she decided, simply the caring, intelligent eyes of the person who was willing to devote his entire life to protect her and Jackie. They were the eyes of someone who'd battled ferociously to break the unfair yoke that her managers had placed on her, who'd fought to ensure that she would be fairly compensated. They were the eyes of the first person who'd realized how ill she was, who'd managed to coax from August the secret of where she'd been hiding in fear, who'd arrived at the West End *Chabad* with Dad to rescue her and bring her back into the family. She would play the prelude for him whenever he asked, with as much love as she had within her.

Listening to her play, Max marveled again at how much genius resided in his little sister. She would have continued with her amazing career as a concert pianist—rivaling the likes of Clara Schumann—had it not been for her illness. He thanked the fates, her lucky stars, *kismet*, everything that now enabled her to create the miraculous new music that she brought forth for others to perform.

As Kayla ended the prelude in that mysterious D-Major broken chord, she felt Max approach from behind, lightly grasp her shoulders, and kiss her on the top of the head.

"Thank you so much, Kayla."

She got up from the piano, turned and hugged him briefly, and said, "It's time for us to go to bed, too. I want to get up early and talk to Rabbi Beck before the minyan."

HISTRIONIC?

Nicky and Helen didn't say much on the drive from West Orange to Highland Park. Nicky was thinking how much he would rather they'd stayed the night in his Manhattan apartment, from where it would have been relatively easy for him to get to work. Staying at Helen's house meant he'd have to get up at five to beat the traffic and still would have an hour and a half drive if he was lucky as opposed to his normal forty-minute commute. But Helen had insisted she needed to get to her own home, something about her family, something about her not having spent enough time there lately. Nicky hadn't wanted to argue. He just accepted that the following morning would be difficult and decided not to talk. He turned his car radio to WQXR, and they listened to Bach's concerto for two violins. It had long been one of Nicky's favorites, and he hummed along. Finally, just as the concerto ended, they pulled into her driveway on Valentine Ave.

He turned off the ignition, but sat quietly as opposed to opening his door. He wanted Helen to understand how much he had been inconvenienced by needing to get her back to Highland Park that evening. The day after was a Friday, and he could have gotten her back the following afternoon in plenty of time for *Shabbat*. Before he could think of exactly how to phrase that complaint, she broke the silence.

"What's wrong, Nicky?"

"Thinking."

"About?"

"Why we couldn't have spent the night in Manhattan?"

"I told you. Naomi's going in for surgery tomorrow morning, and I want to be there with her."

"Yeah, but ..."

"But nothing! You want so much to be in Manhattan tonight? Go now." She jumped out of the car before Nicky could stop her, slammed the door, and marched into her house without a look back.

"*Gamoto!*"

He usually reserved his best Greek obscenities for when he was alone. On this occasion, "fuck!" was directed as much at himself as at Helen. He should have known not to make an issue of their staying in Highland Park one evening when he'd rather have been elsewhere. Shaking his head, he too left the car, walked to her front door, knocked, and waited thirty seconds. Nothing. He rang her doorbell and waited. Another thirty seconds. Still nothing. Now his anger turned more toward Helen. She was making a fool of him, a fool who her neighbors could see standing outside her house, begging to be let in. He turned to the left, half-expecting to see the old man who lived next to Helen poking his head out to see what was happening. But the neighbor's house was dark and quiet. He decided to give her one last chance and was about the press the doorbell again when the door opened and Helen stood before him with a mock uncertain look.

"Yes? Did you forget something here and you're wanting to pick it up now?"

"Helen, for God's sake, please let me in. I'm sorry."

"Do I know you?" Her sarcastic voice hurt him deeply. She was clearly tormenting him and having fun doing so. Well, maybe he deserved it.

"You have known me. In the Biblical sense."

"What a mistake."

"Okay, Helen, please stop this. I'm apologizing. I've been too self-centered."

"Hmm." She frowned, pretending to think deeply. "Well, in that case." She stood back and let him enter. Then he pulled her to him and tried to kiss her. She managed to turn her face away, but he gently turned it back and she finally gave in. That she would kiss him must mean that she'd forgiven him for his selfishness. Yet, she broke away and said, "Sit, and let's talk." She was dead serious.

They retreated to the sofa in her living room. He sat first, and Helen placed herself a few feet away, out of his reach. He tried to steel himself for whatever came and wondered what punishment he'd be expected to endure.

"Maybe there's been too much knowing in the Biblical sense."

"Why do ..."

"Wait. Let me finish, and then you can have your say. Yes, we're sleeping together, yes, I love you, but you seem to take that as a sign I shouldn't have my own life. If that's how you feel deep inside, that my interests, my family, my home here, all this, should be subservient to your convenience, then I think we ought to end it." She sighed deeply. "As painful as that would be for both of us. This has bothered me for weeks."

He waited, not wanting to interrupt, unsure if she had more to say or was merely pausing to regather steam. Best for him to let her get it out. He could play the quiet and attentive psychiatrist, waiting for the patient to continue, all the while carefully taking mental notes. And, indeed, in half a minute she took up where she'd left off.

"So, where we spend the night when we're together has become an issue," she continued, looking away at the family photograph that she always kept on the end table. Then she turned to him and held up a hand in a fist, with the thumb extended. "That's number one. But it's more than that, Nicky. It's ... how shall I say this ... that you're often completely absorbed by your family and its problems, which, I understand, are major problems." She extended a second finger. "As if you don't realize my own family has its problems, as if you're not concerned about my family's issues. For example, Naomi's hysterectomy, the possibility that she has uterine cancer." Again she paused, then turned back to look directly into his eyes. She extended a third finger. "If you loved me, if you truly loved me, wouldn't you be concerned? Wouldn't you be caring about my life and my family as if they were your own? As I try to care about your family?" She put her hand down.

Again Nicky waited, at first sure that these were rhetorical questions only. But no. She wanted answers. She turned again toward him and gestured as if ready to receive his response. What he wanted to say was that she was being histrionic, blowing up his *faux pas* into a much bigger issue than it needed to be. He was to the point of saying just that when he noticed that she'd begun to cry. Damn it, he thought. Her tears, as infrequent as they were, always had the same effect on him. They made him acutely aware of his own guilt. It was unfair that he was so susceptible to her crying, that she could manipulate his feelings so easily. And yet, it was part of her charm that she wouldn't hide her own emotions, that her feelings were so close to the surface they could so readily pour out of her eyes in the form of tears. In that sense, she wasn't intentionally manipulating him. He just felt manipulated.

"You're right, Helen. I have been way too focused on what's going on with Jackie, in particular, Jackie and Max, Jackie and Kayla, and yes I've not been thinking as I should about your own family's problems. I do care."

"That's it?"

"And I've not paid enough attention to your needs about … your house, your home in Highland Park, your need to be here more often."

"And?" She reached for tissues and blew her nose.

"And of course I'm terribly sorry. I'll make it up to you. I want to … change. May I hold you? Please?"

Why was he always needing to admit wrong to her and apologize? Why might almost anything he did make her cry? For a second, he was sure that she'd refuse to let him hold her, that she'd even get up from the sofa and show him to her door. But they did hold each other.

Now he was crying too. He didn't know why, but it seemed right and necessary.

AN OCEAN AWAY

It was in the book of Revelations, Fevronia was sure. Scripture made clear that nothing could be added. Nothing could be said about the Lord Jesus Christ that was not already written in the Bible. If so, Jesus couldn't have returned and be living on earth; such an event would have required a codicil to Scripture, impossible for believing Christians.

She borrowed a few books from the priest in Inousa, not explaining exactly why she was doing so, but, after only an hour of reading, she confirmed other information she'd gleaned haphazardly over the years.

A so-called vision of Jesus on earth—of course, it would allegedly have happened in America—in the nineteenth century led to the formation of Mormonism, a fake-Christian sect, but one with millions of adherents. A similar vision of Jesus later that century led to Seventh-Day Adventism, an even more aberrant cult. Both purported visionaries had drawn souls away from true Christianity, and now it appeared that Theodora might want to do the same unless she was disabused of her delusion. It galled Fevronia, contemplating this possibility, that Theodora's *ethos* would be enhanced by her miracle with the Theotokos, a miracle Fevronia herself had helped to document.

It took Fevronia a bit longer to get materials related to Black Hebrews from Andros, whom she made promise to keep her research secret. She learned that Black Hebrews—there were so many sects of them—were mostly African Americans who believed that blacks were the true Israelites of antiquity. Some of these sects had been deemed hate groups and black supremacists, some viewed all white people as devils. In one sect, the Nation of Yahweh, the founder claimed to be the Son of God. She wasn't sure if that meant he claimed also to be Jesus or a second son.

None of this applied directly to Jackie Covo, who after all was just a child. Seven years old? She didn't recall what Dr. Covo had told her. In any event, he was not an adult and wouldn't be making claims himself that he was Jesus. Nor would he be claiming to be the Son of God, or at least she hoped he wouldn't. Nor did she think that Jackie's father—again, Fevronia couldn't recall precisely—was a cult member. He wasn't even American, if she remembered rightly, but Caribbean, so there was no obvious tie-in to Black Hebrews.

She'd promised to call Dr. Covo again in two weeks, to discuss the exact timing of the trip to America, where she and Theodora would stay and where they might be able to pray. She also needed time to arrange for supervision of the monastery, ultimately deciding to appoint Sister Zoe as interim abbess. Any issues that Zoe couldn't easily resolve herself would be discussed by telephone. But Zoe had asked how long Fevronia and Theodora would remain in America. The honest answer was that Fevronia didn't know. She hoped it might be no more than a week; she would do everything in her power to return as soon as possible, but the trip might be as long as a month. Zoe was unaware of Theodora's strange new belief. Fevronia and Theodora had agreed that the purpose of the trip would stay a secret from the other nuns, at least until, in Theodora's view, she confirmed of the truth of her vision.

Meaningful prayer was impossible for Fevronia in this period, distracted as she was by knowing she'd be an ocean away from the monastery, a home from which she'd never been farther than fifty kilometers since 1953. She'd be abandoning the unfound grave of her brother as well.

Fevronia fully expected to return, but she knew as well she could not foresee God's agenda for her. Where He would direct her and where and when He might lead her to suffer and die were parts of her future not under her control.

PSALM 53

The following Sunday afternoon, Kayla decided she needed to talk to Rabbi Berenbaum, whom she hadn't seen in a year. Was Rabbi Berenbaum now the father of four children or five? He'd helped her return to observant Judaism, accepted her as a *ba'alat t'shuva*, helped her so much through her pregnancy and Jackie's infancy. He would understand what she was going through. Kayla called to set up the meeting.

After getting off the train at Penn Station, she decided to walk uptown to the *Chabad* house where she had lived for a year, as opposed to taking a cab. She needed the extra exercise. Although a cab would have been cooler, it wouldn't have been much faster given the traffic.

Kayla rang the buzzer of the West Side *Chabad*—a new door and lock had been installed since her last visit—and answered with her name to the voice squeaking over the speaker. The rabbi buzzed the door open. She went to his office, where they exchanged greetings and praised *Hashem* for allowing them to meet once more. She sat across his desk from him, as she had done so often. She declined the expected offer of a cup of coffee.

"Makes me too nervous these days, Rabbi."

"Well, yes. Coffee can do that. But I need it nonetheless to keep me going."

"First, let me say I'm very sorry I haven't been in touch as much as I should have lately. But I'm still very involved in the West Orange *Chabad*, with Rabbi Beck."

"Well, I've been busy, as you can imagine."

"Mazal Tov on your latest arrival."

"Kayla," he began, then hesitated, seeming to search carefully for words. "I'm distressed by what you told me about Jackie. And you. And what happened between you. It's hard to understand, so maybe you can ..." There, he drifted off.

Kayla had tried to prepare herself on her long walk for this awkward moment. How do you explain to anyone, but particularly to the rabbi who'd been so important in your life, how you almost killed your beloved child in a quagmire of hallucination, how you believed your son was the Devil? There would be no way to sugarcoat the episode, so she told the story as straightly as possible. She had looked at Jackie and not seen him as her son, but as evil incarnate. She'd brought this evil into the world, it was still part of her, and that part of Jackie which remained inside was killing her, devouring her from a base in her gut. She could feel the pain of his teeth gnawing on her ovaries. She had to stop it, him, the Devil, whatever it was.

So she tried to choke Jackie to death and would've succeeded had not Max found them. And, yes, she'd gone off her meds, unwisely. She chose not to explain that she'd stopped taking them in large part because Rabbi Beck had disparaged the use of any drugs in a woman who was truly *ba'alat t'shuva*.

Rabbi Berenbaum stared at her for a long while before responding. "I am so sorry, for both you and Jackie."

Then she told what she knew of her father's misadventures in New Orleans, with Jackie and his girlfriend in tow.

"So Sorel's back in the picture." He shook his head in dismay. "Unfortunate, to say the least. He should just stick with playing the violin."

"I fear what he might do now. How he might continue to try to get Jackie away from me."

"Let me know what happens. If I can be of help ... If Sarah can help ..."

"Sarah's got her hands full with the kids, I know. But you can help, Rabbi. Which is why I came."

"So tell me."

"Why does *Hashem* want me to have this horrible illness? I've often asked myself. I've asked you before, too, of course. But now, how much worse it's getting. To think that I saw my own son as the Devil?"

"I wish ..."

"That's not my only question. Why does *Hashem* want to bring August back into our lives? Why does He want my father and my son's father to fight each other? Why does He want to put me at risk for losing Jackie? I know you can't answer these questions with certainty, but you can guide me to a better understanding. Tell me what the sources say. What do I have to read?" She paused momentarily, then added, "I've been working hard on my Biblical Hebrew."

Berenbaum paused again, this time folding his hands together and cracking his knuckles as he tried to compose a decent answer. "When you said I couldn't answer with certainty, you should have said 'at all.' Some religions take the view that *Hashem* – they don't use that term of course—gives us *tsouris* to make us stronger people. Well, some Jews believe that too. I don't happen to. It's too convenient a solution. The fact is that the troubles *Hashem* sends our way often weaken us. Some may gain strength in facing down their troubles, but not everyone and maybe not even most of us."

"That's comforting," said Kayla, not intending to be ironic, but realizing after she spoke that she must have sounded that way. Berenbaum gave a short laugh and continued.

"The history of our people is one of repeated trouble and recovery from trouble. Slavery, then freedom and Pesach, to use the most obvious example. Desecration of the Temple, then the Maccabean victories and Chanukah. Destruction of the Temple, then the founding Jochanan ben Zakkai's academy at Yavneh, without which Judaism would not have survived. *Ha Shoa*, then the State of Israel."

Kayla thought of her murdered grandparents and aunt, and she thought of the other aunt, now known as Sister Theodora, lost to Judaism as if she were dead. "And yet the ledgers never add up, do they? The millions who perished in *Ha Shoa*, they're still dead. They still suffered."

"It's true."

"So what are you telling me?"

"As Jews, we have faith in the goodness of *Hashem's* plan. We've talked about this many times before, but it bears repeating."

"And if I go off my meds again and end up killing Jackie, what then? Still part of *Hashem's* plan?"

"You won't. If *Hashem* wanted you to kill Jackie, he would have been dead long ago. If that was *Hashem's* will, Max wouldn't have arrived to save Jackie and you."

Kayla barely suppressed a snigger. "If August takes Jackie from me? Also part of *Hashem's* plan?"

"He won't."

"How do you know, Rabbi?" She assumed he was telling her only what she wanted to hear. Then, she was ashamed of herself, because the rabbi had always been honest with her and was certainly not telling her only things that would make her happy. He was reminding her of tragic events in the history of her people. So how then did he know what August could or couldn't do?

"It's based on what you've told me over the years about Jackie's father. It's based on my experience with people. Those who are most self-centered, so full of themselves they often see other people merely as tools, are least likely to want the burden of taking care of children, even their own. I just sense that Sorel is being disagreeable for spite, but won't pursue what you fear. And, if he does pursue this, I trust you will find a way—*Hashem* will help you find a way—to defeat him."

"I wish I believed you or even half-believed, Rabbi. But I don't. I never thought he'd go to court and file custody papers, but he has."

Berenbaum nodded as if he'd anticipated exactly the argument that Kayla would raise. "Then let's do look at the sources, as you proposed. They might help you believe me."

"The sources didn't know about August or Jackie or child custody cases."

"I wouldn't be too sure. There's a mountain of material about the separation of children from their parents and reunification. Ah, well. You say you've kept up your study of Hebrew?"

"I've tried."

"Then look at this." He reached to his bookshelf for an edition of the Psalms in Hebrew and flipped through it until he found what he wanted. "*T'hillim* fifty-three, verse three." He handed it to Kayla, pointing. Kayla read it easily:

"*Yom i-rah, Ani alecha evtach.* Yes. I've read this psalm before. Let's see. In my day of fear, I trust in you. Trust in *Hashem*."

"Well done."

The rabbi seemed to have a satisfied look on his face, as if all the answers Kayla would ever need were contained within those five words. It looked as well as if he were waiting for her to acknowledge that her problems were now solved. She shrugged her shoulders. "That's it? It doesn't answer my questions, though, does it?"

"Well ..."

"In fact, Rabbi, with all respect to your learning, doesn't this almost tell me I should stop asking questions? That there's no point in asking questions, because there are no answers? That I *should* be in fear, and my fear will point me to *Hashem*, and my trust in *Hashem* will ... will what? Take away my fear? Teach me to live with that fear?"

"More the latter. Yes, the point is maybe not as miraculous as you'd hope, but learning how to live with the fears that constantly surround us is no small thing."

"This doesn't apply to my situation with Jackie," she said, shaking her head.

"Really, Kayla? Why not?"

She turned a page or two in the volume of *T'hillim* and, after a few seconds, read the verse she'd been looking for. "Verse 11. *Ma ya-asseh adam li?* What can man do to *me?* These are the words of David, before he became king. He's in personal danger here, true, but this has nothing to do with his son."

"But ..."

"He is not speaking as a parent here."

"Yes, but I ..."

"If I remember, David's first son Amnon was murdered by his half-brother, Absalom. Maybe Amnon deserved it, but David's trust in Hashem didn't prevent his family catastrophes. And Absalom went to war against David and was killed."

"But ..."

"And what else? Solomon, David's son, had his brother Adonijah executed. Quite a happy family that was. David should have asked 'What can my family do to itself?'"

Berenbaum looked away. There was really nothing else to say.

LET US PRAY

Only with great difficulty did Fevronia make the necessary arrangements for them to leave the monastery.

First, she'd been obliged to seek the blessing of the Metropolitan, with whom she hadn't been completely honest and thus not honest at all. It was important for Theodora to visit her brother, she'd explained, putting aside that it was her brother's grandson Theodora needed so desperately to meet. Fevronia had informed the Metropolitan months before about Dr. Covo, how he was Theodora's long-lost brother, how Theodora and the Theotokos had saved his life during the war. She'd given to the Metropolitan a copy of Dr. Covo's sworn affidavit attesting to these facts. For whatever reason, Fevronia told the Metropolitan, Theodora urgently wanted to see her brother again. Fevronia felt it was important to try to comply with Theodora's wishes, because, for all anyone knew, a trip to America might be the first step in another miracle of the Theotokos. And Fevronia's presence obviously would be necessary to record whatever happened, in honor of Christ the Lord and the Word of God.

But their meeting hadn't gone as smoothly as Fevronia hoped. After Fevronia finished her appeal, she waited in silence. The Metropolitan gazed questioningly into Fevronia's eyes until she looked away.

"Why aren't you telling me everything, Abbess? I sense there's much more to this. Am I not worthy of your trust? You're asking for quite a lot here."

Fevronia wanted to cry in shame, but managed to hold back tears. It was wrong of her, she knew, to hide the monstrous reason Theodora wanted to make the trip. It was wrong of her not to trust the Metropolitan, who had so often supported her against her critics. Yet, she felt too vulnerable to disclose everything, for she knew that she would be found at fault. Although Theodora had been selected by the Theotokos for being saved and for leading a life devoted to Christ, she was still a Jewish girl whom Fevronia had allowed to play the role of a nun for decades before her baptism. Following Dr. Covo's visit, Theodora seemed at times even more of a Jewish girl, one who could recall Talmudic stories taught by her father. The story of Rav Huna and the wine had been only the first that Theodora told her about. Her father had recounted a tale—the accuracy of which he disputed—in which Jesus had been hanged, not crucified. How could such a person—infected as she was with Talmudism—be a reliable witness to Jesus's return? The Metropolitan would believe that Fevronia too had lost her mind in crediting the truth of Theodora's dream. Fevronia had to steel herself to convince the Metropolitan of the importance of their trip without having him wonder whether she was crazy.

"You are correct, Blessed Father, that there's more. And of course I trust you. But I ask if you will trust me." She paused for a minute, collecting her thoughts. "I fear Theodora would leave the monastery for good and go to America, with or without our consent, with or without me. I so much want to keep her in the faith and have her return to St. Vlassius after she makes this visit. And there's great danger in America."

"Then you would be in danger, too. I've heard about kidnappings and shootings and the like."

"There may be such, but I mean the danger of loss of faith. I mean danger that the Devil infuses into the supposed charms of America."

"Again, you would also be in danger."

"Not if I go prepared to defeat the Devil."

"This still doesn't tell me what you're hiding from me. But I shall give you the blessing you seek." He held his hand out to her, and she brushed the back of it with her lips. "In the name of Lord Jesus Christ, I bless you, Abbess Fevronia, and wish your soul comfort as you undertake this perilous journey. And may the Lord Jesus Christ keep you and Sister Theodora in His care and protect you from harm. And may the Blessed Holy Mother ensure your safe return."

Fevronia was almost delirious with relief. She fell to her knees, bent and touched her head to the floor at the Metropolitan's feet, and offered a prayer of thanksgiving to the Lord. After a minute, the Metropolitan touched his hand lightly to Fevronia's shoulder and helped her stand again.

"Now that you have been blessed to make this journey and to take Theodora with you, can you please tell me everything?"

Fevronia hesitated, fearing that a blessing given could be withdrawn in the next breath. Yet, the Metropolitan had never gone back on his word to her. She decided to share more of the truth.

"Theodora believes that she has been given a vision from God and a vision that shows her Our Lord Jesus Christ is alive in America."

The stunned look on the Metropolitan's face was what Fevronia expected. It seemed that he was trying to speak but not finding the words.

"And there's more, Holy Father. In Theodora's vision, Jesus has taken the form of Dr. Covo's grandson. He would be Theodora's grandnephew. A seven-year-old, I think." She paused, knowing she needed to deliver the whole truth. "A seven-year-old who, as it happens, is black."

Now it was the Metropolitan's turn to kneel, gently pulling Fevronia down with him. They bowed their heads.

"Let us pray," he said.

IF GOD SO WILLS

Theodora was awake the whole night before their departure, praying. At times, she felt herself deeply submerged in her prayer, hypnotized, in a warm trance of love and devotion to Christ. She could not see Him, but felt surrounded by Him, as if the very molecules of air in her cell were parts of His body. She felt sustained and kept in life by His presence. Had Christ not given her life? Had He not sent his Holy Mother, the Theotokos, to her rescue when she should otherwise would certainly have died and, by saving her, led her to a life of devotion? And now, she was about to behold Him in His new form, in His new continent. She prayed, not only to gaze upon His earthly form—she would happily die once she saw Him in person—but for the strength she would need to make the long journey. She was afraid of leaving the monastery.

Theodora felt herself unprepared to leave the environment that had sheltered her since the age of six. The outside world was full of danger. The Devil's agents, those evil people who had forsaken God, would swarm around her. Perhaps they would kill her just for the sake of killing, just for her being who she was, as Bulgarian soldiers once tried to kill her. The evil from which she'd sought refuge at the Holy Monastery of St. Vlassios had not disappeared from the world merely with the defeat of the Nazis and their cronies. Those who rejected God had merely retreated. They were there, in the shadows, in their bunkers, waiting for another chance. They would take one look at her, know her mission, and contrive to defeat her.

Theodora did not fear death. She knew that, at the time of her death, she would still live and find herself in the glow of the Lord Christ for eternity. What she feared, however, was that her death would occur too soon and prevent her from seeing her Lord on earth and that her mission would come to naught. Her mission was to help Christ bring Himself into the world's consciousness. She couldn't have said how she came to know this as her mission, nor could she say how she expected to accomplish it. She just knew that God meant for her to try. Evil would fill the dark corners of the earth until the Lord Christ announced His return and the world saw Him in flesh and blood, a man again and yet indisputably God. If the world remained blind, Christ might depart for another two millennia and evil would flourish in his absence.

Very early in the morning, long before *Orthros*, Fevronia and Theodora walked through the chilly night air to the car that would take them to Athens. Ephraim, Andros's son, had agreed to serve as their chauffeur, using his old but dependable beige DIM 652, and get them to Ellinikon International Airport for a mid-afternoon departure on KLM. They would land in America that evening. They watched nervously as Ephraim loaded their suitcases into the back of the car.

Before entering, Fevronia turned to Theodora to ask, one more time, if she was certain that she needed to make the trip. She expected Theodora merely to nod. Each word Theodora spoke seemed to come with a high cost to her. But on this occasion, the words came out as naturally as Fevronia could have wished.

"I am certain, Mother. God so wills. May He bring us safely to America and lead us to success on our trip. And may He bring us again safely to this blessed place."

"Then let us proceed, my dear one. If you need ..."

"And yet ..."

It was so unlike Theodora to interrupt Fevronia.

"Yet?"

"I fear I shall never see this holy place again."

"Then let's not go."

"No. We must go. If God so wills, we will come back."

NOT AFRAID

To Fevronia, the flight from Athens to New York seemed to last forever. Even knowing in advance exactly how long the flight should take, the hours dragged by. She couldn't imagine a less comfortable seat, and yet they were in first class, compliments of Dr. Covo. Those poor people in back, she thought.

She'd brought with her one of Theodora's favorite sacred texts, an edition of the letters of St. Basil the Great. Wholly by accident, she flipped the book open to the second letter. As she read, she regretted her hasty choice. Here, the blessed saint threw a harsh light on distant travels. He likened himself to "travelers at sea, who have never gone on a voyage before, and are distressed and seasick, who quarrel with the ship because it is so big and makes such a tossing."

It was exactly how Fevronia herself felt about the 747 in which she and Theodora traveled. The point of the letter—at least as Fevronia read it—was to emphasize how the unpleasantness of a long journey, indeed, the nausea that such a trip is likely to provoke, lasts long after the voyage has ended. Although Fevronia was not physically nauseous, the trip was making her intensely ill in the spiritual sense. She imagined herself being miserable throughout their time in America, all the way back to Greece, and for months after getting back to the monastery, even if God enabled her return.

She put the book away, then tried unsuccessfully to sleep despite having been warned that it was imperative to stay awake throughout the very long day that flying westward would create. When she gave up sleep, she looked again at Theodora. As she'd been from the moments after they'd boarded the flight, Theodora was praying, fingering her prayer rope, her eyes closed.

Then, without knowing exactly how, Fevronia did fall asleep and dreamed. She had entered Theodora's cell while Theodora was kneeling at her prayer corner. Fevronia was there to confess. "I have sinned against you, my child. I have asked too much. I have disturbed your prayer." The Theodora of her dream took no notice of her. Fevronia attempted to kneel next to Theodora, but could not make her body move. Her attempt at confession had been worse than useless. She had merely embarrassed herself. Then she found herself suddenly kneeling before an icon in the church, alone. Then she was kneeling at the *Microdermis*, still alone, scratching through the rocks and muddy ground in search for her brother.

Only an hour from New York, Theodora nudged Fevronia awake; Fevronia was startled and had expected to find herself in church, not on a plane. Theodora was showing Fevronia her Bible, pointing out the book of Proverbs, Chapter 25. Smiling, Theodora read Verse 25: "'Like cold water to a weary soul is good news from a distant land.' That will be us when we see God in America, don't you agree, Mother?"

Fevronia gently took the Bible from Theodora and read out loud, but quietly, from Verse 2. "It is the glory of God to conceal a thing." She turned to Theodora and spoke sympathetically. "If the Lord Christ has come back, shouldn't it be God's decision alone to decide when and how to reveal His coming? Are you not afraid to announce something that is not yours to announce?" She handed the Bible back to Theodora.

Theodora looked at Fevronia carefully for a few seconds, then said, "No, Mother. I am not afraid."

A WEAK SMILE

Their plane landed at Newark International Airport at about 7:30 pm local time. Fevronia and Theodora watched grimly, both praying silently for deliverance, as their plane descended through rough weather and strong winds, rain beating horizontally against their window, only clouds visible until just seconds before touchdown. The plane seemed to skid, but then righted itself, and the relief was palpable as the brakes took hold and the plane slowed. Hearty applause rang throughout the passenger compartments.

"Is it not clear, Mother? God wants us to be here in America to see His Son."

Fevronia saw Theodora's logic but realized she would have found a way to conclude that God's will had been done regardless of the plane's safe arrival. Fevronia had learned, despite her faith or possibly because of it, that beliefs are not affected by evidence. Rather, one gathers evidence to support beliefs or rejects the need for evidence altogether. She feared that the same thing would happen when Theodora met her grandnephew. Everyone else would understand the Jackie was just a boy, but Theodora would interpret evidence to the contrary proving that Jackie was the Second Coming of Jesus, evidence that no one else saw. Fevronia agonized over what her next move would be.

They were treated politely by Immigration Control, probably because of their black nun's habits. Americans respected religion, she'd come to understand after entertaining American visitors to the monastery for decades. And it was a predominantly Christian country.

Yet, Fevronia felt completely out of place in the vast reaches of the airport. The noise, the crowds, the ten-meter-high continuous wall of windows bordering the long hallways, the massive physicality so at odds with the ambience of the monastery, all contributed to the onset of a dizziness so sudden that Fevronia stumbled to a bench and sat.

"Are you quite all right, Mother?"

"Just give me a minute to catch my breath. Perhaps we sat too long on the plane and should have been walking around more."

"Nicky and Helen are waiting for us."

"And they'll be happy to wait a few minutes more."

Indeed, Fevronia was able to regain her stability after just a short rest, and they continued to walk, finally pushing their luggage cart out of the International Arrival secured area, and in minutes they were face-to-face with Theodora's brother and his girlfriend.

The reunion of brother and sister at the airport was so different from when they'd met in Fevronia's office earlier in the year. Then, at least at its beginning, they each were not sure whom they were meeting, but when recognition happened, and they knew they were brother and sister who'd been separated for forty-six years, the sudden shock of emotion overwhelmed them. Tears flowed freely, not only from Nicky and Theodora, but from Fevronia herself and Helen. At the airport, however, there was no shock, only awkwardness.

"Kal, welcome," Nicky said in Greek. "I'm so happy to see you again." Nicky moved toward Theodora for a hug, but she seemed to push him away after a second, looking not at him but at the floor, crossing herself. "Kal?" Theodora looked up at him briefly, tried weakly to smile, then stared again at the floor.

Nicky turned to Fevronia, extending his hand. "And welcome to you as well, Abbess. I hope your trip was not too unpleasant," he said, glancing at his sister.

"It's so good to see you again," chimed in Helen.

"It is my pleasure as well," said Fevronia. She nodded toward Theodora, who remained silent. "Sister Theodora here is so deep in prayer she's forgotten her good manners. We do have a lot to talk about."

"Yes, but we can save such discussions for tomorrow morning," Nicky said. "It's late, you both must be exhausted, so let's get you out of here. We've decided to take you to Helen's house, where there's plenty of room. Here, let me push that."

MODEST HOUSES

Theodora remained silent on the drive from the airport to Helen's house. Indeed, there was little discussion among the others in Nicky's car. From time to time, Nicky would mention where they were and what they were driving past, as if Theodora and Fevronia had crossed the ocean solely for a tour of Northern New Jersey.

Theodora stared out the window, mesmerized by the Turnpike as it sped by and the still heavy rain, amazed by the sheer size and complexity of America, the oil refineries, the heavy truck traffic even late at night, the bridges and overpasses that seemed to jump over each other from dark meadows and black canals, going nowhere. There was too much confusion around her to even think of praying. The dizzying whirl of her sudden capture by America, as if she were Jonah swallowed by the great fish, made her shiver with discomfort.

When they left the Turnpike, they drove through a city that reminded her dimly of Salonika, her birthplace. Houses and stores crammed into each other, and the world shrank. It was long after midnight, but Theodora sensed thousands of people in these modest houses were awake, aware of her coming, waiting for her, watching.

RESPONSIBILITIES OF BEING A PARENT

The next morning, a Monday, after Kayla had been called by her father and told that Fevronia and Theodora had arrived safely the previous evening, she took her daily two-mile walk. As she returned to her house, Kayla met at her doorstep an Essex County sheriff's deputy, a uniformed woman with a no-nonsense demeanor holding an envelope. The name tag over her badge read "F. Johnson."

"Kayla Covo?"

"Yes. Is ..."

The deputy held out the envelope to Kayla, who took it automatically without understanding what it contained. "I'm serving you with these papers from the Essex County Family Court. Good day, Ma'am." With that, F. Johnson marched off. Only then did Kayla notice the squad car parked in front of the house next door.

Her hands shook as she read the summons at her kitchen table. She was being ordered to attend a status hearing in Newark in two weeks. The papers gave a Newark address for the Complainant, August Sorel—he was renting a house on Ann Street in the Ironbound District—and included copies of the complaint August had filed in New Orleans. Kayla called her father first to tell him she'd been served, then Max. The more she read the papers, the more upset she became, and she cried profusely, thankful that Jackie was at school and couldn't see her.

Kayla's immediate instinct after helping herself to a shot of Max's bourbon was to call August and scream at him over the phone. She could scream until he relented and agreed to drop the custody complaint. She could threaten him with legal action for his having seduced her while she was underage. She'd been only sixteen when they'd begun having sex. Indeed, she'd had to beg her dad not to call the police when he learned she was pregnant with Jackie. But, in retrospect, perhaps that had been unwise. At the time, she was in love with August and was also afraid of the bad publicity that might arise from her pregnancy. She'd not yet come to understand that her concert career was over anyway. Now, the possible sting of bad publicity wouldn't be an impediment. Was there a statute of limitations that prevented her from making a criminal complaint?

Had she known what telephone number to reach August at, she might well have called him, screaming and threatening. The space for a phone number had been left blank on the form that accompanied the Complaint. The local phone book, a year old, showed no listings for an August Sorel or even an A. Sorel. Directory Assistance was of slightly more help: yes, there was a phone number for an August Sorel, but the number was unfortunately unlisted. The only phone number she had was his parents' in Manhattan; she doubted he would be there and didn't want to involve them. Continuing to ponder, she realized she'd waited too long to retain her own lawyer. Max had given her names of people she could trust. She would have to call someone soon.

But the instinct to cry out in anger, although subdued, hadn't entirely evaporated. Before she could even think about talking to a lawyer, she would need to call and vent to Rabbi Beck. She dialed his office number, praying he was in, and luck was with her. She quickly brought him up to date.

"I can tell you're angry, Kayla. But stop and ask yourself whether you can't work out an agreement with the father—August, you say his name is?—that would be to Jackie's benefit."

"With all respect, how can I? Come to terms with someone who's accused me of child abuse?"

"I didn't say it would be easy. But what's in Jackie's best interest? That's what the courts look at." She'd heard that all already. What about her own interests? Were they simply to be disregarded?

"His best interest is in staying in my complete custody, obviously, so I can raise him as an observant Jew, among other things."

"Did you call me to know what Jewish law requires?"

She stopped to wonder why, exactly, she had called Rabbi Beck. In a way, she felt he was responsible for her entire predicament. Had he not urged her to stop her meds, she would never have attacked Jackie, and the problem of whether she was an abusive mother would never have arisen. His advice had been foolish, but she had been more foolish to follow it.

"I called for your support. I called because you know Jackie well."

"You do have my support. I obviously care about both you and Jackie. He's quite an intelligent little guy. If I need to, I would be happy to testify in court as your rabbi that you are a very good mother. But, as a rabbi, I also need to tell you what Jewish law requires, if you ask me to. I don't give such opinions unless asked."

Did she really want his presentation of Jewish law on the subject? She knew that, unless he asked her to do something outrageous again, she would follow his dictate, or at least try to follow it. She could easily answer him at this instant that, no, she didn't want to know the Jewish perspective on the issue. But, if she unmoored herself from Judaism, then what would be her anchor in the world? It was only through *Chabad* and strict observance that she'd been able to find a sustainable and enriching way of life when concertizing had failed her, when her illness had all but overwhelmed her.

"Please tell me what Jewish law requires."

"Fine. You must act as the pious one of our tradition would have acted."

"But, what ..."

"Please let me finish. Then you can ask all the questions you want."

"All right."

"Whatever you do must be pleasing to *Hashem. V'asita ha-yashar ha-tov b'eney Hashem.*"

"You're quoting from *D'varim.*"

"Yes, of course."

"But the Torah doesn't deal with custody disputes, particularly outside of marriage, does it?"

"Most assuredly it does, and the best example is the story of *Shlomo* and the two women who sought custody of the same infant. The true mother is the one who puts the wellbeing of her child first, beyond all personal concerns."

"And I do. I care more about Jackie's welfare than I care about my own life, when it comes to that."

"Good. Then you're well on the way to answering the question you have implicitly asked me, the question of what to do next."

"I will have to go to court and fight for total custody."

"That is an option, but perhaps you haven't been listening closely to me. That fight might not be in Jackie's best interests."

"I have a right to determine my son's future. I've taken care of him without August's help for seven years." She paused, trying to come up with a stronger argument. "Did not *Rivka Imanu* intervene, even use subterfuge, to determine her son *Yaakov's* future?"

"Because it was *Hashem's* will. Here, we don't know exactly *Hashem's* will. So we proceed the best we can, hoping to do the just thing in His eyes. You might be able to establish a legal right to get what you want. I'm not an expert in law or the legalities of custody disputes. But under Jewish law, which you asked me to interpret, being a parent is not about the rights of the parent. It's about the responsibilities of a parent."

"I've been a responsible parent." Even as she spoke these words, Kayla had to stifle the urge to tell the rabbi she would have ended up being even more responsible had he not given her such poor advice.

"Quite so. And responsible you must continue to be going forward. Under Jewish law, a child needs parental guidance from two parents, his mother and his father."

"Max is like a father to Jackie."

Here, it was the rabbi's turn to think before responding. He was sorry that they were conversing on the telephone. He should certainly have urged Kayla to come to his office, where he could observe her demeanor. He'd not asked her because he'd set aside a block of time that afternoon to study *Pirkei Avot*, the Sayings of the Fathers, and hadn't wanted her arrival to interrupt him. How ironic, he thought: here they were, discussing the role of fathers, and that's what he had wanted to spend time studying. Well, a congregational rabbi's life is nothing if not a series of interruptions.

"And I'm sure Max is very good in that regard," he said, even though he wasn't sure at all. "Your father is also an excellent role model for Jackie. But all of that doesn't negate the possibility that August too, in his way, can be of great benefit to his son, if he truly wants that role."

"He doesn't."

"Kayla, I think I've said everything I can say at this point. If you want to talk further, we'll set up a meeting in my office. And, of course, feel free to talk to Rabbi Berenbaum, too. I imagine he'll say much the same."

She sighed, realizing that Rabbi Beck wouldn't be able to provide more help than he'd already provided, the advice to trust in *Hashem*. "*Todah rabah*, Rabbi Beck. *L'hitraot.*"

"*L'hitraot.*"

THE INEFFABLE

Helen sat at her kitchen table, watching Nicky fry finely chopped onions, to begin his preparation of scrambled eggs. As she'd showed Fevronia and Theodora to their rooms, she'd mentioned the possibility of breakfast at nine and received nods of assent, but it was now almost eleven, and her two guests hadn't appeared. At least one was awake, however. Both Helen and Nicky noticed the smell of incense near their rooms, part of their prayer ritual, they'd surmised. Nicky was reminded of the smell of hay.

"So, when they come down, when we're done with breakfast, should we just ferry them to West Orange to meet the rest of the family? Or do we talk first about what Theodora believes? By the way, crack one egg at a time into the small measuring cup and check for blood spots before you contaminate the others."

Nicky turned to face her, an egg in each hand. Then he turned back to the counter, put one egg down, and cracked the other as she had directed. "I know what I'm doing here. But, to answer your question, we let them call the shots. Like we'd let our patients lead the discussion in therapy."

"I've told you before, Nicky. The people I help are clients, not patients, although you're right. We should've also let them decide when and what they wanted to eat."

After a few minutes, Nicky had a low fire under the eggs and turned to Helen again. "I can't believe how different Kal seems from how she'd been in Greece."

"Amazing that she's not talking. Somehow, I'm not surprised, but it must be a shock to you."

"In Greece, that last time when I was with her in her cell, she was the loving little sister she'd always been, as well as Sister Theodora. She talked to me as sister might and got me to talk."

"It's the long trip and the strangeness of being here. I think she'll come around soon. She'll ..."

At that moment, both Fevronia and Theodora walked into the kitchen, cautiously, it seemed to Helen, but smiling.

"*Kalimera*, Nicky."

"*Kalimera, adelon mou.*"

"Good morning, Dr. Covo, Mrs. Blanco."

Happily, there was no problem with the scrambled eggs. Everyone was hungry and concentrated on eating. Helen easily made small talk, asking about the flight, commenting about the previous night's prodigious rain. The others found it easy enough as well to join in a pleasant conversation. Fevronia acquiesced in letting Nicky translate into Greek for his sister. When Theodora said something in Greek, Nicky likewise would repeat it in English for Helen's sake, and then Theodora would also try to say the same thing in English. Theodora hoped that her incense burning hadn't disturbed anyone; she agreed she should have asked first, but it was so much a habit. Yes, the room was lovely and the bed, to speak truthfully, a lot softer than what she was accustomed to—a sentiment to which Fevronia heartily agreed—but it was very nice, she could adjust herself to the new feel and was grateful—hadn't she said so before?—for Helen's hospitality. And, yes, she would be happy to borrow a paperback Greek-English dictionary that Nicky offered her.

As Nicky cleaned up, Helen turned the topic to what their visitors hoped to do that day. Theodora seemed to know what Helen was talking about, if not her exact meaning. Fevronia and Theodora looked at each other for a second, Theodora nodded at her, and Fevronia then spoke in English.

"I know what Theodora wants. She wants badly to meet your grandson, Dr. Covo. You know about her obsession. I, for one, agree we should get this over quickly. She will be disappointed, of course, when she realizes how mistaken she is, but I hope we will get past that and then enjoy this visit for a short time before we return to the monastery."

"We're worried about Jackie, Abbess Fevronia," Nicky said. "His father is making a lot of trouble for my daughter. He wants to take Jackie away from her."

"I am so sorry, Dr. Covo. And we do not wish ..."

"You don't wish to make more trouble, I know. Jackie's also been problematic in other ways lately."

"Problematic? How so?"

"There are family issues. My daughter has a mental illness. She suffers from schizophrenia, I'm afraid. It's caused family trauma."

"That must be very stressful. Although I do not really see what this has to do with our visiting him."

"I'm very concerned that ..." He stopped, not wanting Kal to be offended when she heard the translation. He had to choose his words carefully. "I'm concerned that a visitor who venerates Jackie, who sees in him something superhuman, might throw him back into muteness or perhaps something else bad. Do you get where I'm coming from?"

"Very much so. Yet, that's why we're here. We have to do this, Dr. Covo. Otherwise, Sister Theodora will have no rest. If there's something we can do to make this whole thing easier, please to tell me. In any event, she's not going to see him as a god. She will realize her mistake."

"You're sure? Because I would've never guessed that she'd have such ideas in the first place."

Fevronia hesitated, glancing at Theodora before turning again toward Nicky. "Well, I'm not sure. She constantly surprises me. She's fully invested in her belief. So, we will just have to see."

"Nicky, let's just do this," said Helen. "We'll all be close by, not only you and I, but Kayla and Max and the abbess. There's no way to plan for something as odd as this. But let's have faith in *Hashem*."

"*Hashem* is your name for God?" asked Fevronia.

Helen smiled, reaching out and taking Fevronia's hand. "*Hashem* actually means 'the Name.' It's a substitute for the name that Jews never pronounce, the name too holy to be said by human lips. So, yes, when we use that term, *Hashem*, we refer to the Ineffable."

"Ineffable?" asked Fevronia. "There, I'm afraid, you've got me."

"*Aneipotos.*" Nicky clarified.

At hearing the Greek word, Theodora stood and said, "*Eima etoimos na to ton Theo.*"

"What does she say?" asked Helen.

Fevronia volunteered the translation.

"She says she's ready to see God."

TURNING THE PAGE

Kayla wondered how she would dress Jackie for the occasion of meeting his great-aunt and the abbess. There was no protocol she was aware of, but it occurred to her that, out of pure respect for their visitors and their high religious standing, they might expect to be presented with a boy wearing his best clothes. She voiced her uncertainty to Max, whom she seldom asked for child-rearing advice.

"You've got to be kidding, Kayla. Just tell him to take a shower and let him pick out what he wants to wear as usual. Let's not make this into something even bigger than it is already."

What Max said made sense, she realized. The first problem of the day cropped up when Jackie complained that he didn't need a shower, that he'd taken one "only yesterday," and that he instead wanted to continue his clarinet practice. And, no, he wouldn't change his clothes, either. Those he'd worn the day before and put on again in the morning would be fine.

Pick your battles, Kayla thought. Let him make his own decisions, as long as he's not about to kill himself.

"All right.," she conceded. "But when Grandpa and Helen and the others come, put down the clarinet, wash your hands, and come to meet everyone politely."

He merely nodded at her, the instrument still in his mouth.

"Say: All right, *Ima*."

He continued playing a few measures, then turned to her. "All right, *Ima*. Now can I please practice?"

In the kitchen a few minutes later, Kayla saw Max starting a new pot of coffee.

"What if they don't drink coffee?" she asked.

"There will be more for us. So, I get it. You're very nervous. Just take a deep breath. Things will be okay."

"I don't know."

"Do you want me to massage your shoulders and help you relax?"

"Sure." She sat at their breakfast table, and he began to do as he'd offered, focusing on her upper back around the neck. In seconds, Kayla was purring with contentment. "Ooh. That feels good. I must be even more tense than usual."

"Well, you're not stuttering. That's a positive sign."

"Do you think I should have bought them presents? Something to convey that I'm happy they're visiting?" He ignored the question, continuing to massage her. "Or what if they've brought something for us, and I have nothing in return?"

"Please stop worrying. We can sort all that out. Let's take one ..."

At that second, they heard the sound of a key turning in the lock of their front door and knew that their father was there with the visitors. The anticipated meeting was about to begin.

"Welcome, everyone," Kayla said, smiling, and holding out her hand to the abbess. "I'm Kayla, and you must be Abbess Fevronia. We are delighted to have you visit."

Kayla then turned to Theodora, whom she recognized immediately, from the facial similarities—particularly the cast of her eyes—as her father's sister. She pulled Theodora close for an awkward hug. It was so strange. As Theodora allowed herself to be drawn into Kayla's embrace, Kayla felt an unnatural warmth radiating from her aunt. Then they separated, each pushing back gently against the other. Kayla worried immediately that she had transgressed a rule of monasticism by invading Theodora's personal space. Were nuns allowed by their faith to hug strangers? Jewish strangers at that? She decided that no aunt of hers would remain unhugged in her house unless she was specifically directed to keep her physical distance.

She pulled Theodora to her once again, strangely needing to feel Theodora's warmth. "And you are Sister Theodora. I've heard so much about you, and I'm thrilled to meet you and have you as my guest." That Kayla's words were those of welcome was clear despite the language barrier, but Theodora turned questioningly to Fevronia for a full translation.

"*Efcharisto poli.* Thank you so much." Theodora smiled, took Kayla's hand, and gently brushed her lips against it. "*Anistzia mou.* My niece."

"Yes. I am your niece, and you are my aunt."

"*Eima y thea sou.* I am your aunt."

Kayla settled everyone in the living room, where she'd pulled together a couple of extra chairs to face the sofa. Then, while Max politely asked about their trip, and Nicky turned the conversation to an inquiry about the coming grape harvest and other matters surrounding the monastery, Kayla brought out the coffee and two plates of *rugelach*.

She wanted intensely to converse with Theodora, particularly to ask her about the miracles she'd experienced, but also to find out about the monastic life. She wanted to learn if there was much difference between her own strong belief in *Hashem* and the beliefs of her visitors. Was her strict observance of the *mitzvot* akin to the nuns' daily prayers? She knew that the time for such discussions wasn't right. Indeed, the time might never come, if Fevronia and Theodora were staying only a few days before returning to Greece.

By the time she'd sipped her coffee, the polite conversation had fallen silent. Theodora looked nervously around, obviously waiting for Jackie's appearance. Kayla then noticed that she could no longer hear Jackie's clarinet. He would be listening at the top of the stairs, she thought. He would have to be called down soon. But before she called him, she needed to ask a few questions of the abbess and Theodora.

"Before we have Jackie come in, Abbess Fevronia, please tell us what Sister Theodora intends to do. Jackie has ... had a hard time lately, let's say." Nicky translated into Greek for Theodora, but Kayla had no way of knowing how accurate the translation was. Theodora was surely able to recognize that she was being spoken about.

"So I have heard from Dr. Covo about this hard time, Miss Covo."

"Please call me Kayla."

"Kayla, then. To answer your question, Kayla, I do not know, but I think you are not to worry. Theodora is a gentle person, as gentle a soul as I've ever known. She has great love for God. I'm sure you know what it means to love God beyond all measure, as I've heard you are quite religious. She will do nothing to harm your son."

Kayla nodded thoughtfully, then turned to Theodora. "Nicky, please translate for me. Sister Theodora, I will call you that instead of Aunt Kal, if that's to your liking?"

After the translation, Theodora nodded at Kayla, smiling. "Thank you very much."

"Sister Theodora, my son, Jackie, is just a boy. I know right now you feel differently, but when you meet him you'll see I'm right. We don't want to disappoint you, we want as much as possible to be close to you, as close as family can be, but Jackie ... he's just a human boy. A wonderful boy, but just a boy. I love him very much. We— Max and Dad and Helen and I—love him and don't want anything bad to happen to him. You do understand?"

Nicky provided the necessary translations.

"I understand what you are saying, Kayla, but not your fear. What do you think I might do to hurt your son?"

"It's the fear any mother would have of the unknown."

"I'm not a mother myself, but I've been held by the Holy Mother, She who brought forth Our Lord on his First Coming, She who knew as She brought Light into the world that her Son would die on the cross and yet who with courage gave Him to us sinners. The

Theotokos was special, and I do not expect you to have the courage She had. But Nicky told me about you in Greece, about your own inner strength, how you too brought beauty into the world. I know how you made people happy through your music. I know that you have a beautiful soul, and I know that Jackie is the most precious thing in your life."

"Thank you. Whatever Dad has said about me is just the ravings of a loving father. But the truth is that I have no courage. Without courage, yet I trust that the will of *Hashem* shall be fulfilled."

"I too have such a trust in God's will."

"And I trust you are here with us now because that is *Hashem's* will, that the Ineffable has written this chapter, that we, as *Hashem's* creations, are to proceed and discover what it is we are meant to do and to be."

"Then we share much belief between us."

"But ..."

"I see many things, Kayla, that others do not see. When you hugged me, just minutes ago, I could hear your music inside you, the piano, a sad but strong melody. When I see Jackie, I will know much about him, things that you may not know, even though you brought him into the world."

"But you can't see him as God. That is entirely against our faith. That is what so troubles me."

"I accept that you do not believe. You are Jewish, as I once was. I would have died Jewish, a tiny Jewish girl locked in a closet, except that the Theotokos saved me and showed me the true way."

Try as she might, Kayla could not envision the middle-aged nun who sat before her as a little girl, let alone imagine that a miraculous manifestation of Jesus's mother had freed that little girl from a locked closet in the middle of a horrific war. "I hope we will have time to talk in more detail about that ... experience ... before you return to your home, Sister Theodora. But the true way, as you call it, is your way only and can never be my way. It can never be Jackie's way or the way of the Covo family."

Theodora smiled thoughtfully after hearing the last bit translated. "I've heard it said that 'never is a long time.' I'm not really sure what that means, but please understand that I will not hurt your son. May I now see him?"

Kayla hesitated still. Finally, Nicky said, "It's time, Kayla. Let's turn the page here and get on with the story."

AN EXQUISITE HAPPINESS

"I'll get him. We'll be down in a minute." Kayla left the others and, as expected, found Jackie sitting on the top stair, waiting.

"How much of that did you hear?"

"You were talking about *Hashem*, but I didn't hear much."

"Just as well. Come on, let's meet our guests. Be on your best behavior. Be very polite."

She took his hand and led him down to the living room, where she introduced him first to Fevronia, who shook his hand.

"Very nice to meet you, young man."

"Jackie, this is my aunt; her name is Sister Theodora."

Jackie extended his hand to Theodora. It seemed to Kayla that Theodora was a second slow in reaching out to take it, but she ultimately did, touching it only for a fraction of a second, and then withdrawing. It took a few seconds before her intense stare turned into a pleasant smile.

"I am pleased to meet you, Jackie," she said in halting English. She looked deeply into his hazel eyes. Just as she had dreamed. "Your Grandpa is my big brother."

Jackie nodded. He'd heard repeatedly about the family connection. No news there.

"Come, sit next to me on the sofa, Jackie," Kayla directed. "Our guests would like to talk to you. They might have some questions, too. Please talk to them nicely."

"All right, *Ima*. May I have a *rugelach*?"

"Of course."

While Jackie picked up one of the small pastries and began to munch on it, Theodora watched him closely. He looked to her— sepia skin tone and all—exactly as she had imagined the young version of the black man she'd seen in her message from God. She knew as well what he would look like in twenty years. She watched him lick his fingers after finishing the pastry, then wipe his fingers with a napkin that his mother provided. She waited, not sure what she was expecting to happen. All was silence. The child and the five other adults were looking at her, expecting her to say something. Then, in a flash, she understood what she had forgotten and what she had to do next.

"Kayla, please help me here."

"What can I do for you, Sister Theodora?"

Again, Nicky was required to interpret. "I need a bucket of warm, soapy water, a washcloth, and a dry towel. I must humble myself now, before you and your brother and your son."

Kayla had been half-expecting Theodora to engage in the ritual washing of feet, as her dad and Helen had explained was Theodora's habit. In fact, she'd been surprised when they'd met that Theodora hadn't immediately wanted to abase herself. It wasn't something Kayla wanted to participate in, let alone facilitate, but she schooled herself to comply. She was determined to be a good hostess. Had not *Avraham Avinu* himself welcomed strangers into his tent and provided them with the cakes of the best flower and a meal of the tenderest meat and fixings of butter and milk? She did as Theodora had requested, submitting first to have her own feet washed. Just as her dad had explained that Theodora's touch was unnaturally warm, and just as she'd felt that warmth when hugging Theodora, so too she felt that warmth emanating from Theodora's hands through the washcloth. Then Max, to his great credit, submitted, although Kayla caught his brief facial expression telling everyone he thought the ritual was nonsense, if not pure insanity.

Finally, Theodora turned to Jackie.

"Will you please take off your sneakers and socks," she asked, Fevronia now translating.

"Do I have to, *Ima*?"

"Do as she asks, please."

"All right."

And so Theodora kneeled before her grandnephew, the great-grandson of a famous rabbi. She gently washed his feet, and, as she washed, she felt a glow of an exquisite happiness suffusing through her body. Tears welled in her eyes and spilled down her cheeks. Yes, this was why she'd come to America. The more she touched Jackie, the greater was her certainty that she'd found her God. When she finished drying His feet, she lifted them to her lips and kissed them gently, something she'd never done when washing a stranger's feet.

Jackie was not a stranger. She'd been praying to Him since she'd been locked in that closet in Kavala, since before the Theotokos, His Mother, had come to save her pitiful soul. No one knew it but her, not even Fevronia, but Jackie was indeed Jesus. The truth of the vision that God had given her—and she'd never really doubted that truth—had been confirmed.

But she now knew as well that Jesus was in danger.

VA-ETCHANAN

The foot-washing completed, Theodora handed the bucket, washcloth, and towel to Kayla and returned to her chair, eyes still focused closely on Jackie. As much as she felt with certainty that it was not only Jackie but Jesus sitting in front of her, she knew that the others couldn't see what she saw. Fevronia was still immune to the realization that God Almighty, the Lord Jesus Christ, sat before her. Theodora saw that it would be many years before Jackie Himself realized who He was and proclaimed the Second Coming. God would make sure that the veil would be lifted from Jackie's eyes in due course, in accordance with His will.

Despite this sudden knowledge, Theodora felt that she had an important role to play in God's plan. God would not have given her the vision of Jackie as Jesus had He not wanted her to act. But how? Did she have to act at this very minute or otherwise lose the chance and thereby frustrate God's plan? Was part of the plan to do something to avert the danger she sensed was surrounding Jackie?

She turned to Kayla and asked, "May I speak with your son?" Kayla had seen the tenderness with which Theodora had attended to her washing ritual, particularly as to Jackie. She felt no harm could arise if Theodora and Jackie conversed. So she nodded her assent to Theodora. "Go ahead. Dad will translate as necessary."

"Jackie, I am so very happy to meet you. How are you?"

"All right."

"Do you know who I am?"

"*Ima* and Grandpa told me. And you just told me. You are Grandpa's sister."

"And do you know where I live?"

"In Greece. Grandpa and Helen found you there in the spring."

"Yes, they did. I was very happy about that. It was quite a surprise. Now, another question please. Do you know what I do every day, for most of the day?"

"I don't understand."

"Every day I pray to God. I pray to God more than I do anything else. Do you understand who God is?"

"I pray to *Hashem* too. I say the *Sh'ma* every night before I go to bed."

"Yes. I remember well *Sh'ma*. God the King is faithful. *Sh'ma Yisrael, Adonoy Elohenu, Adonay Echad.* That's right, isn't it?"

"Do you say it, too, before you go to sleep?"

She smiled at the recollection. "I used to, because I grew up Jewish. My Papa taught it to me. He was your Grandpa's Papa too."

"You're still Jewish."

"Well ..."

"If you're Grandpa's sister, and he's Jewish, then you must be Jewish."

"Well, you have a good point there. They told me you were smart, and they were right. Now, tell me please, where do you learn about God, Jackie? About *Hashem?*"

"*Ima* talks about *Hashem* all the time. She teaches me, and Rabbi Beck teaches me at *Chabad.*"

"Do you ask Rabbi Beck questions when he teaches?"

Jackie needed to think. He remembered his last session at the *Chabad* school. They had discussed the Torah portion *Va-etchanan*. *Hashem* told *Moshe* that he could not enter the Promised Land.

"I did ask him a question."

Theodora smiled. It was as she had hoped. "And can you tell me, please, what question you asked Rabbi Beck?"

"Rabbi Beck told us how *Hashem* took *Moshe* to the top of a mountain and let him see all of *Eretz Yisrael*. And I asked how far that was."

She nodded. "A logical question. What answer did Rabbi Beck give you?"

"As far as could be."

"Did you think that was a good answer?"

"No. Not really. It didn't tell me how far."

"Did you ask more?"

"No. I just decided to think about it."

Theodora paused, carefully considering whether she should continue her questions. For someone who had recently been mute, Jackie was speaking as much or more than she had hoped. For that matter, she couldn't recall herself having had as long a conversation as the one she was now having with Jackie.

"Jackie, just a few more questions. You're being very cooperative."

"Okay."

"Do you obey your parents?"

"Do you mean *Ima*?" He glanced at Kayla.

"Your mother, yes."

His instinct was to protest that he always obeyed. But he felt the eyes of all the adults boring into him. They knew. "Not all the time."

"Have you heard of the Holy Mother, the Mother of God? We call her the Theotokos. I pray to Her every night and all during the day too."

Kayla held her breath, apprehensive about what Jackie would say. He looked confused and gave the question a fair amount of thought before answering.

"*Hashem* doesn't have a mother. Rabbi Beck has taught me—*Ima* has taught me too—that *Hashem* ..." Here he stopped, struggling to remember what negated the possibility of a mother for *Hashem*. "They have taught me that *Hashem* has existed before ... time." He looked at Kayla, who nodded encouragement. "Before time. Before there was anything. So, *Hashem* doesn't have a mother."

Theodora felt a warm glow inside, unsurprised, thinking it was what Jesus might well have said had He been asked the question at such a tender age.

Finally, Kayla interrupted. "With all respect, Sister Theodora, are you finished with your questions? I mean, for this afternoon?"

"Just a few more, Kayla, if you don't mind." Kayla shrugged, and Theodora turned back to the boy. "Jackie, is Max your father?" She asked this question in English.

Jackie was now profoundly confused. Why all the questions? Why such stupid questions at that? He was done. He got up, ready to bolt as soon as he had *Ima*'s permission. "No. Uncle Max is white, can't you see? My real father and Grandpa had a big fight and they were both bleeding." He turned to Kayla. "Can I go upstairs now, *Ima*? Please?"

"Go ahead, Jackie. Thank you for answering Sister Theodora's questions."

LIP SERVICE?

"Why in tarnation would you ask him if I was his father?"

Max was more than perturbed. In addition to the question being outlandish—a mixed-race child could not possibly have been produced by two white parents—it presumed the unspeakable, that he and Kayla had sexual relations. Theodora was startled by the harsh tone of Max's question, even though she didn't quite get all of it. "Tarnation" was a word she hadn't encountered. She turned toward Nicky, waiting for the translation, but Nicky decided not to. Enough was enough. He didn't want to have their meeting end up in accusations and recriminations. Theodora turned to Fevronia, who merely shrugged her shoulders; if Dr. Covo wasn't going to translate, then neither would she.

"Max, stifle yourself." The anger in Nicky's voice was palpable.

"No, Dad," added Kayla. "Max is right to ask. I want to hear Theodora's explanation, too. Although Max's question could have been asked in a nicer way."

"Abbess Fevronia, should I put that question to Sister Theodora?"

"That's up to you, Dr. Covo, but I too would like to hear what Theodora has to say. I think I know why."

So Nicky came up with a polite version of Max's question.

"Of course I know Max isn't Jackie's father. I was trying just to get him to say that Max was like a step-father to him. Jesus grew up with a step-father. Then I was going to ask whether Jackie obeyed

Max as well, just as Jesus obeyed Joseph. Perhaps I did not ask properly. I am so truly sorry if I gave offense."

Now Max, in a calmer voice, directed a second question to Theodora. "And what was the purpose of all that?"

Theodora shook her head grimly and turned again to Fevronia. "I cannot speak further to him, Mother. He doesn't like me. I can sense that he wants me to leave. I have nothing more to say."

Fevronia turned to the others and spoke in English. "She's tired, she says, and wants me to answer for her. So I will, to the best of my ability. She's wondering how much Jackie is like, or unlike, the stories of Our Lord Jesus Christ when He was a child. She was hoping to hear Jackie say he obeyed you, Max."

"And Jackie's other answers?" asked Kayla. "Does Jackie fit the description? Does she think his answers support her beliefs?"

"Well, first, let me assure you that I absolutely don't think Jackie is Jesus. You realize obviously that we are only paying lip service to Theodora's ... craziness. But whether the answers fuel her beliefs or not, only Theodora could say. I see reasons why Jackie's answers prove him to be, as everyone knows he is, just a fine human boy—an intelligent boy—with no supernatural element. For example, he admits he doesn't always obey you, Kayla. He repeats his Judaic training—that your God has no mother—as I would have expected him to. Clearly, he believes that the idea of a Mother of God is fanciful."

Kayla looked over at Theodora, who had sat back on the sofa, had her eyes closed, and was fingering her prayer beads. She apparently was paying no attention to the conversation surrounding her.

"Dad, please ask Theodora if she wants to talk to Jackie again on another day. You can see Jackie was getting impatient. After all, a woman he doesn't know, old enough to be his grandmother, dressed in a black habit, has asked him some weird questions."

Nicky conveyed the question to Theodora, if not in exactly the same words.

Theodora took her time to respond, looking first at Fevronia, whose face was impassive, and then at Kayla. Finally, she nodded. "*Nai. Fisika.*" She would very much like to speak with him again, when he felt more up to it.

"Well, then we'll have you back again." Kayla turned toward her father. "*Shabbat?*"

"You know Helen won't travel. And although I can bring Fevronia and Theodora here, I'd really like Helen to be here as well if we're having dinner."

"Of course, Dad. Helen, I'm sorry, I wasn't thinking. Why don't we do it this Sunday evening?"

It was agreed. They would dine as a family, and Theodora could question Jackie if she liked. But if Jackie didn't want to answer, and Kayla doubted he would, that would be the end of it.

THINGS FALL APART

When the phone rang the next morning, Kayla couldn't have anticipated that the caller would be a lawyer and that the subject of the call would be August's effort to steal Jackie from her.

"You are who again?"

"Peggy O'Dell, with the law firm of Batson Redden, the court-appointed guardian *ad litem*. Call me Peggy."

"The court? It's about those custody papers? What's going on?"

"Well, I was hoping you'd tell me. All I know is that the father of your son has filed an emergency lawsuit in the Family Court in Newark. Judge Jill Haney has appointed me to represent ... um ... Jackie. This is Kayla Covo, isn't it?"

"Yes, but this is crazy. August hasn't been involved in Jackie's life for years."

"Well, we can save all that for when we meet."

"What do you mean?"

"I have to investigate and report to Judge Janey. She makes the final decision about custody. I always do a meeting at the home of the child, you know, as part of an evaluation."

"You're k-k-kidding."

"Hardly. I very much need to see your house and also talk briefly to Jackie, there've been allegations, but you know that, we'll go into that later. So, just tell me when I can come and meet you and Jackie at your house and, let's see, there's an uncle ..."

"N-n-never." Kayla slammed down the phone. Her hands shook, her head was suddenly pounding with pain. Had she taken her pills yet this morning? She couldn't remember. The phone call struck her as a bad dream. Maybe it hadn't happened at all, maybe this was just another hallucination, like those visions of the fan who wanted to kill her. But she knew it was real. August had started a custody action and was trying to take Jackie away from her forever. To stop him, she would have to kill him. It was as simple as that. No one would steal Jackie.

She went over to sit at her Steinway and began playing in a trance, composing a melody into which she subconsciously poured themes of fear, disgust, anger, and bewilderment. In her mind, however, a line from a poem she'd read long before kept repeating, growing in intensity as her hands moved over the keys.

"Things fall apart, the centre cannot hold."

NEW LAW

"You have to meet with her, Kayla." Max and Kayla sat across from each other at their kitchen table. "Unless there was a way to get August's custody action dismissed outright, and I'll look into it although I'm not a family lawyer, the judge needs the eyes and ears and reactions of a neutral guardian *ad litem* to make an informed decision. That's how Family Court operates here and in most other jurisdictions."

"How could this be happening to me? To our family? To Jackie, who's the one who'll suffer the most if this continues?"

"I could give you a textbook legal explanation, although I don't think that's the answer you're looking for. You really want to know why God is making you and Jackie suffer."

"I want to know both."

"I can't speak about God."

"Then legally?"

"The state assumes, unless it hears otherwise, that parents take good care of their minor children. Feed them, educate, clothe, and protect them from harm. If something happens to disturb that assumption, then the state can intervene. When parents fight about custody, the state intervenes. It's always a judge who must decide what's in the best interests of the child. I've been through this so many times with Joseph and Rosina."

"August isn't really a parent. A parent doesn't abandon his son."

"Well, that's a point you'll make ... we'll make ... in court if we have to."

"Yeah? But what if this Ms. Butt-in-ski sides with August? We're done for, aren't we?"

"That would be a big problem. Not decisive, but a big problem, I grant you. Which is why it's so important not to annoy her. She'll interpret any resistance on your part as selfishness, not putting Jackie's interests first. That's human nature."

"That's ridiculous."

"Maybe it's ridiculous, but I'm telling you that's what will happen. You have to make her see you're cooperating."

"When she finds out about ... what happened ... what sent Jackie to the hospital ... it's over."

"She probably knows that already, and, no, it's not over. You're being careful to stay on your meds, you have a lot of backup here. There are plenty of good reasons why she might give you a favorable report to the judge."

"I need to get my own lawyer, right?"

"Of course. As I've been urging you. And I can't represent you, not that you'd want me to. And I'd never recommend that crappy lawyer who represented me. But I've given you other names, and you haven't called anyone yet. You can't fight August without proper representation."

"I w-w-will."

"Kayla, if this goes to court, you know that I might be subpoenaed, and I'd have to testify about what I saw that day."

She thought about this for a minute. "There's no privilege? We live in the same house, we both take care of Jackie, and you could be forced to testify against me?"

He shook his head sadly. "If I remember my evidence class, there's a spousal privilege under common law. A husband can't be compelled to testify against a wife, and vice versa, but I think that might be limited to criminal proceedings, which this wouldn't be, and anyway there's never been a brother-sister privilege to my knowledge."

Kayla shook her head in disbelief. "Well, I can't let you testify. That would be grossly unfair to you. We'll have to make new law."

MIGDAL HASHEM

Three evenings later was the appointed Sunday dinner. Theodora was grateful she'd have a chance to observe Jesus once more. She decided, however, that she needed to restrain herself from questioning Him. Her questions had become odious, at least to Max, and maybe to Kayla and Jesus as well. Theodora felt she could learn as much as she needed about Jesus just by watching Him. Let the others converse with Him. Just being in His presence and paying close attention would be enough.

Kayla had also invited Rabbi Beck and his wife, Miriam. She thought that the rabbi and the abbess would enjoy meeting each other and keep the conversation, if still to religious topics, away from Theodora's obsession with Jackie. She told Rabbi Beck that the visitors from Greece were particularly interested in Jackie as a biracial child, but not about Theodora's belief that Jackie was the incarnation of Jesus.

Kayla laid out a simple meal. Fevronia and Theodora would eat only cooked vegetables, and she felt self-conscious about preparing something more substantial for the others, so everyone ate a meal of potatoes, beets, yellow string beans, diced tomatoes, cheese, and the bread she herself had baked earlier that day.

As expected, the rabbi was friendly, but his questions to Fevronia made Kayla feel distinctly uncomfortable, almost wishing she hadn't invited him.

"Abbess Fevronia, if I may? I know you have the holiday *Pascha*, celebrating Easter, the rising of your Lord. But do Orthodox Christians actually have something that resembles a *seder*?"

"No. Jesus transformed what Jews had practiced as the *seder*. He is the sacrificial lamb, of course. For us, what you call *matzah* became the body of our Lord. So, historically, we appreciate that He attended a Jewish *seder* before His crucifixion, but we don't have any ritual meal that seeks to replicate that event, if you will."

"I know who Jesus is," said Jackie seriously. "I mean, I've heard of him."

Abbess Fevronia smiled warmly at the boy, who was sitting just to her right.

"Is that so, young man? How interesting."

"Yet, Abbess," continued Rabbi Beck, as if Fevronia had not been talking to Jackie, "as I understand it, meals at a monastery are often ritualistic, are they not?"

"Yes. What we put into our bodies, we must keep holy, and we often hear Psalms while we eat, Psalms sung by our most talented nuns. It wouldn't violate Judaism, would it, if you came to a Grand Liturgy and listened? The choral singing can be beautiful, the Psalms very moving."

"I'm sure they are very moving. Maybe if you agree to attend *Kol Nidre* services on *Yom Kippur*, we can trade visits, and I can hear what you're talking about."

"I don't think we'll be here in America until *Yom Kippur*, which is in the fall, isn't it? It's only mid-summer. We shall not be staying that long, but thank you."

"*Ima*, may I leave before we *bench*?" Jackie was speaking to Kayla, but looking toward his left at Fevronia and Theodora. "I don't quite feel like it tonight. I can sit in the living room and listen. And maybe they will come with me." He nodded toward the nuns.

"Bench?" asked Fevronia.

"That means we say prayers of blessing after a meal," advised Jackie.

"Oh. We do that too in our church. I'd rather stay here for the blessings, Jackie, but, if your mother will allow you to leave, perhaps you can take Sister Theodora with you."

Fevronia smiled at Kayla, who nodded her assent. It was one thing to be concerned about Theodora questioning her son through an interpreter, when her son didn't care to be questioned. It was quite another to allow them to go off together with no interpreter, when Jackie himself had made the suggestion. And, although she usually insisted that Jackie stay for *benching*, there were times to be flexible, at least before Jackie attained the age of *mitzvot*. "Go ahead."

Fevronia whispered to Theodora, who stood and said "*Efcharisto poli*, Kayla." Jackie, who'd come around behind her chair, took her hand and led her away.

"Come with me."

When they were out of the room, the rabbi looked at Kayla and remarked, "A boy his age should stay at his table and master the blessings in praise of *Hashem*."

Kayla now was mortified that she'd allowed Jackie, almost seven, to leave without first seeking approval of her spiritual guide and was about to call Jackie back, when Max, who'd not been heard from in quite some time, intervened. "Rabbi, with all respect, Kayla's right. I understand *Chabad* has its rules, Orthodox Jews have their rules, but it doesn't make any sense to force a young child into prayer when he's not ready. I know your children are all long grown, and I'm sure you raised them properly, but Jackie's special and ..."

"That's okay, Max," said Kayla. "I can explain. Jackie's been having a hard time these days, and I have to give him plenty of slack. So, with your indulgence, of course, I will let him spend some time with his great-aunt. And I feel it's important that they have a relationship." Immediately, Kayla wondered why she had added that last point. It was as if her fear of Theodora doing something to harm Jackie had evaporated momentarily. Right after *benching*, she would have to peek in on them and assure herself that all was well.

Kayla stood and passed out *benchers*. "Rabbi Beck, will you do us the honor of leading?"

When everyone including Nicky—everyone except Fevronia, reading to herself in English—had finished singing *Migdal Hashem* and had lightly touched the books to their lips and placed them on the table, Fevronia mentioned that she had a request, which she directed to Nicky. She and Theodora were grateful for the fact that he had taken off from work and had shown them around. Their visit to Ellis Island and the Statue of Liberty had been particularly fascinating, as well as the trip to the World Trade Center. But she and Theodora now hoped, if possible, to attend an Orthodox church service in the morning—in fact, every remaining morning.

Kayla mentioned a church she knew of, St. George's Greek Orthodox Church. It wasn't far from West Orange. But then Nicky pointed out that Fevronia and Theodora were staying in Highland Park, and they likely wanted something closer. A quick check of the Yellow Pages produced the fact that another St. George's Greek Orthodox Church was only a few miles from Helen's house, up the Raritan River, and she volunteered to take Fevronia and Theodora there whenever they wanted.

"That's very generous of you, Mrs. Blanco," said Fevronia.

"Helen, please."

"Helen, yes. It's very generous of you, but our services may be long, much longer than you are used to in your synagogue. You will be welcome to come in with us, of course, and observe from the back. But you can just drop us off, if you can arrange for us a taxi back? There are taxis here, yes?"

"Of course. Maybe Nicky and I can both come in with you, though, just to get the flavor of your services. We'll be happy to stay in the back, won't we, Nicky?"

Nicky sighed and went so far as to say that he might accompany them if the occasion arose. More likely, though, he'd be in his Manhattan apartment or stay at Helen's house. "I've had enough of churches for a lifetime," he continued.

"And why have you had enough of churches?" asked Fevronia. "If you please to say?"

"Too many people die there."

HOLD OUT YOUR HANDS

Jackie led Theodora first to the living room, but felt as he did so that they needed to be farther from the dining room. Surely everything he said would be overheard if they stayed in the living room. He enjoyed the feel of her warm hand in his. She was becoming less strange to him every minute they spent together. Still holding onto her hand, he led her to what they called the piano room. The room's main feature naturally was his mom's upright Steinway, next to which was a small desk at which she worked on her scores. At the end of the room were two dark blue upholstered chairs perched on either side of a window, where Theodora and Jackie sat.

For a few seconds, Jackie looked carefully at Theodora, who modestly kept her daze downward. He was intrigued by their visitors. They looked so uncomfortable in their black habits. He was intrigued as well by the questions Theodora had asked him a few days earlier. They weren't like Rabbi Beck's questions. Rabbi Beck asked questions to make sure that his students had learned their lessons. An hour-long class on Sunday mornings on aspects of Judaism, then long questioning the next Sunday in which Jackie and his classmates were expected to say everything they'd heard the previous week. It sounded as if Rabbi Beck had asked the same questions many times before, as if he could teach the class in his sleep.

Theodora's questions were of a different order entirely. He had been annoyed for a while, yes, but then thinking back about it he'd wondered why. She had been polite, even if the questions were strange. It sounded to Jackie as if she didn't know how to ask questions, that she'd never before asked such questions. Her reaction to Jackie's answers was different, too. If Rabbi Beck thought the answer was correct, he just moved on to the next question, as if reading from a list imbedded in his memory. When Jackie's answers had been satisfactory—as he thought all had been—Theodora betrayed a hint of excitement, unable to conceal the delight she felt in his answers. She must have expected him not to answer at all.

And it was doubly strange to be questioned through an interpreter. He couldn't be sure that Grandpa was phrasing his answers exactly as Jackie had intended, nor could he be sure that he was correctly hearing in English everything that Theodora said in Greek. For first time in his life, he understood the great advantage of easily speaking two languages.

"I wish I could understand you better," he said.

Theodora looked up and smiled. "I try to learn English. You learn Greek?"

Jackie pointed to himself and said "boy."

"Boy. I know boy. *Agori.*"

"I am an *agori.* Boy." He pointed to the chair upon which he sat. "That's a chair."

She smiled and said, "You are sitting on chair. *Karekla.*"

"*Karekla.*" He pointed to the piano and gave its name.

"*Piano,*" she said, and both smiled to find that there were words common to both languages.

"Please wait here," Jackie said, pointing to Theodora's chair before running out of the room. Theodora was nice, he'd concluded. She was interested in *Hashem* and even knew the *Sh'ma,* although he didn't quite understand why she'd stopped saying Judaism's main prayer. Yes, she could be annoying, too, as when she asked if he obeyed *Ima* and if Max was his father. As to the latter, anyone could see the answer just using their eyes. But he sensed that the questions hadn't been intended to be annoying. They seemed more like general curiosity, maybe questions asked just so she could hear him speak. Jackie knew that the two nuns had come very far, all the way from Greece, because they wanted to meet him and *Ima*, as well as to see Grandpa again. His instincts told him that Theodora was sincere and wanted to be friends with him.

Quickly up in his room, Jackie looked around for a gift. She knew the word "piano." It had been a year since Jackie's last piano lesson. He looked in a drawer to see if there were some of his beginning piano books that he'd no longer need, but found nothing save a jumble of crayons and pencils. Then he looked at the top of his bookshelf and spotted the 3-D wooden puzzle, a model of a grand piano, that Jackie had assembled months earlier on a rainy afternoon when nothing else was going on. He stood on his desk chair and was able to reach the piano. He would give it to Theodora and tell her he'd made it.

Back downstairs, he saw that Theodora had obliged him by staying seated in her chair. He walked in with a big smile and presented her with the piano. "Sister Theodora, this is for you."

"*Piano. Ya mena?* For me?" She took the gift from Jackie and gestured toward herself.

"Yes, for you."

"For me. *Efcharisto poli*, Jackie."

Now that he had her attention and goodwill, he needed to question her, but his only language was English. Yet, he had to try. Maybe, when he saw her again, he could teach her more English.

"Why are you all dressed up like that in that costume?" He pointed to her black habit.

"Costume? *Then katalaveno*." She had foolishly left the dictionary at Helen's house.

"If you were Jewish once, if you were Grandpa's sister, why did you stop?"

"*Then katalaveno*."

Theodora didn't understand. The English had gotten beyond her. She wished she'd had the foresight to ask Fevronia to accompany them, badly wanting to understand what Jesus-to-be was asking. As long as she stayed in America, she would continue to work on her English, but for now she virtually was lost in the language when it got beyond basics. For now, she could either continue to protest her lack of understanding, in which case Jackie would soon give up asking questions, or she could request Fevronia or Nicky to interpret. Or, she could think of an alternative course of action. Then she hit suddenly on what she could try before asking for assistance. She gestured for Jackie to stand in front of her, which he did.

"*Aplete ta cheria sas.*" She reached for his hands, and he held them out as she had asked.

Theodora's hands were very warm to the touch. Jackie imagined that she might have a fever, although she didn't look sick.

"*Efcharisto. Tora, se parakalo klise ta matya sou.*" She leaned forward to show him how she wanted him to close his eyes.

He complied, wondering where this was all going. "Like this?"

"*Nai.*" It sounded at first like "no," and he opened his eyes, but Theodora's remained closed, so he closed his again.

"*Hashem?*" she asked.

He kept his eyes closed and thought about the word, but was not sure what he was being asked to do. What about *Hashem*? Did she want to talk about *Hashem* again? If so, why did his eyes need to be closed? Then he remember Rabbi Beck telling his class one day recently that *Hashem* could never be seen. Was she teaching him what Rabbi Beck had taught him or a new way of thinking of *Hashem*? *Ima* covered her eyes, of course, when lighting the *Shabbat* candles, until the *bracha* was over, so was this the same thing?

"*Hashem,*" she repeated, but this time not in the form of a statement. "*Pou esai Hashem, agori mou.*" (Where is *Hashem*?)

"What's going on here?" He opened his eyes to find *Ima* standing next to the Steinway, Nicky and Fevronia directly behind her. *Ima* didn't look mad or even concerned. She was smiling at them.

Theodora released Jackie's hands, turned, picked up the wooden model that Jackie had given her, and showed it to the other adults.

"*Piano mou.*"

EVERYONE DECIDES

Kayla understood at least part of what had happened. Jackie had given Theodora a present, the wooden piano puzzle he'd so painstakingly assembled. And they had been holding hands, or at least Theodora had held Jackie's hands. Jackie hadn't felt threatened at all. In a magical way beyond words, a small link had been created between her son and her aunt.

"It's very nice to have given Sister Theodora your little piano, Jackie."

"I tried to ask her questions, but she doesn't understand."

"She will soon, Jackie, because she's trying to learn English," volunteered Nicky. "What did you want to know? I can ask in Greek for you."

"Dad, I think we should ..."

"Wait, Kayla." Max had now joined the group. "She gets to question Jackie, so isn't it fair if he gets to question her?"

"Well ..."

Jackie addressed his grandfather. "I wanted to know why she dresses like that, in this black robe, and why she stopped being Jewish."

"Dad ..."

"I will ask her," said Nicky.

Theodora listened to the questions and wondered how to respond. A grown-up Jesus had to know the answers to both questions and wouldn't have needed to ask. But Jackie was still figuring out His own role in the world and couldn't yet see that He was the Son of God. Jackie was curious. Jesus was curious. Jesus insisted on honest answers to good questions, and Jackie would obviously do likewise.

She nodded at her brother. "I will answer. Please tell Him exactly what I say, Nicky." Then she turned to the boy. "Black is a symbol. It symbolizes humility and repentance. Do you know what those words mean?"

"No."

"To be humble, to have humility, is to see that a much greater power is above us. God is above us. You would say *Hashem.*"

"Yes, *Hashem* is above us. And below us. And all around."

"So wearing black helps me remember who I am compared to Our Lord. And repentance means that I am sorry for the bad things I did."

"What did you do that was bad?" Just as Jackie thought he'd begun to understand Theodora, he was now confused again. She looked like a good person. Really good. She was sweet. He could tell that she really liked him.

"Every moment when I am not thinking only about God, and what God wants us to be, I am a sinner."

"What's a sinner?" He'd heard Rabbi Beck use the term and thought he understood it, but wanted to hear her explanation.

"Someone who misses the mark. Someone who aims themselves not where they should be aimed."

"Do you mean like a pitcher that throws balls and not strikes?"

Here, Nicky couldn't help but chuckle. He tried to explain to Theodora the baseball analogy Jackie had come up with, but could tell immediately from her expression that she was confused. Of course, she would have had no conception of baseball. But she smiled at Jackie and continued.

"I think I know what you're asking. Maybe you've got it. Even when we try to be good and do as God wants us to do, we never quite get there. And, to remind us of our failures, to help us feel sorry for missing the mark, we wear black. Does that answer your question?"

He tried to imagine the Mets pitchers wearing black uniforms when they'd walked too many opposing players. It didn't exactly make sense, but he understood that Theodora wasn't really talking about sports. So he nodded.

"Yes, all right. But why did you stop being Jewish?"

"When I was a little girl, about your age, bad people wanted to kill me because I was Jewish. You know that terrible things like that happened?"

"*Ha Shoa.*"

"Then the Mother of God saved me. I know you've told me that God doesn't have a mother, but this is really what happened to me. She led me to believe in Our Lord Jesus Christ, and I became a Christian."

"Grandpa was in *Ha Shoa* too. But he stayed Jewish."

"The Mother of God, whom I call the Theotokos, saved him too."

"But he stayed Jewish."

"Everyone, Jes ... Everyone, Jackie, chooses what they will believe and what they won't. Everyone decides for himself if he will see the light of Our Lord. Everyone decides for himself if he believes he has been saved by Our Lord or not. You will decide too someday." Then Theodora realized she'd spoken too soon. Jesus would never have to decide if He believed in Himself. "What I mean is, some day you will understand better what I mean."

"I decide I'm Jewish." He looked hopefully at Kayla. "Right, *Ima*?"

"Totally right. It's your decision."

THE METS PITCHING STAR

Jackie lay in bed, unable to sleep, replaying in his mind all that had transpired between him and Theodora. He thought first about the last half-hour of her visit, when he had insisted upon pulling her upstairs, into his room, to play her tunes from his Artie Shaw CD. That, too, had created a problem. After conversation in Greek among Grandpa, Fevronia, and Theodora, Grandpa explained that nuns weren't supposed to listen to music, but that Fevronia had given Theodora a blessing in this one instance. Jackie wasn't sure what it meant for a person to be given a blessing, as he understood blessings were things that Jews gave to *Hashem*, but all the same, he was grateful that he could share his favorite music with his new friend. The language barrier wasn't a problem, as the first few songs on the CD were instrumental only.

As they listened, Jackie pulled his clarinet from its case, assembled it, and handed it to Theodora, indicating when Shaw's solos could be heard. Theodora seemed to understand. In a few minutes, however, Theodora handed the clarinet back to Jackie and took his hands in hers again. The position was awkward, because they sat side-by-side on his bed, half-turned toward each other. Jackie was willing to let his hands be held, though, as he liked the touch of Theodora's white skin on his black skin. Too soon, Grandpa reentered—he wondered whether Grandpa had been listening from the other side of the closed bedroom door all the while—and announced that Theodora had to leave. Helen needed to get back to her house and get to sleep, and Fevronia was tired too. Jackie reluctantly let go of Theodora's hands.

"Good night, Aunt Theodora." As soon as he said it, he wondered where that had come from; no one had told him to call her "aunt."

"*Kalinichta*, Jackie." Then, after a moment's thought, she added with a warm smile, "Good night."

"Good night. *Kalinichta*."

She gave him a big hug before she left.

When she was gone and he turned out his light, he mulled over the issue that had been troubling him since Grandpa and *Ima* told him of Theodora's intended visit. He'd overheard enough to understand that a mistake had been made, and Grandpa and *Ima* confirmed the odd mistake. Of course he wasn't Jesus. He knew that. He knew who he was. Jackie Covo. And Jesus, he'd learned, had lived long ago in Israel, where Jackie had never been. And, as it appeared, Jackie wasn't a grown-up and thus couldn't be Jesus, a painting of whom he'd seen around Easter in the *West Orange Chronicle*. Grandpa and *Ima* had assured him that Theodora would soon understand the truth and then would go home, back to Greece, still very happy to have met him. Everybody makes mistakes, he was reminded, and Theodora had made a mistake, a serious mistake at that, but we would love her just the same.

Anticipating her visit, Jackie concluded that she must have been a very stupid person to make such a mistake. Or, perhaps a better way to think of her might be like the fourth child mentioned at the *Seder*, the simple one who doesn't know how to ask a question. You have to lay it all out for them, from the beginning to the end. So he'd been prepared to lay it all out for Theodora.

And, yet, when he met her, everything he'd thought before quickly disappeared. She was neither stupid nor simple. In fact, it was quite the contrary. She was a very smart person, full of energy and light. More significantly, he understood that she was a person filled with love. She loved him. She cared deeply about him. He could feel that love as she washed his feet. And he could sense as well her love for the others in the family, Grandpa primarily, but also for Mom, Uncle Max, Helen, and the older woman she came with, Fevronia. He didn't know then how to lay it all out for Theodora. She didn't strike him as a person he could set straight, even if he wanted to, even as fundamentally wrong about his identity as she was.

He tried to remember what he could of their conversation. The ideas were confusing him; they swelled together to the point where it was hard for him to recall who had said what. Black clothes were an issue he could visualize, though, because Theodora and Fevronia were massively black in front of his eyes, in their garb if not their skin. He remembered Theodora said it was a symbol that *Hashem* was above, but not why. Then he vaguely recalled Theodora saying she was sorry for bad things she'd done, but what bad things? She hadn't been specific, and Jackie could not envision this gentle, loving woman having the capacity to do anything bad. And what did that have to do with baseball, anyway? Dwight Gooden was the Mets pitching star and struck out so many batters, but even he would walk a few, unable to get the ball over the plate consistently. But how could that be a sin?

The main thing that troubled Jackie, as he lay in bed fighting sleep, was why Theodora stopped being Jewish. You were born a Jew and stayed a Jew. There was something about *Ha Shoa* that made her stop being Jewish. He recalled insisting that he himself was Jewish, but that's where memory and understanding stopped and gave way to the sweet oblivion of slumber.

He remembered nothing about Theodora's mentioning the Mother of God.

THE BEST REPRESENTATION

Late on the next afternoon, Kayla and Max were ushered into the Newark office of Rebecca Friedman, of Ferrick and Friedman, who had been referred to Max by one of the partners in his firm. At first glance, Kayla thought Rebecca seemed too young to be competent and convincing. She couldn't have been a day over thirty. What persuasive power would such an attorney carry in a court of law? That she was very good looking, wore makeup, and wore a dress that revealed bared shoulders did nothing to recommend her, in Kayla's view. She should have asked Rabbi Beck for a referral instead of going with the attorney at the top of Max's list.

"Your brother's told me a bit about the case, Kayla. I'm very interested in helping if I can." Then she glanced at Max. "The thing is, for us to maintain a confidential attorney-client relationship, Max can't be part of this meeting. I should have made that clear earlier."

"But he's my brother. I live with him. I trust him."

"Of course. Yet, legally, I need to be very careful. The father's lawyer, Ken Greavey, is someone I've come up against before. He's tough and he leaves no stone unturned. Max is going to be a witness, whether he likes it or not, if this case ever comes to trial. Unless you want Max to be forced to testify about everything you and I say to each other in our meetings, he has to leave. I hope you can see why."

Kayla was about to protest again, but Max rose before she could get words out. "You're absolutely right, Rebecca. I should have known and never have stepped in here. I'll wait outside, Kayla. Take as long as you need." With that, he left.

"I wish you hadn't done that."

"Kayla, trust me, it's the only sensible way to proceed. You've come to me as an expert in family law, and I know what I'm doing."

The meeting lasted well over an hour. Friedman meticulously went over each allegation in August's complaint. No, there had not been parental abuse, save for the one instance—admittedly disturbing—in which Kayla, hallucinating, had placed her hands around Jackie's neck. Well, yes, there was more than placing; there had been squeezing, too. There was no denying the photographs—apparently obtained by Sorel from the police and attached to a supplemental pleading—of the bruises. But it was well-established, and Max, if he was to be a witness, could certainly testify to this as well, that Kayla had been good thereafter in taking her medications. Her psychiatrist would testify in conformation and offer the opinion that, as long as Kayla complied with her medications, she would not endanger Jackie. Yes, Jackie had developed a behavioral problem, and his own psychiatrist would likely say it was related in part to Kayla's attack, but the muteness had come and gone; it was now just an unhappy memory. Yes, she had in fact entrusted Jackie to her father and her father's girlfriend on a trip across the country, and, yes, during that trip her father had punched August, who had come upon them suddenly and been obnoxious, and yes, the blow had caused an injury, but to her father had been hurt as well as August, and, yes, her father had been served with papers in New Orleans, and, yes, they had fled the jurisdiction.

"That was the only reasonable thing for them to have done. New Orleans has absolutely no connection to Jackie or me or August, for that matter, and it was pure coincidence they ran into each other there. Don't you agree?"

"Well, if I'd been in your father's position, I might have absconded the same way. Still, it doesn't help his credibility much, if he takes the stand, to have him admit he fled from lawful process."

"Aren't you supposed to be helping me here?"

The lawyer sighed. The look on her face was one of resignation and recognition. Kayla sensed that Rebecca Friedman was looking at her as a type of client she'd had many times before. Maybe she was older than she looked. Kayla would have to investigate.

"One way I help you," Rebecca said, "is by telling you the truth, the real lay of the land. You need to know what will likely happen when any particular witness takes the stand. Now, you can find lawyers who will be only too happy to tell you what you want to hear. If that's the way you want to go."

"How many of these custody cases have you tried, if I may ask?"

"Three."

"Oh, great."

"But you see, it takes a smart lawyer to know when to fight in court and when to work for the best possible settlement. And to know when to fight, you need to evaluate credibility."

"Then let's talk about the credibility of August Sorel."

"Let's do."

"He abandoned me. Necessarily, he abandoned his son."

"Did you expect him to bring Jackie around the world with him as he gave concerts? No, of course not. You don't have to answer that."

"When he was in New York, except for the first few months of Jackie's life, he never even visited his son."

"We'll use that against him, if we have to."

"What do you mean 'if we have to'? We absolutely have to."

"What I mean, Kayla, is that we need to have a strategy, one that we both agree on, and I strongly suggest that the best strategy is one which minimizes the downside risk to you. Now, I've settled a score of these kinds of cases, and that's almost always a better way to go."

"The downside risk? Settle? Just please talk to me in plain English."

Rebecca picked up the folder on the desk before her. "These papers say he wants to take Jackie away, period. If the judge agreed, August would have full physical custody, and you'd be lucky to get supervised visitation once a month. That's the downside."

"I can't believe it."

"Well, you have to believe that it's a risk. I am telling you now that it's a risk, and I don't want you ever in the future to complain, to me or anyone else, if things go badly, that you weren't warned this was a possibility."

Kayla gritted her teeth and counted silently to ten, then twenty. "In those three cases you tried, did you win?" She fought unsuccessfully to keep the sarcasm out of her voice.

Rebecca put down the folder and carefully placed her hands in front of her on her desk. "Maybe, Kayla, you'd like a different attorney?"

"I just want to know if you won."

"I will answer you, but in my own way. Winning and losing seems to be a big concern, not only of clients but of everyone in the world. Well, in the three cases, there were both winners and losers. In every case, the child at issue was the loser. Even in the two cases in which full custody was granted to my client, the kids were the losers. Were my clients the winners in those two cases we won in a technical sense? They got what they wanted, or thought they wanted, which was to hurt the opposing party. Did they want their children to be hurt? Go ask them. They'll confirm what I just told you, that they ended up hurting their kids in the process of winning."

"Do you think Jackie's going to be a loser if I keep him with me as we are presently set up? That's going to be a loss?"

"No, not necessarily, in terms of his overall care, wellbeing, guidance."

"It's critically important for me that he be brought up Jewish."

"You say 'important for you,' but that's not a standard the judge uses in custody cases. The judge is required by law *not* to worry about what's important for you. The judge must consider only what's in the best interests of the child. Here's my point. Even if you win a contested hearing and even though you continue to take good care of him, what long-term effect will it have on him to be at the center of a big custody fight?"

"He wouldn't have to testify, would he?"

"He very well might. That's up to the judge. Imagine being put on the stand at age—how old is he?"

"Seven next week."

"Okay. Seven. Imagine being put on the stand at seven and essentially being forced to testify for or against one parent slugging it out with the other. Think that's easy?"

"I don't ..."

"And imagine if one of the things Jackie has to testify about is that his mother tried to strangle him."

Kayla started to cry. Oh shit, she thought. This is the last thing I wanted to do in front of this so-well-put-together lawyer. But she couldn't help herself. She cried because the things that she was being told now by Rebecca were the very things she had already figured out. There was no way she could really win, if winning meant putting Jackie through more trauma than she'd already put him through.

"I'm sorry, Kayla. If you want the best representation, which I can give you, I have to be brutally honest. I'm going to step out for a minute and chat with Max while you pull yourself together."

A DEGREE OF SECRECY

On the following evening, the day after her meeting with the lawyer, Kayla called Helen and asked if she could visit. Kayla valued Helen as a friend, as someone with good judgment, as someone whose professional experience as a social worker provided her with a fund of practical, helpful advice. And she knew that Helen loved Jackie as she loved her own grandchildren. Privacy wouldn't be a problem, either, as Helen was dropping off Fevronia and Theodora at the local Greek Orthodox church for an evening Bible study group and Nicky was staying the evening in Manhattan.

Their conversation didn't start out exactly as Kayla had imagined, though. During the usual pleasantries, Kayla could see that Helen looked depressed and tired, as if she'd not slept the night before, an assumption that Helen glumly confirmed when Kayla asked.

"I do have a lot on my mind."

"Well, that makes both of us, but you first. What's going on? Is it Dad? Is he being his usual jerky self?"

"I wish that was all. No, I mean, I love your dad. He can be trying at times, but what's on my mind now is Naomi." Kayla had met Helen's older daughter at Helen's house when she, Max, and Jackie had been invited to dinner on the Sunday evening shortly after Helen and Nicky had returned from Greece. "She does have uterine cancer and will have to start undergoing chemotherapy. She's taking it hard, of course. So many complications."

"I'm so sorry to hear that."

"And Catherine, my sister, is dying of breast cancer. It's spread to her bones. Her doctors say maybe a month or two. Maybe less. I may have to fly out there soon, maybe this week, maybe tomorrow."

"That's terrible. What's her Jewish name? I will add a *refuah shlema* for her to my daily prayer."

Helen thought for a second. "*Keturah bat Sarah.* Thank you for that."

"*Keturah bat Sarah.* Got it. That's going to be a tough trip. I can't imagine how difficult. I'm so sorry."

"We have to say our goodbyes. We have to try to forgive each other for whatever wrongs we did when we were kids."

"And here I was thinking you'd be able to help me with my issues."

"I want to hear them, and I'd be glad to help if I could. I can't help my daughter or my sister with the kind of help they really need. Only *Hashem* and their doctors."

"You can give them spiritual help, a mother's love, a sister's love. They need that more than anything."

They fell silent for a moment, each lost in her own thoughts. Then Helen remembered why Kayla was in front of her. She'd come to talk, and Helen was ready to listen.

"So, it's about Jackie and Theodora, I presume? How's Jackie reacting now that he's met Theodora and been subjected to her questioning?"

"That isn't the primary thing I wanted to discuss, but, to answer you, I don't see any clear harmful effect. *Baruch Hashem.* He's asked me a few times why Theodora's not Jewish anymore, and I've tried to explain, but he keeps insisting you can't just change your mind about what religion you are. I leave it at that."

"They did seem to have developed a rapport."

"Yes. So strange he gave her his model piano, but that gesture is the kind of thing Jackie would do, come to think of it. So I agree they've exhibited what you call rapport. Bonding. *Achadut*."

"Unity, yes. Then the real problem is not Theodora but ..."

"This custody suit. I know you've testified in custody cases a few times ..."

"Probably close to twenty. Never fun."

"Can you tell me anything useful?"

"Each case is different, Kayla."

"So I've heard. The thing is I'm being pressured on all sides to just give up, as I see it. August—biological father, although not a real father—has rights. So I'm told. The judge can be an asshole. So I'm told. Jackie would be better off having August in his life, in addition to Max and my dad. Max could be cross-examined, even though we live together. And if I fight, if I do what is clearly best for my son, I risk losing custody altogether and putting Jackie through the mill at the same time. He can be forced to testify."

"I'm not surprised by anything you're telling me. There's a lot of truth in what you've been told."

"Max could be forced to testify about how I hurt Jackie on that awful night."

"If it comes to that, Max would tell the truth but couch it in the least objectionable way. Max would do nothing intentionally to hurt you. He loves you dearly and he loves Jackie equally and takes great care of him."

Kayla sighed, lost in thought. After a minute of silence, she went on. "My case for complete custody and control is very weak, I'm told, because of what happened. I'm lucky I didn't kill Jackie. I'm lucky I wasn't thrown in jail. I'm extraordinarily lucky that Jackie doesn't seem to be suffering major consequences at this point, thanks to you and Dad, in particular, in getting him past that muteness thing."

"Are you asking me to testify for you, about what a good mother you actually are to Jackie? Because I most definitely will, if you want me to. Not as an expert, of course, but as a close friend, someone who's seen you and Jackie in action constantly over the past half year. And it can't hurt that, by profession, I'm a social worker."

Kayla smiled and leaned over to hug Helen. "Thanks, Helen. I wasn't asking that you testify, or at least I don't think I was, but if we go to trial, I probably will ask you. Makes sense. You're sweet for suggesting it."

"But ..."

"What I think I really need is advice. Do I have to listen to all these naysayers, my lawyer in particular? And Rabbi Beck, who tells me that Jewish law highly values children having two parents, not one? You'd think he'd value Max's presence more. You'd think he'd feel otherwise in regard to a non-Jewish father, but that point doesn't seem to be important to him at all."

"They're not asking you to give Jackie up."

"No. Just that I compromise somehow. But I can't see myself compromising with someone who's acted as badly as August has acted all these years."

To Helen, it was clear that Kayla wanted something that she wasn't quite able to express. Helen's offer to testify had been welcome, but hadn't been the reason Kayla came to visit and talk. And what advice could Helen possibly give, when both of them knew that Kayla would most likely have to do what her lawyer told her was prudent? Try to help Kayla accept that outcome? The truth was that Helen's own experience in testifying in custody cases made her hesitant to give even that much advice. In many of the cases in which she'd been involved, the party for whom she was testifying had relied upon attorney advice and things had not turned out as well as they had hoped. Lots of judges turned out to be assholes. Power went to their heads.

"These are tough cases, Kayla, and there's no right or wrong answer. You'll make the best judgment you can make when you need to, and, however things turn out, you know that your dad and I will be there to support you. And Max of course."

"If only …if only I could persuade August to drop everything. I don't have much to offer him, but maybe the full rights to the CD we recorded together. That's not worth very much, though. If I could only make August see how difficult it would be for Jackie, to have him suddenly pop up and interfere in Jackie's life. About how important it would be for Jackie—forget about me—to have a unified Jewish upbringing."

"You can't talk to August?"

"His phone number in Newark is unlisted. Plus, we're not supposed to have off-the-record discussions. Now, any communication between us has to be with the lawyers present. So I've been commanded."

Then it dawned on Helen what Kayla was asking of her. "You want me to talk to August, don't you?"

"Would you try, please? If it doesn't work, we've lost nothing, have we?"

"I didn't quite like the looks of him, when I saw him those few minutes in New Orleans. And someone who makes the reckless allegations he's made is definitely unstable."

"I know this would be asking a lot. If you say no, I'll understand."

Helen saw that Kayla needed to hear a positive response. Against her better judgment, she agreed to think about talking to August. She'd have to keep this whole thing quiet from Nicky, of course, even Kayla's visit, a degree of secrecy that bothered her. It wasn't that Nicky could command her not to engage. No one would command her as to anything. It was just that Nicky would be extremely unhappy and take it out on her in other ways, by withdrawal, silence, snide comments, and more.

If she decided to try something along the lines Helen suggested, Nicky would be the last to find out.

SAINT DYMPHA

After being dropped off at the Holy Apostles Greek Orthodox Church, by then the third church they had visited in America, both Fevronia and Theodora felt uneasy. Surprisingly, they entered to the stares of other congregants. Had the worshipers never seen nuns dressed in traditional habits? After the Divine Liturgy, the priest, the Venerable Arthur Sastrikos, walked over to introduce himself. Discovering where his visitors were from, he happily conversed with them in Greek.

"Yes, I did see everyone turn to look at you. Sadly, it is not often that we have guests here from a Greek monastery. Please do sit down for a bit, now that the service is over."

Fevronia did not want to get into any extended conversation with the priest, but felt compelled to follow his lead. He was, after all, in charge of all that happened in his church.

"So what brings you both here to honor my church with your presence?" he asked.

Fevronia tried telepathically to convey to Theodora that she was not to discuss her motivations. "Sister Theodora has a close relative here, her brother, and this is a family visit."

"Really? Is her brother a congregant here?"

"Hardly," Fevronia continued. "Her brother is Jewish. He lives in Manhattan, but we're staying in New Jersey with her brother's girlfriend."

Sastrikos looked puzzled, first waiting for Fevronia to continue, then turning toward Theodora, whom he likewise assumed would provide more detail. Theodora looked at Fevronia, seeking a silent blessing to allow her to answer further. Again moved by her interest in being polite, Fevronia nodded briefly.

"Most Reverend Father, thank you first for welcoming us to your church. I don't speak English very well yet—although I'm learning—so I couldn't fully appreciate those parts of your service. But the service was lovely."

"Very nice of you to say so. I take it then that your brother converted to Judaism?"

Theodora smiled, then shook her head. "We were born Jewish. I never thought of myself as having converted, but, from your point of view, I can see that's how it must look. It was the Holy Theotokos who brought me to the monastery where I've lived ever since."

Sastrikos nodded agreeably, happy that Theodora also seemed now ready to talk. "Ah then, you were inspired by the Holy Mother of God to ..."

"No, no, no. You don't quite understand. The Theotokos Herself literally carried me to the Holy Monastery of St. Vlassios after we flew across Greece to save my brother's life, which was right after the Theotokos rescued me from the locked closet where I was left to die. And would have died without Her intervention."

Sastrikos forced a weak smile, convinced that these nuns were either playing an ill-advised practical joke on him—one he didn't find funny—or that Theodora was delusional, but then the sudden change in Fevronia's expression, the look of despair, told him they were not trying to get him to laugh. It had to be the alternative. He remembered a study conducted in the United States in which exceedingly high rates of schizophrenia were found among cloistered Catholic nuns. He would have to find that study again, he thought, if these two nuns continued to visit his church. He didn't want any untoward behavior to disrupt his congregation.

"Most interesting." After neither of his guests offered to continue the conversation, he rose. "Would you excuse me please, while I say good evening to some of the others?" Without waiting for a reply, he walked off, silently praying to Saint Dympha, considered the patron for those poor souls suffering from mental illnesses. Her relics rested in Belgium, he thought, and could cure the most severe disorders. He would have to find a way to remind Fevronia of these cures. Perhaps the nuns might stop in Belgium on the way back to Greece. Born Jewish indeed. That must also have something to do with the fantastic story he'd heard.

"Why did you have to say all that?" Fevronia asked after the priest was out of the range of hearing. She couldn't suppress the urge to chastise, even though she knew Theodora had meant no harm. They stood, ready to leave, and made their way outside.

"I am sorry, Mother. I thought you were giving me a blessing to share. You've spread the truth about my encounter with the Theotokos in Greece, and I ..."

"Well, we're in America now, and we don't really know this priest, and this is not the kind of thing that one can just bring up casually."

"I am so sorry. I knew you didn't want me to tell him that we had found Jesus."

"My dear child: We found a boy, a lovely boy at that, but ..."

"You're going to tell me again He's not Jesus."

"I hoped, after your having met Jackie, you'd see it my way."

"But that hasn't nullified my vision, although I realize the boy doesn't know quite who He is yet."

The taxi they'd arranged rolled up, and the two got in, momentarily suspending their conversation as they provided Helen's address.

Fevronia was of two minds. In one mind, she could continue to chisel away at Theodora's beliefs, perhaps again invoking the concept of the Devil being at the root of Theodora's dream, but she saw how futile that attempt would be. Theodora had merely ignored her previous efforts to warn her that she was falling victim to the Devil's tricks. In the opposing mind, Fevronia began to feel a degree of awe at the steadfast way in which Theodora adhered to her vision. It was a degree of stubbornness Fevronia had seldom encountered in anyone, based on the same determination that led Theodora to devote so much of her time and energy to prayer.

"All right, then." She lowered her voice and leaned closer to Fevronia in the back seat of the taxi. "You've seen whom you believe is Jesus. Or will grow up to become the Jesus we know from Scripture. But the Second Coming hasn't occurred yet, as our holy books described it."

"No, you're right."

"Our Lord hasn't marched down from heaven in glory." She paused to clear her throat, the better to lecture. "And the Mount of Olives is still the Mount of Olives, all of which I've outlined for you before."

"Yes, you have."

"So I have to ask then, Theodora, what do you plan to do now? Certainly, I hope you're not thinking of staying in America to watch Jackie grow up? It might be twenty-five years before he reaches the age at which Jesus performed His miracles. You're not waiting here for that, are you?"

"I haven't made any such plans. I've promised to come back with you to the monastery. Whenever you return to the monastery, so shall I."

Fevronia sighed. "And I don't want to pull you back across the Atlantic until you're ready, but when might you be ready?"

"Not now. Please?"

As the taxi pulled up to Helen's house, Fevronia and Theodora could see that Kayla had visited; she was walking down Helen's front steps, and Helen was on her porch, smiling, saying goodbye with the slight wave of one hand.

"When, though? I can't stay here and abandon St. Vlassios indefinitely."

"You're not ordering me back?"

"I've thought about ordering you, yes, but I would rather you were fully ready to return of your own accord. "

"I will let you know. But, I just feel ..."

"What?"

"Something has to happen before I'll be ready." They paid the driver and got out of the taxi.

"What has to happen?"

"Another message from God."

"And what would that message be?"

"I don't know."

They stepped up onto Helen's porch. Helen and Kayla both greeted them with hugs.

WHERE OUR TRUE CALLING RESTS

It was a warm, humid night. Fevronia was anxious to enter Helen's air-conditioned house, but the four women lingered on the porch. Helen asked how well they had liked the church service, and Fevronia had been forced by politeness to answer pleasantly, if noncommittally. Very nice. The priest had sung with a very appealing baritone voice. And they had chatted with him after, ever so briefly. Would they return? Perhaps, but perhaps instead they might return to the other Orthodox churches they had visited before.

Then Theodora noticed that Kayla was wearing a gold Star of David necklace. It was not the one that Kayla had been given as a child, which she still wore under her clothing, but a new Star of David that Max had given her on her last birthday, larger, of better quality, and one that Kayla seldom wore. She'd worn it that evening, for reasons she couldn't have explained, after deciding to visit Helen. Theodora reached to finger it gently as it lay on Kayla's chest.

"*Parakalo?*"

Kayla smiled and nodded, letting Theodora do as she pleased. Then Theodora stepped back and spoke to Fevronia in English.

"Mother, may I stay with her? At her house?"

"To sleep there?"

"Well, yes, to stay there with her and Jackie until we leave America." She glanced at Kayla, then looked once more at Fevronia. "Will you please give me a blessing to do so, Mother?"

Fevronia saw that things had gotten completely out of hand. Once Theodora had left the monastery, she was more subject to the Devil's wiles. Her bizarre and dangerous requests would never stop. Fevronia felt a flood of adrenalin. She was sure something terrible would happen if she assented. She imagined Theodora dressing Jackie up with a crown and parading him down the streets of West Orange, singing praises to him as if he really was the Lord God Jesus Christ.

"Jackie does seem to like Theodora so ever much," Kayla observed, before Fevronia had a chance to object. "And he's most curious about her. I do have the extra bedroom, but wouldn't you want to come, too, Abbess? The room has two twin beds, you'd be more than welcome, and I know it would mean a lot to Jackie. He has a new friend." Then she turned to Helen. "Would you mind very much if Jackie, Max, and I stole your two guests for ..." She turned back to Fevronia. "For how long exactly?"

"I don't know even if I want to allow it." Fevronia turned toward Theodora. "My child, you are asking me for a lot. I've already acted outside my best judgment in bringing you to America. I will give you the blessing you seek on one condition."

"And that is?"

"We leave a week from today. Whatever experience you've sought by coming here, you've had. Whatever you think has to happen will either happen in the next week, or it won't, but that's my condition. I've been trying to explain that I can't wait forever. The monastery needs us. That is where our true calling rests. Sister Zoe needs me to take back the responsibilities of my job. Can you accept that condition?"

"Two weeks, Mother."

"You are sorely trying my patience, Theodora."

"I can accept two weeks, and if you grant me those two weeks, then I shall certainly thank you and the Lord Jesus Christ for your blessing. If my expectations or hopes haven't been met by then, I will know it's God's will."

Fevronia barely suppressed her anger at the nun she loved as a daughter, but she sighed and agreed. The women entered Helen's house—Fevronia was most grateful to get out of the heat, which had been making her sorely dizzy—to call the airlines and make return flight reservations.

No one thought to call Max or Nicky, to ask them for their consent or opinions.

GATHERED

Helen was deep in thought the morning after her houseguests had departed for West Orange. Perhaps she had agreed with the plan too easily, but then who was she to tell Fevronia and Theodora where they had to stay? If Kayla was happy to host them for two weeks, Helen would wish them well. When she'd later called Nicky to explain what had happened, he was aghast.

"But my sister needs someone like you around her. I love Kayla and Max and Jackie dearly, but that's a troubled household if there ever was one, and now Jackie and Kal will have unlimited contact. I wish you'd called me first. Maybe I could have dissuaded Kal."

"Kal or Theodora, whatever you call her, was determined. Like you, Fevronia hated the idea, you could tell from her expression, but went along with it because Theodora agreed to go back to Greece in two weeks. And they made their reservations already."

"Holy cow, as Phil Rizzuto used to say."

"What?"

"Just a baseball expression. I guess David couldn't bring himself to watch the Yankees after the Dodgers left. Anyway, I'll call Kayla to make sure everything's okay, but I must say things are moving along so quickly in a way I can't control."

"We never control these kinds of things. They just happen."

"Yeah, I know. And we roll with the punches."

"Talk to you tomorrow. Love you."

When her phone rang, Helen thought immediately that it was Kayla, wanting to reverse the process and send the nuns back to her. Or perhaps, she thought as she picked up the receiver, it was Nicky again, calling to further complain about the recent developments. But it was neither. Instead, a nurse was calling from the Rush University Medical Center in Chicago. Helen's sister was failing quickly, and if Helen wanted to see her, she'd better come now. That afternoon if possible.

She'd known Catherine was gravely ill and that, at best, had only a few months to live. She'd intended to visit her sister soon, yet with the drama of Fevronia and Theodora, she'd put off that depressing trip to Chicago. It appeared that she had waited too long; it was almost too late. She called Nicky and fortunately found him between patients. Nicky agreed they would both fly to Chicago at once. Ten minutes later, he called back with their flight information. They would meet at Newark International and could be in Chicago by five that afternoon.

In too much of a rush even to pack a suitcase, Helen called a cab, threw her toothbrush into her bag, walked outside to wait. The airport was crazy with summer holiday travelers and, it looked like, kids on their way back to college. She had with her a paperback that had been in her bag, but found it impossible to concentrate on reading, knowing that she was about to see Catherine alive for the last time, and then only with luck. The whole trip would have been wasted if not. Or maybe they would just stay in Chicago and wait for the funeral. But if Catherine was still alive, would they wait in Chicago for her to die? That was absurd. Neither of them would have funeral clothes or any other spare garments for that matter.

Midway Airport was only a tiny less congested than Newark International, and Helen fumed as they had to wait an inordinately long time on the taxi line. Finally, they got moving and made it to the hospital by six. They rushed to Catherine's room. Unbelievably, she was sitting half propped up on her bed. She looked terrible, her eyes were closed, her skin was yellow, but she was happy know that

Helen had come. She opened her eyes at the sound of Helen's voice, seemed to recognize her sister, and then noticed that Helen had brought a man with him.

"Who's that, Helen?"

"Why Catherine! That's Nicky. Nicky Covo? Don't you remember I told you we were seeing each other?"

Catherine closed her eyes again, tired from the exertion of having opened them. She grimaced through the pain that could not be managed with morphine. Nicky? She tried to process the name. She knew it must be an important name. She'd known a Nicky once. Was this the same person? The Nicky she'd known was little more than a boy. Tall, though. Cute. The same Nicky?

Nicky looked over at Helen, shaking his head sadly. He'd not seen Catherine since his wedding to Adel three decades earlier. Or had Catherine actually been there? Now he wasn't sure. Maybe the last time he'd seen her was in '46, when he moved out of the Saltiel family house, where Catherine, Helen, and their sister Irene had grown up. As he stood over the dying woman, he felt the room almost tilt with vertigo. To steady himself, he had to reach out to hold the edge of the night table next to Catherine's bed. This was the woman who'd seduced him, the woman to whom he'd lost his virginity, but oh so different now. That woman was strong, full of life in every sense of the word, even though a war widow, but the woman in whose presence he now found himself was a shell of what she'd been. She wouldn't remember their one-night affair. She wouldn't remember how scared she'd been later that she might have gotten pregnant. Fortunately, that hadn't happened. He took her hand gently. It was cold.

"It's Nicky, Catherine. I'm so sorry to find you ill."

She opened her eyes then and focused them on Nicky. "You are the same Nicky."

Same as what? he wondered.

"I came here with Helen because ... because she wanted to say how much she loves you. I mean ... we wanted to say how much we both love you." Now where did that come from? Deathbed visits were always full of inanities, like declarations of love to dying people you hadn't seen in many years. What you said didn't really make a difference, though. It was just the being there and the knowledge of the dying person that you were present near the end. He hoped, however awkward their meeting might be, that it brought some solace to Catherine.

Helen could perceive the barest of smiles on Catherine's face. Was she smiling because she recognized Nicky and remembered their tryst? Was she smiling because she'd succeeded in lasting long enough to see Helen again? Or was she smiling because she sensed how very close she was to the end of her suffering? The Bible spoke about death as if one was gathered thereby to one's "fathers." Putting aside the male chauvinist aspect of those who'd written the stories, the concept of gathering with one's family after death had always appealed to Helen. She'd decided long before to believe that she, too, would be gathered in this way when she died, and so felt that this would not really be her last meeting with Catherine, that somewhere beyond, in *Hashem*'s book, they would once more be words linked together in a well-constructed sentence.

"I do love you Catherine. I always looked up to you. I wanted so much to be like you."

Catherine's response was barely above a whisper. At first, Helen couldn't understand what Catherine had said. She leaned over close to Catherine's mouth and asked her to say it again. It seemed that Catherine pulled together her last bits of strength to speak louder and clearer. It was the last thing Catherine said.

"I'm glad you and Nicky found each other."

They decided to fly back to New Jersey and return two mornings later for Catherine's funeral. Her ex-husband and oldest son would make the necessary arrangements. It would be a gravesite service, quick and as painless as possible. They'd decided there would be no formal eulogy, but attendees could make a remark or two before shoveling dirt over the plain pine casket. Both Nicky and Helen would take their turns with the shovels.

Helen, too numb yet to feel the first pangs of grief, sat quietly and thoughtfully next to Nicky on the plane back to Newark. *Hashem* had been good to her. To them. He had allowed them to see Catherine one more time in this world and to let them hear her last words. Things like this didn't happen just by chance. There was a purpose behind everything. Often, one couldn't discern the purpose, but on this occasion *Hashem*'s purpose was obvious.

"Nicky."

He turned from the window, through which he'd been looking over the Appalachian hills.

"Yes, my love?"

"You asked me once, back in Greece, if ..."

"If you would marry me. As I distinctly recall, you said no, and I haven't brought it up since. I decided, if you ever did want to, you'd let me know."

"Well, does the offer stand? Would you still have me if I said yes now?"

He leaned over to kiss her. Then, pulling himself upright, he looked in the direction of the flight attendant call button, as if something there might tell him what do say. "Do we have time for a quick drink to mark our engagement?"

She fought the urge to laugh. "We're too close to landing, but maybe tonight. The thing is, though, I don't feel like celebrating now."

"I know."

"And, can we not tell anyone for a while? It'll cause a ruckus, to say the least, and I don't think I could take it, everything else going on. Let's get through the funeral and *shiva*. And *shloshim*."

"Of course. We can wait a month, as long as you and I know. I will leave it to you to say when we announce. You'll want us to be married in a *shul*, right?"

"I think so. If I decide yes, can you do that?"

"I'm pretty sure I can."

"Great. How do you say in Greek 'I love you'?"

"*Seyaro.*"

"I will try to remember. Please say it again."

DIVINE CONSCIOUSNESS

Fevronia watched Theodora pray in the corner of the bedroom given them in Kayla's house. She'd been sitting on one of the twin beds, staring at her younger colleague, for about ten minutes, apparently unnoticed. It was time they'd had another heart-to-heart talk about the status of Theodora's delusion. Because a delusion it clearly was. Fevronia had known both nuns and laypeople with mental illness, some of whom heard things that no one else could hear, some of whom saw things that weren't there, but never had she encountered anyone with as fixed a delusion as Theodora's.

She was also confused by Theodora's interactions with Jackie. Theodora's questions to him had mostly made sense, if Theodora was trying to find parallels between Jesus's childhood and Jackie's. But the question about whether Max was Jackie's father had rattled Fevronia's understanding. If Fevronia had been in Theodora's position—something impossible to imagine—she would have asked a question like "Do you realize that God is the father of us all?" That would have brought together the concept of God and fatherhood in a more appropriate manner.

And talking about repentance to a seven-year-old? What child could really understand those concepts? What child could really understand that all human beings were sinners? That it was in human nature to be a sinner, for which forgiveness needed to be constantly sought? Yes, surely Jesus as a child would have understood immediately, and Jesus as a child would have been able to lecture the adults on the subject. Jackie's response was what one would have expected only from a normal human boy of his age. Maybe this was the point Fevronia needed to make, to help Theodora realize she had been living in a self-made fantasy.

Theodora rose slowly from her kneeling position and sat next to Fevronia on the bed. "You've been here watching me, Mother. You wish to speak. Please tell me what is on your mind." Theodora knew that Fevronia was about to question her and had been praying for Divine insight into what she must say in response.

"How do things stand with you now, my child? And I mean, of course, with respect to the boy?"

"If you're asking me whether I still believe Jackie is Jesus come back to us, then the answer is yes, absolutely."

"Very well. I had hoped perhaps for a different response, that you now see him simply for the very human and lovable boy that he is."

"And should I lie to you and forsake my Lord?"

"No. I'm not asking that you lie. If you honestly feel as you do, then I won't challenge you on that belief, even though I don't share it."

"I know you don't believe me, even though my vision comes from God. I think I've come to accept that no one will believe me, Mother, as much as it hurts to admit that." Theodora paused and looked suddenly into the corner of the room, as if noticing for the first time that someone else was watching her from that vantage. Fevronia half-expected Theodora to welcome another person into their conversation. The gesture harbored some painful disclosure, a confession perhaps, a plan that Theodora was about to put into action. Would it be that, despite the absence of belief in those around her, Theodora was determined to announce to the world that Jesus had returned? Would she obstinately invite everyone to share her delusion? Would Theodora divorce herself from Fevronia's tutelage, settle herself at another monastery, maybe one here in America, now that they had irreconcilably different beliefs on this fundamental question? Would she even abandon Orthodox Christianity altogether and join one of the cults that Fevronia had studied?

"I'm sure it must be painful, to feel that you're the only who sees the truth."

"Nothing like the pain of our Lord Jesus Christ on the cross, however."

"There is no pain like that." Here, at least, was one important idea upon which they could agree.

"But this ache I feel, let's call it a burning ache, tells me I must do something extraordinary."

"For which you will seek my blessing?"

Theodora had never done anything outside of the monastery's daily prayer regimen for which she'd not sought a specific blessing. That Fevronia asked at all betrayed her doubt about her continued influence over Theodora. As the silence grew, Fevronia's anxiety grew with it.

"I'm not sure yet, Mother. Because I'm not sure yet what it is I'm meant to do. God means me to do something. I sense that He wants me to put matters ahead somehow. To make a beginning, and thus to make an end. To bring things around. To find the holy ground."

"I don't understand. What can you do? What are you thinking of doing?"

"My English is getting better. I could become His teacher."

Here, Fevronia thought she saw an opening based on logic. "But Jesus doesn't need a teacher, Theodora. Jesus was the teacher. He taught us, and He still teaches you. Do you see how off the mark you are?"

"Jesus does need a teacher now. I can teach Him."

"You are sadly mistaken, my dear child, although I love you as much for your mistake as I ever loved you for your miracles. Jesus is the Son of God and is as perfect as the Father. Jesus is God and needs no one to teach Him. No one did teach Him. Jesus has possessed all knowledge from before the beginning of time. If you feel that Jackie, your grandnephew, needs a teacher, then logically he cannot be Jesus."

"I thought you would argue that. I have thought for a long time about what you would say to me."

"Well?"

"Far be it from me to correct you, Mother. That has never been my role, and I know you are wise and learned beyond my comprehension, and I owe so much to you, for how you have taught me and let me be the person I needed to be, but ..."

"But nothing. You need to trust me when I tell you that your own thoughts prove that Jackie is just a boy. God does not need to be taught."

Theodora stood, walked to a corner of the room, the corner to which just minutes before she'd looked as if someone was watching her. She turned. "When I pray—as do we all—I pray for a share of the Divine consciousness, a glimmer. At times, it's almost a oneness with God."

"Yes."

"I trust my feelings. When I joyfully encounter that state of being, even if it's just for a few seconds, I know myself and my capacity as a human being better than at any other time. I know myself as an instrument of God's will."

"Yes, but ..."

"If I could not trust my feelings, I could not begin to share in God's consciousness. That's how I know that Jesus needs a teacher now. A guide. My feelings, my recognition, cannot be displaced by your logic, as loving as you are to me. Logic has no role when it comes to knowing and understanding God, what God wants and what God needs."

"God needs us to open our hearts to Him, but does not need to be taught."

"We are characters in God's book, and He's written this book to hear us speak. Just as we need God to guide us, God also needs us to guide Him, at times. I'm sure of what I'm saying."

Fevronia felt physically ill as she contemplated the true meaning of Theodora's words. Theodora was quickly slipping away from Orthodoxy. She was, in a moment of supreme individual hubris, positing the fantasies of her mind as truth and, in so doing, rejecting the two-thousand-year teachings of the Church. Theodora didn't realize it, but her assertions starkly contradicted the humility that she otherwise embraced. God needed no one, not even a devout nun, to take Him in hand.

Fevronia could see the grave jeopardy into which Theodora's life as a nun, her ability to continue as a nun, had fallen. Had any other nun engaged in the kind of blasphemy that Theodora now voiced, that nun would be put out of the monastery and instructed to retake her normal life as a layperson. But Theodora wasn't any other nun. She had performed miracles with the Theotokos. She was destined—or should have been until this recent turn of events—to become a saint herself. Fevronia could not just dismiss her without first trying to undo the damage already caused by Theodora's fantasies about Jackie.

Fevronia also realized that she wasn't going to make any progress with Theodora in this conversation. The issues she faced now seemed well above her ability to address alone, but her own religious father, the Metropolitan, was thousands of miles away. She would have to think things through very carefully before doing anything. She would need to seek counsel, but from whom she was unsure. Theodora's brother, Dr. Covo? Her niece, Kayla? They had no idea about what it meant to observe Orthodox Christianity. But talk to a priest in America she barely knew? There wasn't anyone with whom she felt she could seek the necessary counsel. It was imperative they return to Greece.

One key question remained now, however.

"I have tried to teach you to embrace that Divine moment, although again I fear you are being misled by the Devil. And how can you possibly teach Jackie? I have to call him by what I know to be his real name. How can you possibly teach him when you and he don't speak the same language of faith? He's Jewish. He believes there cannot be a Divine Trinity. The task you've set out for yourself is hopeless from the start."

Theodora smiled and nodded slightly. It was another argument of Fevronia that Theodora had already anticipated.

"Oh, we do speak the same language of faith."

"This has got to stop, Theodora. We have to get ready to return to our monastery. Nothing will change in the next two weeks."

"That is for God to decide."

ADJOURNED

Judge Jill Haney's courtroom in the Essex County Courthouse was tiny and windowless. There were two small tables facing the bench. At one table sat Kayla and her lawyer. At the other table sat August and his lawyer. Behind the low wood bar, in the spectator area, Peggy O'Dell sat next to Nicky, Max, and Helen.

The judge's clerk called the case. "*Sorel v. Covo*, Emergency Motion for Custody Order."

"Make your appearances for the record, counsel," ordered Haney in a no-nonsense voice. Nicky had been in many trials as an expert witness during his career and had heard many judges address lawyers, but wasn't sure he'd ever heard a judge sound as impatient as Haney now sounded.

"Ken Greavey for the complainant, Judge."

"Rebecca Friedman for the respondent."

"I've read your papers, counsel," Haney said, looking at Greavey. "Is there anything you need to add?"

Greavey stood and approached the podium between the small tables. "Time is of the essence. The minor child, Jackie Covo, should be removed from his mother's physical custody at once. She's a danger to his life, and ..."

"I read all that already, Mr. Greavey. No need to repeat what you've already written. Anything else?"

"No, Your Honor." The chastened Greavey resumed his seat.

"And you, Ms. Friedman, you haven't filed papers yet?"

"That's right, Your Honor. We were only served with this emergency motion yesterday. I reserve the right to file a written response, but I have three witnesses here who will testify that my client, Ms. Covo, is not a threat at all to Jackie, and Ms. Covo is prepared to testify about Mr. Sorel's non-involvement in his son's life for seven years."

"I see Ms. O'Dell is here as well. Thanks for coming on such short notice." The judge fumbled for a second at the papers on her desk. "I don't think I've received any report from you yet. Have I?"

The guardian-ad-litem stood and spoke from behind the bar. "Not yet, Your Honor, but I have only recently talked to the principals, and briefly at that. I can share what I know if necessary. But I see absolutely no reason to change the present arrangement. Jackie is very well cared for where he is."

"Very well. Mr. Greavey, put on your case. What's your evidence?"

"It's in our papers, which include a certified copy of the hospital record for Jackie's admission after his mother tried to strangle him. Did strangle him. And Mr. Sorel can testify about how he's prepared to make a home for Jackie in Essex County."

"Ms. Friedman."

"We object to the hospital report as evidence, as it's clearly hearsay. We don't dispute that there was an incident, but the statements about what Ms. Covo was or wasn't trying to do can't be considered because ..."

"Stop right there. In the best interests of the child, I can and will use any information, whether formally hearsay or not. Is that clear?"

"Very clear, Your Honor. In which case, Ms. Covo and my other witnesses are prepared to testify and refute the allegations."

"Ms. Odell. Does the complainant have the facilities and wherewithal to take care of the minor child?"

"He claims he has an apartment in Newark, but I've not seen it. We met in my offices last night at my request. He also claims he has a housekeeper who will look after Jackie while he's away on his concert tours, but I've not met her, so I can't verify that or evaluate what type of caretaker she would be."

"Concert tours? August Sorel? This is the violinist I've read about?"

Greavey stood quickly. "Your Honor, Mr. Sorel can explain fully what his arrangements are. And we can ...we can maybe bring in the housekeeper at some point."

"At some point, counsel? You're the party that requested this emergency hearing, which by the way is keeping me from a meeting. You could have brought the housekeeper if she was going to be part of your case."

"Here's her phone number." Greavey wrote something on a slip of paper and held it out as if the judge could reach ten feet and take it from his hand.

"Give that to the clerk, please." The judge whispered something to the clerk, who got busy on his telephone.

"No answer at that number."

"Put on your evidence, Ms. Friedman. And it better be quick."

Kayla took the stand, a determined look on her face. Nicky had often seen that look, one of extreme focus and dedication to the task at hand. If Kayla was nervous, Nicky saw no evidence of it. He noticed, however, that she was holding the smooth stone that she'd taken from near Adel's grave.

Friedman stood at the podium without notes. "What happened that night, Kayla? Please tell the judge."

"I am ill with schizophrenia, Your Honor, and I had stopped taking my medication for about a week. It was a bad mistake, for which I will always be sorry, but since then I have faithfully stayed on my medication, and there's been no recurrence."

"How can Judge Haney be sure you won't go off your medication again? How can you be sure?"

"I know I hurt Jackie. I know now, painfully so, what the consequences could be of not caring for myself properly. I doubt that there's any mother in the word who's as aware as I am."

"Have you been through counseling about this?"

"Yes. Jackie and I have seen a therapist, we've met as a family, including my brother Max, with whom we live."

"Has the counseling ended?"

"We stopped going two months ago because we felt that we'd obtained the full benefit. And there's been no recurrence. I've continued to take my medication as directed, and Jackie seems comfortable around me, as always. I still bring him to his psychiatrist once a month. She would notice if there were any continuing problem."

"Mr. Sorel here is Jackie's father, right?"

"Yes."

"How old were you when you were impregnated by him?"

"Just sixteen."

"Did he stay around New York for Jackie's birth?"

"No. He was on tour."

"Did he visit his new son when he came back from that tour?"

"Only once."

"Did he pay or offer to pay for your medical expenses, hospital, doctor's care, things the baby needed?"

"I received a check once for two hundred dollars. That's it."

"But you didn't file a motion for support, did you?"

"No, I didn't."

"Why not?"

Here, Kayla paused, seeming to collect her thoughts. "Honestly, my father had money. He's here in the courtroom." She glanced Nicky's way. "But, probably more important, I didn't feel Jackie or I needed anything from August, and August was obviously happy that way because ..."

"Objection. Speculation."

"Overruled. Mr. Greavey, don't waste my time with frivolous objections."

"My apologies, Your Honor."

"Ms. Covo, please continue."

"From everything he said, from everything he did, I could see August wanted to move on, from both me and from Jackie. And I didn't want to tie myself to someone who had so little interest in his child. And for these seven years, he's not made efforts to visit, he's not sent money, he's not sent presents to Jackie, not even a card on his birthday. He's not called. He's not even sent a CD of his recordings."

"No further questions."

"Cross? And it better be brief, Mr. Greavey."

Greavey stood and took his place at the podium. He banged a fat file down onto its top.

"You've had paranoid schizophrenia for years, Ms. Covo, have you not?"

He picked up from his table a copy of the Diagnostic and Statistical Manual and read portions to her. "Delusions? Hallucinations? Disorganized thinking? You've had all these?"

"At times. When I'm not properly medicated. Most of the time— all the time now that I'm keeping up on the meds—I function perfectly well. I'm a composer now. My work is ..."

"You know there's no cure for schizophrenia, don't you?"

"If there was, I wouldn't still have the disease."

"And medications can have unpleasant side effects, can't they?"

Kayla paused for a second and stared at Greavey as if he were the Devil himself. "Yes, they can."

"You don't like those side effects, do you?"

"No, I don't."

"And when you stopped taking your medications, even though you knew you'd be close to your son, even though you knew you still had the disease, it was because you just got tired of the side effects, isn't that right?"

"That's not right."

Greavey suddenly seemed unsure of himself. "That's not right?"

"She answered that already, Your Honor." To Nicky's ear, Friedman's voice carried much the same tone of annoyance as the judge's. Of course, she was reputedly a very good lawyer who would channel the judge before whom she stood. The voice said that somewhere there was a lunch to be eaten, a call to be made, a meeting to attend, an opinion to write.

"You're on Abilify now, correct?" Greavey continued.

"Yes."

Greavey picked up another document. "Dizziness, lightheadedness, drowsiness, nausea, vomiting, tiredness, excess saliva, drooling, blurred vision, weight gain, constipation, headache, trouble sleeping. Quite a list of severe side effects, isn't it?"

Nicky was pleased that Kayla refused to answer. She had been well coached.

"Haven't you had those side effects?" he continued, feigning anger.

"As anyone does occasionally, I've been dizzy. But that's because I sometimes sit up too fast. I had nausea when I caught a stomach bug. And ... I walk miles every day to keep off the weight."

"You're wasting time, counsel," sniped Judge Haney. "Anything else?"

"Not at this time."

Judge Haney took a sip of water from a plastic bottle and cleared her throat. "Here's what we're going to do. The hearing's not over. We'll set a date about three months down the road for a continuation. There's no need for an emergency order to take custody of the minor child from Ms. Covo. Ms. Covo, I urge you to use the assistance of the guardian-ad-litem to work out a settlement in which the father, Mr. Sorel, can get visitation with his son. Let's see. We'll set a date in November for the next hearing, a status conference." She consulted momentarily with the clerk. "All right. Be here at noon on November 28. Anything else?"

"One thing, Judge." Friedman took a place at the podium as Greavey picked up his file and sat again. "We don't want contact between Jackie and Sorel at all until the Court hears the full evidence. As we've pointed out and as has not been contested, he's had no contact at all for Jackie's entire life. If the Court decides, after a full hearing, to grant some visitation, of course we'll want that to be supervised visitation."

"Yes. I agree. Most certainly, I agree. Mr. Sorel. No contact at this time, whatsoever. Is that clear?"

"But ..."

"No contact. Did you hear me?"

Greavey whispered in Sorel's ear. They seemed to argue for seconds. Finally, Sorel answered. "Yes, Your Honor, I do hear you."

"Good. Then we're adjourned."

A LIGHT DRIZZLE

Except for one particularly cool spell, it had been sizzling hot for most of August, and when Jackie stepped out of the *Chabad* auxiliary building, where he attended school, he wasn't surprised at the heat. What surprised him, however, was how dark the sky was. A thunderstorm had just passed through. His classmates could hear the thunder as they were wishing Jackie a happy seventh birthday, when the cupcakes from the Papa Ganache kosher bakery had been distributed and were half-consumed. What surprised him also was that he couldn't see his mother's blue Dodge. She was always waiting for him in the queue, sometimes a bit farther back, sometimes closer, but now as his classmates met their rides, she was nowhere to be seen. He would find out later that evening that she had been delayed by a flat tire.

"Your ride's not here?" asked Rabbi Beck on his way out, snapping open his black umbrella.

"She will be."

The rabbi looked doubtfully about, then turned once again to Jackie.

"Well, our secretary's still here. If you need to make a call, go inside and tell her."

"All right."

"And *yom yoledet sameach* again."

The rabbi walked off down the street toward his house. Watching him depart, Jackie wondered if he should have asked to walk along, sharing the umbrella, because at least the rabbi was walking in the right direction. But Jackie then would have had to navigate about a half-mile to his own house, would have had to cross busy Orange Avenue where there were no traffic lights, and would have been thoroughly soaked by the time he made it home. *Ima* would surely be along to pick him up soon.

Then an unfamiliar car—a bright red convertible—drove up and stopped in front of him. From it emerged a tall, good-looking, black man, a man who sported a mustache, goatee, a diamond earring in one ear, and a black leather cap pulled low over his forehead. He was smiling at Jackie, approaching, holding a paper bag in his hand. There was something familiar about him. Jackie wasn't scared at all.

"Hi. You're Jack, aren't you?"

Jackie smiled and nodded, curious. "I'm Jackie, not Jack."

"Oh, right. Well, I'm your father, Jackie. We met in New Orleans."

And then Jackie remembered. It had been about two and a half months since the JazzFest. The man who had had a fight with Grandpa. The man who Grandpa and Helen and he had run away from. But the man in front of him didn't seem threatening at all.

"Do you remember me?"

Again, he nodded.

"Well, you can call me Dad."

"Okay Dad."

"I see you're quite alone here and the weather is bad. How would you like a ride home?"

Jackie looked up the street again to see if perhaps *Ima* had arrived. But she hadn't. He could go inside again and ask Mrs. Rosenberg to let him call home, but what if no one answered? He had his own key, after all, had possessed one for over a year, ever since he was allowed to play outside by himself, so getting into the house wouldn't be a problem.

"And I have a present for you." The man—his dad—held up the bag and opened it so Jackie could peek inside. He could see a Star Wars action figure.

"Okay."

The man put his hand on Jackie's shoulder and nudged him to the sleek red car, opened the door, and gently pushed Jackie inside. Then, in a second, the man was around to the driver's side and sped away from the curb even before Jackie could fasten his seatbelt. The man reached under his seat and clicked a button. Jackie wondered what that could have been.

"Hey, mister ..."

"Dad ..."

"Hey, uh ... Dad. You missed the turn for my house."

"Don't worry. I know where you live, because I've been there myself, and for sure I'll take you home in a minute. I just need to make a quick detour."

They turned left on Bloomfield Avenue. Jackie knew the name of the road, had always paid attention when *Ima* or Uncle Max drove him anywhere. Then they made a right, and Jackie knew this led to a steep hill and wooded area called the conservancy. This afternoon, the road was not heavily travelled. The persistent rain would keep hikers away. Now he was getting a bit scared. What if *Ima* had come for him after he'd left and had not seen him waiting as usual? She would go inside and talk to Mrs. Rosenberg, who surely wouldn't know where he had gone. Now the man parked at the side of the road.

"I want to ask you a few questions, Jackie, before we go home. The sooner you answer me, the quicker you'll get there. All right?"

"All right."

"Last February, do you remember when your mom attacked you?"

Finally, he understood what had happened. He'd known, even without being told explicitly, that his dad wanted to do something to hurt *Ima*, something to do with lawyers and judges and official papers. Something to do with him. This was a part of his dad's plan. But surely his dad wouldn't hurt him. Would he?

"When your mom attacked you ... hurt you ... do you remember?"

He closed his eyes to help himself think. He did remember something. But it was hard to explain.

"Tell me what happened, and I'll take you home."

"I couldn't breathe for a while."

"How did you feel?"

"I was scared." Now that he was talking, the words started to come more easily.

"She could kill you next time."

He understood and was frightened. Was there going to be a next time? Certainly, if this man, his dad, said so, then there had to be. He felt himself gasping for breath, struggling. He tried to grab and push away the imaginary hands around his throat.

"But don't worry, Jack. If you're with me, no one will try to kill you. No one will strangle you. When the judge asks, you want to live with me. Do you understand?"

At once, as if by magic, the sense of being unable to breathe had disappeared.

"Okay."

"Say: Okay, Dad."

"Okay, Dad."

"And your uncle. He's hurt you too, hasn't he?"

He remembered being very angry once with Uncle Max. What had Uncle Max done to him? Grabbed him. That was it. So unfair.

"Uncle Max tells me to stop practicing when I need to practice."

"He hits you, doesn't he?"

"I don't know. Maybe?"

"You can do better than maybe. He hits you, doesn't he? He makes you miserable, right? He's only pretending to be like a father, right?"

So many questions. So confusing. He had to get home. *Ima* would be worrying about him now.

"Right."

"What right? Yes is your answer? To all my questions?"

"Yes, Dad."

August reached under his seat, and again Jackie heard a click. "Now I'll take you home, and don't tell anyone about our little visit. I'll save that as my surprise. Say you decided to walk home and got lost for a while. Do you understand?"

"Yes."

"Say: Yes, Dad."

"Yes, Dad."

Four blocks from his house, August let Jackie out of his car and told him to walk the rest of the way. Jackie, anxious to get home, left the Star Wars figure in the car. A light drizzle had returned, but did not dissipate the warmth of the day. The steam bath through which Jackie plodded up the hill sapped him of energy. Then he noticed that a police car, its lights flashing, was parked outside his house, and a policewoman was there, talking to *Ima* and Uncle Max. In the driveway, *Ima*'s car was up on a jack and the right front tire was missing.

He called out to them. Kayla looked his way and ran toward him, screaming in relief.

SERIOUS PATHETIC PSYCHOLOGY

"Where have you really been, Jackie?"

Ima was angry. Uncle Max was angry. He'd not meant to do anything wrong. He'd been careful to tell the police officers exactly what his dad had instructed him. He'd decided to walk home and had gotten lost. The police officers had frowned and shaken their heads though, not believing him. Nor had *Ima* or Uncle Max, but he stuck to his story, and, when they decided he was unhurt and didn't need medical attention, the officers left, warning *Ima* and Uncle Max to keep a closer eye on him. The officers rolled their eyes when *Ima* accused his dad of deflating the tire on her car.

Now that the police had left, he was being grilled again. *Ima* and Uncle Max had not believed him for a minute.

"I said ..."

"I know what you said, but it's ... it's a sin to lie. It's one of the Ten Commandments, not to lie. *Lo ta-aneh b'reacha eyd shacker. Hashem* hates it when someone lies. Particularly little children, who should know better." *Ima* paused for a second, and it looked as if Uncle Max was about to speak, but *Ima* put her hand up into a stop sign.

"I don't want *Hashem* to be angry with me," he said glumly.

"And it's also a sin not to treat your mother with honor. And to lie to your *Ima* is a compounded sin, violating two of the commandments."

Now there were two commandments against him? He'd lied because his dad had told him to. Wasn't there also the commandment about honoring a father? He was sure that Rabbi Beck had said "You must honor your father and your mother." Did *Ima* forget that?

"So what really happened?"

He broke down and told all he remembered, afraid that he'd be punished. It hadn't turned out that way, though.

"All right, Jackie. Thank you for telling me the truth."

Uncle Max asked *Ima* whether they should call the lawyer. Yes, it was all about the court papers.

"And the guardian, too, don't you think Max?"

Who was the guardian? Wasn't it enough to have *Ima* and Uncle Max and Grandpa and Helen looking after him?

"I think that's a good idea, but talk to Friedman first," Uncle Max responded. They talked almost as if Jackie was no longer in the room. "And, you know, even before you do that, talk to Dad. There's some serious pathetic psychology going on here with Sorel. Get his advice first."

"Good thinking. Will do."

CHANA AND SHMUEL

About a week after Fevronia and Theodora moved to Max and
Kayla's house, Jackie had what he would years later describe to his
therapist as "the weirdest experience of my young life." Max had
stayed late at the office, and Fevronia had convinced Kayla to drive
her to evening services at St George's Greek Orthodox Church in
Piscataway. Kayla would never have left Jackie alone, but Theodora
had not wanted to join Fevronia; she preferred to pray at home. So,
because Kayla knew Theodora would hustle Jackie out of the house
in the event of a fire, she had no concerns about leaving him in her
care. Besides, Kayla thought, she'd be gone for only thirty minutes
or so, depending on traffic. She warned Jackie to behave himself
while she was away and reminded him to practice his clarinet.

"Sure, *Ima*."

He did indeed begin warmup scales until he was confident that
his mother and Fevronia had driven away. Then he put down the
clarinet and listened for sounds that might tell him where Theodora
was praying. By this time, a pattern had developed, one that Jackie
observed even if no one else in his house did.

Theodora had taken to praying in different rooms at different
times of day. In the early morning, well before breakfast, Theodora
prayed in the piano room, kneeling before the very same blue
upholstered chair that she'd sat in when she and Jackie had had their
first interaction there. Jackie discovered her quite by accident

because he'd woken up ravenous at four in the morning and had come downstairs for milk. He'd been very quiet, noticed Theodora praying, then took his milk upstairs. He was sure she'd not known that he'd seen her.

After breakfast, Theodora would kneel in the bedroom that she and Fevronia shared, praying with the abbess. Although the door to that room was always closed, *Ima* had told him they were praying, and he'd been careful not to disturb them. Prayer was important, not only to *Ima*, but to Rabbi Beck and to Helen and obviously to the visitors from Greece. That they had to pray so much, though, did bother him. If you pray, you say a series of *brachot* to *Hashem*, *Hashem* hears these prayers, and you're good, at least for a day. Sure, before going to sleep you have to say *Sh'ma* and when you wake up you have to say *Modeh ani l'fanecha*, but even the very religious Jews who went to *Chabad* didn't pray more than three times a day. Yet, it appeared to Jackie, the nuns had to pray all the time. Well, except for eating and talking occasionally. But when they used the bathroom, he imagined, they were probably praying then too.

Was it that their God wasn't listening closely enough? Was it that they had more to say to their God than Jews had to say to *Hashem*? If so, he wondered what else could be said, other than repeating the standard *brachot*. Or, he thought, maybe this was another form of punishment, just like Theodora had said having to wear black robes was punishment. That this was a practice imposed upon them because of their having done something bad was possible, but they were good people and had always been very nice to him.

With these questions in mind, Jackie thought he knew where Theodora would be praying. It wouldn't be in the bedroom, because she knew by now that Jackie's practicing could be heard there. She'd be praying elsewhere in the house, and the only place that made sense, where she could be alone, was the finished basement. The room was sparsely furnished. There sat the family's only television, seldom used. The room was sparsely furnished. Besides the television, there was a threadbare sofa and a bookshelf, whose contents included a few dark-green bound volumes of plays by William Shakespeare— Jackie had recently tried to read *The Merchant of Venice* but found it way too difficult—and volumes from The Book of the Month Club that Uncle Max had collected. Jackie had browsed one day and begun to read *The Pillars of the Earth*, but *Ima* had caught him while he was still on the first page and chastised him for reading garbage. He never again looked at these books, and it seemed that within months Uncle Max stopped receiving them. *Ima* was the boss. And finally there was the ironing board, used while *Ima* watched TV in the afternoons. "Soap operas," she said, as if that was supposed to mean something, but Jackie wasn't allowed to watch with her. If they were bad for him to watch, then why was *Ima* watching them?

Jackie quietly opened the door at the top of the steps to the basement and saw light at the bottom. He smelled the piney incense that Theodora had lit. That was another thing that puzzled him. Why burn incense when praying? What good did that do? The incense that Jackie and *Ima* smelled at *havdallah* service, as they reluctantly said goodbye to *Shabbat*, was sweet-smelling. It was to remind them of the sweetness of *Shabbat*. But the incense that Theodora burned did not smell sweet. It smelled sharp and prickly. Was it part of the prayer? Was smelling it part of the punishment? He wished he could ask Theodora those questions, but wasn't sure they could communicate well enough without either Grandpa or Fevronia to translate.

Jackie inched his way downward, as quietly as possible, yet he knew that he would inevitably interrupt Theodora. He would kneel next to her and try to pray. As it turned out, he was unable to conceal the sound of his footsteps on the linoleum-covered floor. Theodora turned her head to see who had come into the room, then smiled at Jackie and, by the gesture of patting the floor, invited him to join her. "*Ela edo se, parakalo.* Please to sit."

It was exactly what Jackie had wanted. He drew near, then kneeled himself. Theodora kissed a small, rectangular gold box that

Jackie now noticed for the first time. In a small window of the box, he saw the picture of a woman and baby. He understood immediately—perhaps he had seen something like that before—that the baby was the Jesus to whom Christians prayed. Some of their neighbors at Christmas time put up displays of little people and farm animals on their front lawns, and there was always a cradle with a doll baby, and the figure of a mother leaning over the cradle, and the other people around the cradle paid a lot of attention to the baby, some kneeling just like Theodora and Jackie at that instant. Now he finally realized who that baby was supposed to be.

Jews didn't kneel when they prayed. Rabbi Beck had told him that this was a too-Christian thing to do. After kissing the box, Theodora made that cross sign at the top of her chest and lowered her head in prayer. He could see her lips moving but couldn't hear anything. Looking at her pray like that reminded him of a story that Rabbi Beck had told last *Rosh Hashana*, a story that had made a big impression on him and about which he'd talked to *Ima* a few times. It was the story of *Chana*, a Jewish woman who had prayed for a son and was granted one by *Hashem*. As he understood the story, the woman couldn't have had a baby herself for some reason, but with *Hashem* a miracle had occurred. And the baby, *Shmuel*, had grown up to be a prophet and a judge. He wondered if Theodora, too, was now praying for a son or any baby at all.

Jackie closed his eyes tightly and tried to pray to *Hashem*. At first, all he could think of was *Shmuel*, coming into the world because *Hashem* had heard *Chana*'s prayers. What did Jackie really want from *Hashem*? What was there that he needed so badly that he could disturb *Hashem* by praying for it? *Chana* had prayed for a son. Should he pray for a father? Uncle Max acted like a father for Jackie, had even helped coach Jackie's rookie ball team in the Little League the previous summer, but real fathers were supposed to love their sons, and Jackie didn't feel that Uncle Max loved him enough. But the man in New Orleans, the man they'd run away from, was his real father. That father didn't love him either. Then he had an idea about what to pray for. He would pray that *Ima* would find a father for him and marry this father. This would be a father who loved him. Maybe a father who loved him as much as Grandpa loved him.

As the idea took hold, Jackie began to feel a swell of happiness. He would pray, *Hashem* would hear, and Jackie would eventually get what he wanted. Without being aware of what he was doing, he reached out with his left hand and placed it on Theodora's arm as it peeked out from under her robe. Skin to skin, he again felt Theodora's intense warmth. Then Theodora took his hand in hers and squeezed, and the happiness exploded. He felt so at one of with the world, so at peace—this is how he later described it—that he couldn't help but cry.

How long did that sensation last? Years later, he couldn't say, but he knew it had lasted not nearly long enough, because what he remembered next was a vision that drove him immediately from happiness to fear. He saw Fevronia lying cold and still on a bed. She had died.

WHERE IS FEVRONIA?

He opened his eyes, but the vision of a dead Fevronia stayed before him. He'd never seen a dead person, but he knew what death was. There had been dead birds in the backyard. There was the story of Abraham needing to buy a cave in which to bury Sarah. When he asked his mother about death, about why people had to die, the conversation had led to her telling him about how her mom—whom she had not called *Ima*—had died from a heart attack. It was *Hashem*'s will, that people had a chance to live one life and when that person's time came, it came regardless of what you wanted, regardless of what anyone wanted. And it was never possible to understand why. That kind of understanding was not for human beings.

But Fevronia wasn't dead. He'd just seen her within the hour. He closed his eyes again. Still, the image of her lifeless form was there. Then he prayed to *Hashem* to erase Fevronia from his sight. Slowly, all too slowly, the image faded, and ultimately Jackie saw only the dark purples and aimless wandering yellows that usually tracked with his eyes closed.

He'd had enough of prayer for that evening. When he tried to stand, however, he couldn't move. Something immensely powerful was holding him down on the floor, pulling him even lower. Then a total blackness enveloped him and he passed out.

He wasn't sure how much time had elapsed before he started to regain awareness. He could hear *Ima*'s voice calling to him. He heard Theodora as well, saying something excitedly in Greek. Then *Ima* was asking Theodora what had happened, but there was no response. He carefully opened his eyes.

"J-J-Jackie, *Baruch Hashem*, are you okay?"

He felt weak, but nothing particularly hurt him. "I'm all right, *Ima*."

"What happened to you? Why are you down here with Theodora?"

His immediate instinct was to clam up. He'd be punished for trying to pray next to Theodora. It's not where Jews were supposed to pray. He had been kneeling. Jews were not supposed to kneel. He sat up slowly and saw the deeply concerned looks of both *Ima* and Theodora. He would have to convince them that he was all right. Maybe *Ima* wouldn't press him on what he'd been doing.

"I got tired of practicing and decided to visit with Theodora. And so I don't know what happened. Maybe I got dizzy."

"I've got to get Dad on the phone," Kayla said. "Both of you, please come with me." The nearest phone was on the first floor. Kayla took Theodora's hand, perhaps not too gently, to make sure she followed.

"I will come," said Theodora.

Once Kayla had gotten Nicky on the line, she explained the weird situation she'd found. Upon reentering her house—Max's car was still not in evidence outside—she'd heard Theodora anxiously calling Jackie's name. She'd rushed to the basement to find Jackie flat on the floor and Theodora kneeling over him. She feared he'd died, and, almost worse, Theodora had been making the sign of the cross over Jackie's forehead. But Jackie now seemed fine, if subdued.

She'd put Theodora on the phone with Nicky and listened to Theodora's side of the story in rapid, excited Greek. Theodora seemed upset, and who wouldn't be in that situation? When she got the phone back from Theodora, Nicky explained.

"She was praying, Kal says. Jackie appeared at her side and kneeled too. She thought he was trying to keep her company. At one point, he'd grabbed her arm. That confused her, but Jackie seemed fine, so she kept on praying. In a few minutes, though, he cried out for Fevronia of all people and collapsed. That's what she says. And you came in only a minute later, when she was trying to revive him. Does any of this make sense? Where is Fevronia?"

"I just dropped her off at the church. Jackie said 'Fevronia'?"

"That's what Kal says. Do you need me to drive up there?"

"I don't think that's necessary. Wait a second, Dad. Jackie wants to talk to you." She handed the phone to her son.

"Grandpa?"

"Yes, Jackie. Are you okay? You had everyone worried."

"Grandpa, something bad is going to happen to Fevronia." Jackie could hear *Ima* gasp beside him.

"Something bad? What are you talking about?"

"She's going to die, Grandpa. Or she died already."

Kayla grabbed the phone away from Jackie, as if the phone had spoken an obscenity and had to be punished. Jackie feared he was in danger of *Ima* striking him with the phone as she stared at him uncomprehendingly. Theodora looked from one to the other again in confusion and took the phone from Kayla.

"*Parakalo.*" She spoke to Nicky on the phone and to Kayla beside her at the same time. "If Jackie says Fevronia will die, then she will die. *Tha pethane.*"

SPIRITUAL CONNECTION?

But Fevronia had not died. She returned from church an hour later to find that Jackie had been put to bed, that Theodora was sitting in Kayla's kitchen looking glumly down at the table, and that Kayla herself was on the telephone with Dr. Covo, with Max standing nearby, looking entirely perplexed. The partial conversation she overheard made no sense.

"This is the last straw, Dad. You've got to do something."

Then Kayla listened, nodding her head as if accepting instructions.

"I'll talk to them and get back to you." She gave the receiver to Max, who hung up, and only then did Kayla notice that Fevronia had returned. "I see you're quite alive, Abbess."

"Alive? What in the holy name of the Lord Jesus Christ is going on?" Fevronia gestured toward Theodora.

"I'm sorry, Abbess, but we have a problem here with ..." Kayla's glance toward Theodora left no doubt as to where the issue lay. "I should never have left them alone together."

"Left who alone?"

"Theodora and Jackie. When I took you to the church. It looks like they decided to pray together. Then Jackie had, I don't know, a seizure? He passed out for a short time and, when he came to, he said ... Maybe you had better sit down first, Abbess." After Fevronia sat in the chair next to Theodora, Kayla continued. "He said you had died or would die or something about your dying."

Fevronia asked Kayla to repeat herself, to tell as much of the story as she knew, which Kayla did. Then Fevronia interrogated Theodora, who likewise told as much as she knew. No, she'd not invited Jackie to pray with her. She'd never thought of such a thing. That would clearly have been an insult to her hostess, an insult that Theodora had no intention of perpetrating. But when Jackie appeared at her side, obviously wanting to kneel next to her, she felt it would have been equally rude to push him away. She'd not encouraged him, she'd not said even a word to him, and for minutes they kneeled next to each other, and, yes, she assumed Jackie was praying, or trying to pray, because what else could he have been doing? And then there was this strange moment when Jackie whispered Fevronia's name and fell over, and, when he recovered and spoke to Dr. Covo, that was the first time Theodora ever heard of his vision of the abbess's death.

Fevronia could not suppress her anger. She felt as if every muscle in her body was shaking in rage. "Do you see what your coming here has done to this boy? Do you see how unwise this trip has been?"

"I see only that I'm not wanted here. And so we must go. I will not stay where I'm not wanted."

"Fine for you to say that now, when you insisted on leaving Mrs. Blanco's house."

Theodora shrugged. Although she was disappointed and hurt that everyone was against her, she knew that she'd done absolutely nothing wrong. She greatly regretted that she'd have to leave, because she felt that she'd been growing even closer to the young boy, Jackie—who someday would be Jesus—and that they shared a spiritual connection. Exactly what that connection was she couldn't say, but it was there. She had felt that connection strongly once again, as he had touched her hand when they were kneeling. And if she had more contact with Jackie, that connection could only strengthen. That must have been what she'd been waiting for, the thing that was supposed to happen before she could return to Greece. There was a reason God had granted Jackie that vision of Fevronia, and it must have been the result of their proximity as they prayed. That Fevronia had not died yet, but would nonetheless die soon, was of little moment.

"I will stay in a hotel until our flight leaves. I'm sure Nicky would pay for a hotel."

"And for me too? And how would I keep an eye on you?"

"You need not keep an eye on me, Mother. I am a sinner, but I have not sinned here."

Fevronia shook her head in exasperation, still trying to suppress her anger, and felt dizzy and nauseous at the same time. She felt like her body was squeezing itself, as if wringing out the life force within. How exhausting it had been trying to understand and deal with Theodora. Long seconds elapsed as she tried to come to grips with the strange sensations in her body. There was a stab of pain behind her eyes. Losing all sense of needing to keep up appearances, she laid her pounding head on the kitchen table. Someone soon pressed a cold compress against her forehead.

"Abbess Fevronia, are you okay? Was it the shock?" She recognized Max's voice. In the background, she heard Kayla.

"Dad. You'd better come now."

Fevronia cautiously picked up her head and looked around at the others, who were staring at her as if she'd arrived from another world. "I'm fine. No need for alarm. Just a bit of dizziness."

"We could call 9-1-1," Kayla said uncertainly.

"No. I'm fine."

SHE'S HAD HER CHANCE

The week of sitting *shiva* ended, with Helen taking a long walk around Donaldson Park to mark the end of the first grieving period. All throughout the week, which Nicky took off from his practice to remain at her side, she harbored the uneasy feeling of her unfulfilled promise to Kayla, one that she still didn't disclose to anyone. Freed from the obligation to remain at home, she begged off on Nicky's invitation to visit Kayla and her family. As soon as his car was out of view, she got into her own and headed toward Newark, only a fifteen-minute drive.

The Ironbound District on Newark's East Side was one that Helen had visited only seldomly. It had at one time been a largely Italian American neighborhood, but had transitioned long past to mostly African American and Hispanic. Sadly, it was one of the sites of riots in 1967, a time that Helen remembered with some fear as the "Summer of Rage." Racial tensions were at an all-time high, the riot had started upon untrue allegations that white police officers had beaten a black taxi driver to death, but poverty, corrupt municipal leaders, and poor housing strategies clearly contributed to a sense of disenfranchisement and constituted a fertile ground for violence. In the years after the riot, however, the once-ruined community was back on the rise. Now, the long-time residents complained about gentrification.

Helen found Sorel's address as well as a barely sufficient parking place on Ann Street. It was a townhouse, which looked like it might be comfortable if renovations had been done on the inside. She sat and watched while she thought. What was it she was going to say to August Sorel, even if she lucked out and found him at home? They'd never met each other, except on that one occasion at the JazzFest. That had been less than a desirable encounter.

It was getting late, and she wanted to be done with the meeting, back in her car, and out of the neighborhood before it got dark. Few people were on the street, just a young mother pushing a baby carriage and a group of teenagers chatting together across from Sorel's house. They looked innocent enough; one or two had glanced at her before going back to their conversation.

What would a social worker want to know from this man who sought full custody of Jackie? Where the nearest school was? Who would get Jackie to and from school? What were Sorel's intentions with respect to a religious upbringing? She wondered if he would even talk to her about anything, knowing that she was Nicky's girlfriend. Still studying the front door of Sorel's house, she began to feel it had been unwise to come. Yes, Kayla had begged her, and she wanted to alleviate Kayla's suffering and anxiety, but at that moment Helen felt powerless to do anything more than irritate Sorel. It had been a bad idea. She was about to start her engine when she heard two hard raps on the passenger window. Startled, she turned to see the man she'd come to visit. Only *Hashem* knew how long he'd been watching her watch his house.

"Looking for me?"

She couldn't tell for sure, but he sounded angry. She thought of pulling out abruptly, even though he seemed to be leaning against her car, then realized how much trouble she might get into, and she didn't want to hurt anyone, even a jerk like Sorel. It wouldn't do to talk to him through the car window, however. She opened her door and stood across the front of the car from him.

"Mr. Sorel, yes ..."

"And you, I've learned, are Mrs. Blanco."

She reined in the impulse to tell him to call her Helen.

"What do you want with me?" Definitely hostile, although he managed to keep a brittle smile on his face.

"Why are you doing this to Kayla?" No, that wasn't the right way to start, she thought even as she spoke. Much too aggressive. He came around the front of the car to stand nearer to her. She sensed that the conversation among the teenagers had been suspended and that they were looking on, curious. Perhaps they were ready to jump to Sorel's defense. Maybe they'd met him already. Maybe they knew he was famous.

He smirked. "I don't see how that's any of your business, Mrs. Blanco." Overly polite. Just barely keeping himself from slugging her, she felt.

"They're a very good family, sir. She takes great care of Jackie, and Max looks after him, and ..."

"I don't give a shit."

Unused to hearing profanity directed toward her, she winced and was immediately embarrassed for the wince. "I thought you loved Kayla at one point."

"I did, but it was clear she didn't want me around after Jackie was born. No, she was going to shack up with big brother and he was gonna play father to my son. And I could tell how Max and your boyfriend looked at me, like I was some kind of ... oh, let's just say a black spot on their lives. I had sullied their little girl. You think I wanted to hang around then?"

Helen had no way to judge whether any of what Sorel said was true. Kayla and Nicky loved Jackie, whose skin color was irrelevant to their love. She'd never heard either make a racist joke. Max ... well, she couldn't really be sure about him, but he'd been careful when within her hearing, so she had no evidence that he was a racist either, and he did generally take good care of his nephew. Whether Sorel believed any of what he said was unclear as well, but he was saying it. It had to be dealt with.

"Whatever happened, happened. You bowed out. Now you're trying to force your way in. Not only that, but you're trying to force Jackie's mother out of the picture. Why?"

"She's had her chance with him. Now's my chance."

"That doesn't make any sense."

"The boy is afraid his mother and uncle will kill him."

"That's pure baloney."

"What do you want from me?"

"Drop the lawsuit. Stop trying to get custody."

He laughed and turned to enter his house. "Drop dead, Mrs. Blanco."

SILENOS

No other sleeping arrangements were practical immediately. Fevronia had told the others that she would feel much better with just a good night's sleep. She quickly retired to her bed, not admitting what she knew to be the cause of her unwellness, the stress brought about by Theodora's behavior.

The more she thought about the situation, the more she felt that she'd been manipulated at every turn. If she hadn't loved Theodora as much as she did, if she hadn't believed that Theodora was destined for sainthood, if some part of her hadn't wanted to share in Theodora's miracles, as crazy as they might be, she would have stopped the nonsense about Jesus at the very beginning. If she'd been a smart spiritual mother—one who trusted her own instincts and greater knowledge of Christ and the plans of the Heavenly Father—she would have required Theodora to undergo counseling, perhaps with the Elder Porphyrios, who had once met Theodora at Fevronia's request and had immediately sensed her uniqueness.

Now, Theodora had put Fevronia in a very difficult situation, one which apparently threatened the life of that dear boy, Jackie. Everything Theodora had done during their visit embarrassed Fevronia one way or another. And in front of a family of Jews, no less. Yes, the immediate embarrassment would end soon—they would be on a plane back to Athens before the end of the month—but the memory of that embarrassment would linger. And how would she explain the whole trip to the Metropolitan, who had trusted her to bring Theodora to America? How could she and Theodora ever resume the close relationship they had had at the monastery?

The room seemed to spin around her, even though her eyes were closed, even as she grabbed the sides of the bed to keep from falling out of it, even as she prayed for the dizziness to fade. Very gradually, the spinning subsided. She could now hear the faint murmur of conversation from downstairs after Dr. Covo's arrival.

She opened her eyes to see Theodora's shadow on the wall, thrown there by the light of the candle in the small lampada. So, even as Fevronia mulled over the situation, Theodora was back at prayer. Fevronia remembered the outrage in Theodora's voice when she protested that she hadn't sinned in Kayla's house. The memory renewed Fevronia's anger. What effrontery! God knows everyone's heart, and it was for God to say when someone had sinned. The essence of asceticism was humility, and yet Theodora had been anything but humble. The Devil had gotten to her and made her arrogant. Fevronia could see it so easily, yet Theodora—surely praying now that she was a sinner—couldn't see her own sins even though they were in front of her face.

What lay at the root of Theodora's delusion, because it was a delusion, was that otherworldly link between Theodora and her brother. It was that link, so strong when they were children, that had prevailed upon the goodness of the Holy Virgin and enabled Her to save the life of the teenage Nicky. It was the beauty of reforging that link, which had been broken by the horror of war, that had motivated Fevronia herself to bring them together again. Was she sorry now that she had done so? Should she have left well enough alone and not sought with all her energy to reunite them?

But reunification with one's brother had been Fevronia's longstanding obsession. How much she still missed Silenos, long decades after his murder. She cried at the remembrance of a time when they were both children, when she had fallen at play and scraped a knee, and Silenos had been there at once to pick her up and comfort her. She had loved him so. If the Holy Mother could only have stopped the slaughter at the monastery, perhaps Fevronia could still be with Silenos. But the Holy Mother had chosen to save Theodora instead. That was the only way in which Theodora's claim that she had killed the monks herself made sense.

Fevronia closed her eyes again. She could see Silenos before her now. A bright white light surrounded him. He called to her. She heard his voice so clearly. Couldn't Theodora hear it as well? Wouldn't she be startled to have this strange voice in the bedroom they shared? Silenos reached out to her, telling her that the time had come for her to join him. He was so good, so loving, always looking after her. Eyes closed, she reached out her own hand to take his.

Then he took her to a new bed and made her to lie down on it next to him.

KADDISH

Nicky's head ached with the multiple confusions arising from Fevronia's death. She'd not been under a doctor's care, so, despite his sister's frantic objections, an autopsy couldn't be avoided. The medical examiner's opinion was that Fevronia had suffered from a heart attack brought about by complete blockage of the left anterior descending artery. Her death was deemed natural, not unexpected for a woman her age. Privately, the medical examiner told Nicky that stress might have been a factor, perhaps the stress of international travel alone might have done it, but there was nothing to be added to the autopsy report.

Even more complicated, however, was the issue of what was to be done with Fevronia's body. Cremation was out of the question, totally against Orthodox Christian beliefs, but what cemetery? Theodora insisted that Fevronia's body be returned to Greece, to the monastery. That much should have been simple enough, and Nicky had no hesitation paying the expenses. But here Nicky was thwarted by another demand of Theodora. She was not ready to end her visit, she had in fact agreed to continue to stay at Kayla's house—at Kayla's urging—but she would not send Fevronia's body back to Greece unless she could personally accompany it. Nicky, Helen, and Kayla all tried to argue Theodora out of her resolve, but the more they argued, the firmer was Theodora's opposition, until they gave up and accepted that things had to be the way Theodora wanted them.

While Theodora prayed one evening and Jackie slept, the three conferred quietly in the piano room.

"Kal says her mission here isn't over," Nicky said. "Her mission as to Jackie, of course."

"And that's what scares me about her staying. She'd never harm him deliberately, of course, but so much turmoil is already hurting Jackie. Who would have imagined that ...?" Kayla stopped herself from continuing what was to have been a diatribe against August. She'd explained to her lawyer and to the guardian-ad-litem exactly what had happened.

"It's hard to be angry with your sister, Dad. She's been through so much. She's suffered from possibly the greatest shock that one can suffer, when her mentor dies suddenly in the same bedroom during the night. And you can see how depressed she is. Right now, I think she needs counseling."

"She probably does, but I'm the only psychiatrist I know who speaks Greek, and I couldn't be her therapist anyway. I actually mentioned to her the possibility of counseling, and she said, as I anticipated, that all the counseling she'd need would be found in her prayer. And then, what she always says, that she must pray to be forgiven because she's a sinner."

"And the sin this time ...?" asked Max.

Nicky shrugged. "Although she hasn't said so directly, she probably considers herself responsible for Fevronia's death. She kept saying 'If I only hadn't made her come to America.'"

Kayla asked, "To which you responded ...?"

"What could I say? I reminded her about the autopsy report. A simple heart attack that could have happened anywhere. That would have happened anywhere. Kal obviously wasn't convinced. Just more of that I'm-a-sinner garbage."

They sat quietly, each unable to come up with a better solution than to let things play out the way they would, each concluding that Theodora/Kal would decide when it was right for her to return to Greece with Fevronia's body. As they thought, Theodora entered the room. They could see she'd been crying. Theodora put her hand on Kayla's piano to steady herself and spoke to Nicky in Greek.

"Am I interrupting?"

"No, of course not. Please sit down."

Theodora sat next to Kayla on the small sofa. She put her hands in her lap and looked down at them for a long minute. Then she continued in Greek. "Nicky, what do Jews do during the period of mourning? I remember little, although it seems that we had a death in our family when I was a young girl. What do we ... I mean ... what do Jewish people do? What Helen's been doing in regard to her sister?"

"There's *shiva*. Seven days of mourning, the most severe restrictions. Then, if the person who died is a spouse or child or sibling, the mourning period is extended to thirty days. They say *kaddish*. They don't do anything for fun, they don't cut their hair, they don't listen to music, even. We call that *shloshim*, meaning thirty."

"But if the person who died was a parent, a mother in particular?"

"For a mother or father, the same restrictions for *shloshim*. But, mourning for a parent, one says *kaddish* for eleven months."

"And what is *kaddish*? I'm sorry I don't know. It's a term I only vaguely remember."

"*Kaddish* is a prayer that praises God. It asks that the name of God be revered. It affirms that the greatness of God is beyond all human comprehension. It's an affirmation of faith even in the face of death."

"And did you say it when your wife died?"

"No. Only Kayla said *kaddish* for Adel."

"I see. So, am I allowed to say this *kaddish* even though I'm not Jewish?"

Nicky wasn't sure he'd heard correctly and asked Theodora to repeat her question; then, he was unable to answer. He turned then to Kayla and Max, summarized the conversation, and asked Kayla what she thought the Jewish view would be. Kayla turned toward

Theodora and answered in English, knowing her father would interpret if necessary.

"The answer is yes, Sister Theodora. Non-Jews may say *kaddish*. No one can stop you from praising *Hashem* in any way you want to. The one condition, however, and this is very important, is that you can do so only in a *minyan*, which in the case of my religious tradition means that there are at least ten Jewish men there constituting the religious community."

"Fevronia was my Mother-in-Christ," Theodora continued in English. "May I say the *kaddish* for that kind of mother?" Her question now was directed only to Kayla, obviously the family authority on Judaism.

"There's tradition on one hand, which would say no, it's not typically done. But there's also *halacha*."

"*Halacha?*"

"Literally, 'the way,' but it means 'the law.' For that, although I don't know for sure, I would bet anyone who wanted to praise *Hashem*, in memory of anyone close, would be welcomed to do so, again, only if there's a *minyan*. We can ask Rabbi Beck to be sure."

"I would like to talk to Rabbi Beck then. But why must there be the *minyan?*"

"To remind us of community, that for the most important prayers and rituals we need a community of believers to approach *Hashem*. To remind us that we face *Hashem* together."

Theodora turned again toward her brother. "Nicky, when we were children, you taught me a lot. You helped me learn to read. Now, I wonder, will you teach me this *kaddish?* If I promise not to say it until there's ... *minyan?*"

FROM WHEREVER HE WILL COME

They gathered in the vestibule of the West Orange *Chabad*, where Rabbi Beck had pulled extra chairs, set opposite a built-in bench with dark green upholstery. Although Nicky doubted the wisdom of bringing Kal to a meeting with Rabbi Beck, Kayla truly wanted to learn what her spiritual leader would say. Thus it was on a Sunday evening—from which the summer's warmth had had temporarily fled, to be replaced by the slight chill of approaching autumn—they faced each other, Nicky again interpreting as necessary.

"My deepest condolences for your loss, Sister Theodora."

Theodora responded with a simple "*Efcharisto poli. E matera mou en Christo enai me ton curio mas*," then translated for herself, "Thank you very much, my mother is with our Lord."

"Kayla has told me you wanted to ask questions asked about Jewish traditions regarding the death of a loved one." She nodded somberly at Rabbi Beck. "Well, Kayla has interpreted our laws correctly. You may say *kaddish* here, if there's a *minyan*. Though you were born Jewish, you obviously converted away from our faith, but that can't stop you from praising *Hashem*. I should think, though, that the other nuns at the monastery where you live and—shall we say—the hierarchy of your religion would find it curious, if not a repudiation of your Lord, were they to know?"

"Curious, perhaps. But it's my affair entirely and not anyone else's business."

"Quite so. It is a personal decision, and your choice speaks highly of how devoted you were to the abbess."

"But, if I can't say this prayer out loud without a *minyan*, would I be prohibited from whispering it to myself? Or thinking it to myself? Is that a violation? Nicky has taught me the words. Well, he's written them out for me, in Greek letters, so I can make the right sounds. I once knew the sounds of the Hebrew letters, but have long forgotten. I'm working on my English right now, as you can obviously tell, but not my Hebrew."

"No problem using the Greek letters, if that's easier for you. It's obvious you are dedicated to *Hashem*, although you see Him in a different way than we Jews see Him. I would never presume to tell you how to pray or how to praise the Supreme One. But, if you whisper, please make sure that only your own ears hear it."

"Thank you. Then, until I return to Greece with my Mother-in-Christ, may I come here with Kayla to say *kaddish*?"

"I will allow it, although there will be some members of my congregation who won't understand. I may take a lot of flak. Frankly, I fear many *Chabad* rabbis would say no. But I say yes, in respect to Kayla and her family, as well as to your religious devotion."

"That is most kind of you. *Efcharisto poli.*"

"But now, if you don't mind, may I ask you some questions?"

Theodora thought for a second. "I'm a simple nun, and I've been at the monastery since I was six years old. I've no formal education beyond first grade. But I will try to answer your questions."

"The Messiah. You believe that your Jesus, the Messiah, has returned. I ask, politely I hope, how that can be? The world is so far from perfect that it's less ready for the coming of the Messiah—at least in my personal view and the view of many Jews—than it has ever been."

"The Messiah returns to *make* the world perfect by His return. And it is most necessary that we, the faithful, watch and pray for this. We pray, before communion, that our sins should be consumed in

His holy fire, to make greater His two comings. We are very sure about the two comings."

"And Jackie?"

"I still feel Jackie is Jesus, although He's unaware now. Although His holy fire has not yet been lit, the time will come."

"Then let's put Jackie aside for the moment and speak of what *Hashem* wants. We Jews believe that the purity of *Hashem* is within each of us. A tiny spark, if you will. We pray to *Hashem* to help us make a place for Him in our daily lives. *Hashem* needs us to do this for Him and waits for us to enlarge that space until He can occupy it. *Hashem* will wait for thousands of year more, millions of years if necessary, until we are ready to receive Him. Only then can our *Meshiach* announce the end of time."

Theodora nodded. "I understand what you're saying. There is much in common about our systems of belief, is there not? I try to make that special space in myself for God, when I pray to Our Lord Jesus Christ that I am a sinner and ask Him to forgive my sins. We have all sinned, we continue to sin every day, and we must recognize our sinfulness to make the proper space for God. I am a sinner. I pray to the Lord Jesus Christ to forgive me, a sinner. But Jesus cannot wait for the world to be made perfect before He returns. He returns in order to make the world perfect. And He's here now, in this very imperfect world, waiting for His time."

"There can only be one coming of the *Meshiach*. Such is the foundation of Judaism."

She crossed herself and lowered her gaze to the floor. Rabbi Beck glanced at the others. He seemed almost surprised that others were there to witness his strange interchange with the nun.

"Sister Theodora, your prayers for forgiveness derive directly from our daily prayers, prayers that existed long before Jesus was born." He waited a second, until she looked up at him again. "*S'lach lanu, ki chatanu*. We human beings have many sins. We pray about them collectively, if you will. We say 'forgive *us*.' We say '*we* have sinned.' We say this every ordinary day. And we say it because we know that the *Meshiach* won't come to us, from wherever He will come, until we have put away those sins. We must all work at that. But, from what I've heard of your life, from having observed you and spoken to you, I honestly cannot conceive of any sins for which you need to be forgiven." For the first time in the conversation, a smile crept onto Rabbi Beck's face.

Theodora nodded, a tear of thanks rolling down her cheek. This rabbi was a kind man and reminded her of Papa. An image flashed through her mind: sitting with Papa at his Talmud and listening to a story. There was a warmth she knew, there, quiet and comfortable with him in his study, a warmth she felt almost nowhere else as a child, except perhaps when Nicky sang a lullaby to her. The memories made her somehow want to confess her sins to Rabbi Beck, to set him straight. But that would never do.

"I'm ready to go back to your house, Kayla. Thank you, Rabbi. Perhaps we will have a chance to talk together again about God before I must return to Greece."

ROSH CHODESH ELUL

Since visiting Rabbi Beck, Theodora had elected not to accompany Kayla to the *Chabad* on the Monday and Tuesday mornings that immediately followed. She explained that she wanted to pray in her traditional way but would add in the *kaddish* in a whisper that only she could hear. Kayla had no desire to coax Theodora into attendance. If Theodora wanted to pray at the *Chabad*, or just attend there to say *kaddish* out loud, she would let Kayla know she was ready. On the next morning, however, when Kayla again politely asked if Theodora would like to join her, she pointed out that the day was a special day, the first day of the Hebrew month of *Elul*, marking one month before the holiday of *Rosh Hashanah*, the Jewish New Year.

"And what happens at your synagogue on this special day?" asked Theodora.

"We sing the *Hallel*, special praises to *Hashem*, from *T'hillim*, Psalms."

"I remember a tiny bit of *Hallel* from when I was a little girl."

"You do?"

With that, Theodora hummed a simple melody, then sang, in a soft but pure voice, the one phrase she could recall: "*Ram al kol goyim Adonai.*"

"*Hashem* is above all the nations. Beautiful, Theodora."

"It's okay that I sang this?"

"Of course. You have a lovely singing voice."

"*Efcharisto poli.*"

At the *Chabad*, as Rabbi Beck had expected, everyone noticed the arrival of a middle-aged nun in a black habit. Theodora and Kayla sat at the very rear of the women's side. The rabbi matter-of-factly introduced Theodora as Kayla's aunt, having come from Greece to visit, and then proceeded with the service. Theodora had half-expected Kayla to whisper to her in explanation of the service, but Kayla was too devout and too much engaged in her own spirituality to do so. Left to her own devices, and having no ability to follow along in the Hebrew, Theodora paged through the prayerbook, *Siddur Tehillat Hashem.* At least, she recognized "*Hashem,*" a term that Kayla used often enough.

In the preface, Theodora's attention fastened on information of great interest. The Kabbalah taught that each of the twelve tribes of Israel owned its own distinct spiritual quality, and each tribe had its own gate into heaven. One could not get into heaven except through the particular gate meant for that person's tribe. How odd, she thought. How would a Jew know today what tribe he was from? That was all lost thousands of years ago. But then, as she read further, she learned that a rabbi had deduced that there must have been a thirteenth gate. Why? Exactly because one might not know to which tribe he or she belonged. Theodora smiled as she continued to look through the book for more English she could understand. She knew that there was only one gate, and that was the gate of Jesus Christ the Lord.

Then it seemed everyone was standing and singing. Theodora stood as well and hummed along as best she could. This must be *Hallel,* she thought, and at one point she definitely heard chanted— in a melody strange to her ears—the words "*Ram al kol goyim, Adonai.*"

Finally, there came a place in the service where Rabbi Beck addressed the congregation in what he called a "*d'var Torah.*" It was all about the special month of *Elul* that had just begun. The essence of this month was that Jews were called upon to take stock of their spiritual nature. This was the special month when *Hashem*—the King—came down from his throne and stood in the fields, ready there to welcome anyone who would approach Him. But, in order to see and greet the King, one must leave his house and go out to the fields. This was the opportunity to prepare for *t'shuvah*—she would have to ask Kayla later for a translation—and to correct what had been wrong in one's life during the preceding year. Knowing that the King was in the field would be enough to encourage the pious Jew, the Jew who sought *t'shuvah*, to rush out and meet the King, but the Jew had to be willing to leave his comfortable house. The trip to meet the King wouldn't be comfortable.

Indeed, thought Theodora. How amazing a coincidence. The coincidence of hearing this "*d'var Torah*" that so directly applied to her own life could only be another message from God. God was telling her, through Rabbi Beck, that Theodora had done the right thing in leaving the monastery and traveling far afield to meet Jesus. She had met him, this very human, very lovable, and very intelligent black boy who was only and especially Jackie Covo.

And then there was the *kaddish*. Kayla nudged Theodora to stand with the other mourners, and Theodora whispered the transliterated words from the piece of paper Nicky had given her. She whispered loudly enough for Kayla to hear her, but no louder.

CHOL HA-MOED SUKKOT

One day, not very long before, the idea of marrying Nicky was at best an unlikely possibility for Helen. There was no need in 1990 for two consenting adults to be married in order to maintain an intimate, loving relationship. Even if one was truly in love—and she was, not sure still what that meant, but committed to the idea—and felt that love returned, marriage was a public statement, sure to lead to embarrassment. Why display to family, friends, and acquaintances alike that her devotion to her deceased husband, David, had faded so thoroughly she could once again take the solemn vows of perpetual union? David, by virtue of his death, had left her, but she had not left him. Helen was still alive, and David's memory lived strongly within her. Their lives together had not ended except in the purely physical day-to-day sense. Their children and grandchildren were all very much alive for her as constant reminders of David, David lived within them, and she could not imagine how they would feel, watching as she stepped under a *chupa* with Nicky.

Yes, they seemed to support her relationship with Nicky. They had no illusions. Sure, their mother and grandmother slept with this man. He was like family. It was good for Helen to have companionship, especially with someone almost her age. But marriage was special. That would, in the eyes of Helen's family, put Nicky at the same level as David, and that's where they would draw the line. So one main reason that Helen had declined Nicky's initial proposal was that she didn't see how her family could accept a marriage.

There were other reasons, too. She'd had a lifetime living with a husband traumatized by his wartime experience. It had been difficult. Likewise, she knew that Nicky—despite his protestations—was still haunted by his own goblins. The phantom former comrade-in-arms whose family name was Raptis but whose *nom de guerre* was Churchill still followed Nicky. She could see it in his eyes, as they often shifted quickly around him when they were out, almost as if Churchill's ghost was just at the edge of Nicky's peripheral vision. She could feel it in his body when, during sleep, he shuddered and seemed to claw into the mattress, dreaming of yet another horrible confrontation with this nemesis.

Finally, how could she not be concerned about Nicky's quick changes of mood, how he might act rashly, with no thought to consequences, as the moments unfolded? She didn't fear that he might hurt her, at least not on purpose. But there was some great instability within him that could be dangerous. She often felt at the mercy of something deep in his core that could not be explained. She was sure it had to do with his rejection of *Hashem*. Following their trip to Greece and as a result of what he had learned from Kal—how both of them were saved by miracles—his absolute rejection of *Hashem* had become less absolute, but it was still rejection. To marry him, she'd thought, he would first have to come around completely to accept the God that he'd been raised with, and she could not see him doing that.

Then everything changed at once; Catherine's death immediately caused her to reconsider. It naturally brought to her mind death itself, hanging right over her shoulder, or Nicky's, waiting to consume either or both of them in an instant. No miracles could negate death forever. The time they might have together was unknown. It might be over in a day. What would her life mean, in that case, if she'd never completely committed to the relationship? If Nicky died, never having had her as his wife, as he so badly wanted, what would that say about her? Or if she died and Nicky, again deprived of what he most urgently wanted, had to live decades knowing she'd rejected him? What would her family think then? What would Kayla, Max, and Jackie—when old enough to understand—think? And Catherine's last words, expressing her joy that Helen and Nicky had found each other, pushed her over the edge. Of course she wanted to marry Nicky.

Then Fevronia's sudden death, more shocking than Catherine's, caused Nicky and Helen to put off their wedding planning, but increased in her mind the urgency of tying the knot quickly. As soon as it seemed appropriate, they formalized their plans. The wedding would take place not in the *shul*, in deference to Nicky's atheism, but in her backyard during *Chol Ha-moed Sukkot*, and the *sukkah*—with minor changes—would serve as the *chupa* too. She would have the rabbi from *Aish Ahaim* marry them. And Sister Theodora would be there. Amazingly, Sister Theodora wanted to linger for another month or two before her return to Greece.

Thus, Helen, with her two daughters in tow, began to search for the perfect wedding dress, starting at Bridal Atelier in Montclair.

BIG STORMS

Something bad had indeed happened, based upon the whispering that began as soon as he walked into a room. He had no memory; it was as if an entire month had passed while he was in a fog. The only visible change was that Fevronia, the kindly old nun, Theodora's friend, had gone back to Greece. That's what he'd been told by everyone, and he had no reason to doubt it. The mental picture of her that had been in Jackie's mind—the sun-wrinkled brown face and small squat stature—faded. He hadn't thought to ask why Fevronia had cut short her visit. And it didn't matter much to him, as fascinated as he was by Theodora.

The other change was that he and Theodora had begun to speak to each other much more in English. She was so eager to learn and so happy to spend hours with him as he taught her after school. She was so smart. In no more than a week, she'd mastered his third grade books and *Ima* had been required to take them both to the library on Mount Pleasant Avenue. Then he noticed her reading books in their basement. When he saw her with *The Pillars of the Earth*, he'd remembered *Ima*'s complaint and tried to warn Theodora that the book was trash—he even learned the Greek word *apporimata*—but to no avail. Theodora simply smiled warmly and said "*ochi*." He knew this meant "no." The book wasn't garbage after all. She would read as much as she could, dictionary close at hand.

He vaguely recalled the time he had joined Theodora in the basement to pray, and passing out, and thinking that Fevronia would die. He had been wrong, but Fevronia could just as well have died, because she'd gone back suddenly to Greece. Now, Theodora confined her prayers to her bedroom. Jackie knew he was supposed to leave her alone completely when she prayed. He was forbidden to kneel next to her as she prayed.

She would pray in the morning well before he rose and continue until he left for school, and for how long thereafter he couldn't be sure, but she was always there to greet him in the afternoons when *Ima* drove him back home, and while the weather was still warm she'd taken to sitting on the front porch in a folding garden chair with a book. One day, a week or so after she'd put back *The Pillars of the Earth*, he saw her with *The Merchant of Venice*. He waited until *Ima* went inside, helpfully carrying his heavy backpack in for him, and asked Theodora how she liked the book.

"It's sad, Jackie."

"Sad?"

"It makes me sad, too, these days."

He waited quietly, expecting her to explain. Yes, now that she mentioned it, he could see that she was sad. Her eyes didn't quite have the same glow that he recalled from when he first met her. Perhaps they were a bit red, too. Perhaps she'd been crying just before *Ima* and he had driven up. But why then read a sad book?

"Listen: here's how it starts. 'In sooth, 1 know not why 1 am so sad. It wearies me …'"

"What's sooth?"

"1 don't know. 1 can't find it in this dictionary. But let me read the rest here. 'It wearies me; you say it wearies you; But how 1 caught it, found it, or came by it, What stuff 'tis made of, whereof it is born, 1 am to learn; And such a want-wit sadness makes of me, That 1 have much ado to know myself."

She handed the volume to him and pointed so he could read the words himself. From the characters' names and following speeches, he was reminded that all the Shakespeare books contained plays.

"Where's Venice?"

"In Italy, a place I have not been."

The book must hold a clue to Theodora's sadness. He tried to read the first page, but many of the words were strange. "Argosies" reminded him of arguments. "Flood," "sea," and "ports" caused him to guess that this had something to do with ships, although that word wasn't used. He wondered if Theodora was thinking of going back to Greece by ship instead of plane and almost asked her. He didn't want to contemplate that she was, in fact, intending to return. Her date of leaving had been put off; that much he knew. He didn't want to hasten the time when she would leave him.

"Do you understand?" she asked.

"Some of it. But there are words I don't know, like 'misfortune to my ventures.' Do you understand?"

Theodora took the book back, sighing, thoughtful. "A little." She read to herself on the first page, then checked something in her dictionary. "On this page, we learn that a man named Antonio is worried because his venture—the very important thing for him that he has tried to do—may be a ... *katastrophe*. Wait." She looked again at her dictionary. "Oh. Disaster. He was worried about a disaster."

"Disaster" was a word he'd mastered at age five. "Like Mount Vesuvius erupting."

Theodora's further consultation with her dictionary led quickly to her assent. "He was thinking that big storms would sink his ships. Yes. We all fear disasters."

"Misfortune?"

"Yes. Some say 'bad luck.' Others say 'the work of the Devil.' But I suppose it all ends up the same thing."

"You are sad, too, Theodora. Aren't you?"

"Is it so easy for you to see?"

"Did you have a venture, too?"

A weak smile briefly crossed her face. "I am still having my venture. When we left the monastery, that was the beginning of a venture and, for me, it hasn't ended yet."

He thought of asking another question. What was it about her venture—that had to be a small kind of adventure, he posited—that was making her sad? But *Ima* was calling. It was time to get started on his homework. After that, practice. Homework was important. Practicing the clarinet was important. We do the important things that *Hashem* wants us to do first, then we have more time for fun. He knew he would be able to talk to Theodora later in the afternoon and in the evening.

He turned to go, but then Theodora asked him to wait. He turned toward her. Tears streamed down either side of her face. Just a second earlier, her cheeks had been dry, but now they were wet. She made the sign of the cross. It's what Christians did. Then she leaned forward in her chair and kissed him gently on his forehead.

"Now go do what your *Ima* wants you to do, Jackie."

SOMETHING ABOUT THE SUPREME COURT

Judge Jill Haney was not a happy judge when she took the bench again, during what should have been her lunch hour. "Mr. Greavey, this had better be good. You were here only a month ago on your last emergency motion. I set a hearing date in November, as you well know. So now what is it?"

"Your Honor, we have new evidence. We have the statement of Jackie himself about how his mother almost killed him and his uncle ..."

Rebecca Friedman jumped to her feet, livid. "Objection. There's no evidence. There's been no testimony taken from Jackie."

"Mr. Greavey?"

He pulled a sheaf of papers from his file, handed a few pages to Friedman, who by this time seemed barely able to control her courtroom warrior's instinct to fight. "Here is a transcript of an interview that Mr. Sorel did with his son recently. May I hand a copy to Your Honor?"

"An interview?"

"Objection, objection, objection. Totally outrageous. Improper contact with the minor child. Violates the Court's order. Child abuse."

The guardian-ad-litem had also stood quickly, moving beside Kayla's lawyer. "And I object as well, Your Honor. There was no notice of any interview, no court reporter present, no sworn testimony, no ..."

"Patience, patience, please, all of you. I understand the objections. The record is replete with your objections." The judge read the papers that had been handed her, then read them again, shaking her head. When she put them down, she looked at Sorel. "Stand up, Mr. Sorel. In fact, come up here and be sworn as a witness."

He rose as if he was entering a concert hall, ready to perform. In his mind, he could hear parts of the Sibelius concerto, his exuberant virtuosity, the audience ready to leap to its feet in a thundering ovation. The clerk perfunctorily administered the oath.

"How did you come to be talking to the minor child?" asked Haney.

He explained how he'd happened to be driving by the West Orange *Chabad* just as the school happened to be closing and how he happened to notice Jackie standing outside, looking around, and how it was raining, and how, well, one thing led to another. He had a duty to protect his son. And, yes, he had questioned him. Any loving father would have done the same. He needed to see how badly his son was hurt by the violence perpetrated by his mother, was still being hurt. The judge heard him out. When he was done, she took a minute to type something on her word processor. Then she looked again at Sorel.

"You were here in court a few weeks ago, sir, when I specifically ordered that there be no contact between you and the minor child before the next hearing?"

"But ... that couldn't have meant I'm not allowed to give him a ride home when I see him standing out on the street. In the rain."

"I see. And, it just so happened, to use your expression, that you had a tape recorder handy in your car?"

"I use it in my profession, to listen to recordings I'm fond of. I'm a concert violinist."

"You do understand English, correct?"

There was no response. He figured he'd now get some kind of tongue-lashing, but it would have been worth it since he'd been able to produce what he thought was compelling evidence against Kayla.

"You must answer me. Do you understand English, Mr. Sorel?"

"Yes, Ma'am."

"That's Yes, Your Honor."

"Yes, Your Honor."

"Very well. You heard and understood my order of no contact?"

"Yes, Your Honor."

"Fine. Excellent. Then listen to what I have to say now." She leaned over to whisper something to her clerk, who got on his phone. "You're in contempt of this Court. You're being remanded into custody of the Essex County Sheriff's Office. You'll spend thirty-six hours in custody as punishment for violation of my order. I'm entering a new order right now. Listen carefully. Make sure you understand every word. You are to have no further contact, by phone, by letter, in person, by intermediary, including your lawyer, with the minor child, Jackie Covo. This no-contact order will be shared with the relevant sheriff's offices and local police. This order is in effect permanently, until modified, if ever, by this Court. The hearing previously set for November is to be reset for such time as I choose, but not sooner than a year from now. Mr. Greavey, if Mr. Sorel is still your client a year from now, you may file a motion for a new hearing. But if he violates this no-contact order, I will consider holding you in contempt as well. Have I made myself perfectly clear?"

A few seconds passed. Finally, Greavey said, in a low voice, the voice of the vanquished, that he understood. Two sheriff's deputies had entered the courtroom while the judge spoke. They walked to the witness stand, put the stunned Sorel in handcuffs, and led him away.

"Judge, you can't do this," Sorel finally protested, as he was being led by the deputies toward the door. "I have a concert tomorrow evening."

"You'll miss it."

As the courtroom door swung closed behind him and his entourage, the judge thought she heard him yell something about the Supreme Court.

"Ms. Covo, will you stand please?"

Kayla complied.

"Have you continued to take your medication?"

"Yes, Your Honor."

"See that you never stop. Good day. We are adjourned."

MORE THAN THE UNIVERSE

The holidays were glum in the aftermath of two deaths. Kayla was naturally upset that her houseguest had died and worried that Fevronia's passing might have been the result of something she served for dinner. Max was unable to get Kayla to see that such fears were unreasonable.

Nicky agreed to attend the first day of *Rosh Hashana* services with Helen at *Aish Ahaim*. He insisted, however, that he return to his practice on the second day, a Friday. Theodora, who begged to be brought along, would attend *Kol Nidre* services with them there. Making late arrangements for Theodora to have a seat wasn't a problem, because the membership of the synagogue had declined in recent years; there were plenty of tickets available.

Kayla's job on the Friday afternoon before *Kol Nidre* was to drive Theodora to Highland Park, where she would spend the solemn day. Kayla brought Jackie along for the ride. On the way, Theodora raised an issue that had been perplexing her.

"So we can talk about your holy day?"

"Yes, of course."

"Jews pray to be forgiven of sin, *nai*?"

"We do. This whole period, from Rosh Hashana to *Yom Kippur*, we admit our sins and pray that *Hashem* will forgive us."

"I pray every day to be forgiven to my sins." Theodora put clear emphasis on every.

"You mean ...?"

"Not just on a special week of the year. It is something that fills me up every day. Not enough hours to say enough prayers. If I could live without sleeping, then there would be more hours to pray, more chance of forgiveness."

"And you pray alone most of the time."

"But always, every day, also with others. Please to tell me. You say 'admit our sins.' You say 'forgive us.' Rabbi Beck has made this point, too. To me, each person must pray for his own sin. Each person is different. Each sin. Each has his own ... how do you say? *Pisti?*" She took the dictionary from a pocket in her habit and found the word. "Faith. Each person must look inside for his own faith to pray. Our God, the Lord Jesus Christ, can forgive just one at a time."

"We have our individual sins too. If I sinned against a fellow human being, I must ask that person to forgive me. *Hashem* cannot forgive me until I have made it right by the person I hurt." It occurred to Kayla just as she spoke that the individual she'd hurt most in the preceding year was sitting right behind her. "So now I will ask for the most important forgiveness of all. Jackie?"

"Yes, *Ima?*"

"Can you possibly forgive me for how I hurt you this year?"

Seconds passed, during which Kayla was certain that her solemn request would be denied and during which she feared that, as a result, she could not find forgiveness from *Hashem* either.

"Could you say that again? I couldn't hear you."

She repeated the question, louder, trying to keep the exasperation out of her voice. She glanced at Theodora, whom she could tell was listening attentively.

"Yes, I forgive you."

"And do you know that hurting you is the last thing in the world I would ever want to do?"

"I love you more than the universe, *Ima.* Even more than the solar system. It's an expression."

Kayla couldn't help but smile. In all the time since the incident with Jackie, she'd not once formally asked for his forgiveness. But it was better that she asked late rather than never at all, she thought, particularly because *Yom Kippur* was still ahead, and her prayers to *Hashem* could emerge from a clearer heart. The gate through which prayers traveled upward to *Hashem*'s hearing had not yet closed.

"And now, Theodora, I've done what I should have done months ago. I'm happy you started talking about forgiveness."

"It is good you have done so, Kayla."

With that, Kayla pulled into the driveway of Helen's house. It was a warm, pleasant day, and Donaldson Park across the way was filled with kids throwing and kicking balls, running in circles it seemed, screaming in joy, the younger ones, roughly Jackie's age, watched by doting parents and guardians, who would soon call them back to their houses to prepare for *Shabbat* and the holiday.

A BIG BLACK BULL

After Kayla explained to Theodora why Jews fast on *Yom Kippur*, Theodora decided to fast as well. Kayla showed her the verse in Leviticus. "*T-anu nafshotechem* ... You shall afflict your souls. We do this so we can concentrate fully on our prayers for forgiveness."

Theodora checked the verse in her Greek Bible. "ταπεινωσατε?" (*tapeinosate*) She then checked her dictionary. "Humble. Is that right? You must humble yourselves? That is to afflict your souls?"

"*T-anu* could be translated as to make oneself poor. Humble? Yes, that would work."

"Is this to be a punishment for the sins of the past year?"

"We don't think of it that way. But we strip away from ourselves everything that might divert our attention from the main job of the day, to seek *Hashem*'s mercy."

"So does it say that Jews should not eat? Or drink?"

"No, but that's how it's always been interpreted. And the fasting is more important, according to Rabbi Beck, than attending the services. Indeed, if we were weak from fasting and could not get to the synagogue other than by eating, it would be better to stay home, lie in bed the entire day, and neither eat nor drink."

"I dreamt last night that I was in a desert, being chased, thirsty, hungry, alone. I had been fasting. Do you mind me telling you this dream? It's something I would have mentioned to Fevronia ..."

"*Zichrona l'vracha*. May her memory be for a blessing. Yes, of course, you can share with me. Who was chasing you?"

"It wasn't a who. It was an animal. Or two animals. Different animals at different times in the dream. At times it was a big black bull, raging with anger. At times it was a terrified goat. The bull wanted to kill me. The goat wanted me to protect it. That's how I remember them. And then ... and then ..."

"Then what?"

"Suddenly, I was sitting in a barn, I guess. Straw was all over the place. That's how I knew I was in a barn. And I was holding Jackie next to me. Afraid for him, afraid for me. And that's it."

Kayla rose from her chair, moved next to Theodora, sat on the sofa, and hugged her fiercely. She could tell that Theodora was trying not to cry. The memory of the dream—or perhaps its recounting—had struck a deep emotional chord. Kayla was, for a full minute, speechless.

"Dear Theodora. I'm not much of a dream interpreter. As it says in the Torah, the interpretation of dreams is solely for *Hashem*. But thank you for sharing all that with me."

"Do you believe that the Devil plants dreams in our minds, to lead us to evil?"

"Evil is always inside of us. We don't need to be led there. Do you feel that the Devil was in this dream?"

"I don't know. Are you upset that Jackie was in my dream?"

"Of course not. He's your grandnephew. He's been a big factor in your life recently. Why shouldn't your dreams encompass him?"

"He was so warm in my arms. In this dream."

"As well he should be. He's a human being."

"Why would this bull want to kill me?"

"I don't know, but it can be something you can think about during *Kol Nidre*. Maybe this is not the Devil playing around in your mind, but a message from *Hashem* Himself. Let's get dinner ready so we can leave for the *Chabad* on time."

SEYARO

Helen and Nicky agreed that theirs would be a small wedding. Only the immediate families would be present. They gathered on the Sunday evening of *Chol Ha-Moed Sukkot*. The forty days mourning period of Orthodox Christianity that Theodora observed for Fevronia had expired as had the thirty days of *Shloshim* that Helen had observed for Catherine.

Nicky and Helen saw that their wedding had the dual purpose of helping, not only Helen, but also Theodora, to push slightly past their respective griefs. *Sukkot* was supposed to be a time of happiness and, even though there was to be no party, no dancing, no hilarity, there could still be a moderately good time. Following the wedding, the entire group would walk to Soshiana, the Kosher Japanese restaurant where Nicky and Helen had enjoyed their first date early in the year.

Theodora sat next to Jackie during the ceremony on folding chairs in Helen's backyard. This was the first Jewish wedding that Theodora could recall having attended. Naomi, who was recovering from chemotherapy and who wore a dark brown wig over her bald head, sat next to Theodora and tried to explain, using simple English. Theodora thought she understood. There were blessings in Hebrew, which no one bothered to translate; there was the spectacle of Helen walking around Nicky seven times; and there was the ring transferred to Nicky from Helen's brother-in-law, Morris. Naomi had helped Helen find a rose floral print dress, which, in Theodora's opinion, nicely accentuated Helen's slim figure. Then, although someone had tried to tell Theodora about this custom beforehand, there was the shattering of glass, which startled her and made her feel sad at the same time. Why destroy something so beautiful as a small glass to start a wedding? What kind of *karma* is that? She would have to ask Nicky when she had a chance.

After the ceremony, but before the group departed for the restaurant—it was only a three-block walk—Nicky and Helen disappeared back into her house. The guests drank cups of punch that had been set on a small table. Kayla and Max sat close to each other, talking. Helen's children and grandchildren came up to Theodora, introduced themselves for the second time, and kept wanting to hug her, then Jackie, then her again. She was happy to oblige. She couldn't remember anyone's names, but Helen's large extended family seemed awfully nice. She smiled at the realization that Nicky would have this family as his own for the rest of his life. It would be good for him. He'd confided to her that he'd been very lonely before getting involved with Helen.

And she loved that Helen's outgoing grandchildren took immediately to Jackie. Perhaps it was partly because he was black, and they thought it so unusual for a black person to be Jewish. Yet, maybe not. Jackie was friendly, sociable, talkative but not too talkative, and seemed interested in what Helen's grandchildren wanted to tell him. She picked up only a bit of their conversation while they waited outside for Nicky and Helen to return from whatever they were doing. A lot to do with baseball, that uniquely American sport, which Max watched in the basement from time to time. There was a lot of talk about a darling who was a pitcher, whatever that meant. Again, she figured she would have to ask Nicky to explain, baseball being one of his main interests. Of course, she knew that a Greek should care much more about *podosphairo*, but that applied to Greeks in Greece, and Nicky had turned completely

American. It was all right. Why shouldn't he be entranced by the odd customs of his adopted land?

Nicky and Helen returned after about fifteen minutes, holding hands, beaming. Theodora supposed they had gone off to have an alcoholic beverage, as she knew that Jews drank a lot of wine. Papa had loved wine. Just as well Nicky and Helen hadn't tried to served wine to everyone. Theodora would have had to decline; she would partake only of holy wine, the Lord's blood.

She went up to hug Nicky and Helen again. Kayla, Max, and all the grandchildren had crowded around them, so at first Theodora couldn't get close enough, but then Helen saw her, reached out, drew her through the group, and soon the three of them embraced.

"*Seyaro.*"

"*Seyaro.*"

"*Seyaro.*"

Seconds later, Kayla, Max, and Jackie joined the hug. In another two seconds, Theodora felt almost that the breath was being squeezed out of her as Helen's family joined in. Only Morris stood aloof, having picked up another glass of punch.

A HARSH RELIGION

He'd been sent to bed at nine in the evening, after a full hour of practice. Uncle Max had knocked on the door of his bedroom to announce, rather formally yet still pleasantly, that the evening had to come to an end. They would be up early the next morning to say their goodbyes to Sister Theodora. Grandpa would be there to take her to the airport and wait with her until her plane left. Jackie was supposed to get a good night's sleep.

"So it's time to brush teeth and then lights out, Scout."

The nickname, which Uncle Max had begun using only a week earlier, seemed normal now to Jackie. At first, he'd been puzzled. Why Scout?

"It's a term of affection. And there's a Scout in my favorite novel about a lawyer. I'll stop if it bothers you."

"No, it's okay. Call me Scout if you like."

In truth, he much preferred "Jackie," but wanted to be agreeable. He thought Uncle Max had been awfully nice since Grandpa and Helen's wedding. That had been a happy time for almost everyone, and maybe the happiness had lingered for Uncle Max. But Jackie could tell that not everyone was really happy. Sister Theodora had been praying less and finding ways to hang around him more, and when she moved toward him for a hug, not necessarily a hug he wanted but a hug he felt obliged to endure, he could see she'd been crying. Once he'd asked her what was wrong, but she'd pretended all was fine. He knew better.

Now, Sister Theodora's visit was almost over. She'd come a long way in learning English so that they could talk to each other without Grandpa having to be there. Fevronia had also interpreted for them, but then she'd departed abruptly. For a while, he had wondered why so much was being made of Theodora's departure, yet nothing had been made of Fevronia's. Not even a chance to say goodbye.

Finally, it struck him. Fevronia couldn't have said goodbye. She must have died, and the grownups were keeping it a secret. He had told them that would happen, and now they were scared to admit he'd been right. They were treating him like a small child, and it angered him, but he held in his anger. They had their reasons, he supposed, but he was seven, he had a right to be told, and they could have trusted him to deal with whatever happened. He was dealing with it now. On this last evening, he would talk to Theodora about Fevronia. About anything else that she wanted to talk about, too. He knew she'd be going far away and didn't know when he would see her again.

It had been his plan to pretend to sleep, then quietly tap on the door of Theodora's room. He hoped she'd be awake and invite him in. But he was tired and actually fell asleep. When he woke, hours later, it took him a minute of trying to remember what had been so important, something he had to do. Finally, he remembered his plan. He slipped on his Batman bathrobe and left his room, careful to close the door quietly. It was but four steps to Theodora's room, and her door was ajar. She was praying in the twinkling light of her candle, and he would have to interrupt her. That would be rude, but she was leaving in the morning. This would be his last chance to be alone with her. He knew that he'd promised to leave her alone as she prayed, but the promise couldn't possibly apply to her last night with them.

"Come in, Jackie," said Theodora, having noticed him in the doorway. She was dressed, as usual, in her black habit. "You should be sleeping. Did you want to talk?"

He nodded, not sure how to proceed.

"Please, sit here on my bed next to me." He did so; then she took his hands in hers. They were almost hot. Her warmth was comforting. "What did you want to talk about?"

"You're sad, aren't you?"

"Yes, I am sad. Sad to be leaving in the morning. Sad because I'm going to miss you very much." She glanced briefly at the empty twin bed in front of them.

"No. I know what happened. You're sad that Fevronia died." Theodora didn't seem surprised at his statement and nodded. "Why did she die?"

"Our Lord called her to His side."

"Where?"

"Some people call it heaven. You've heard of heaven?"

He nodded. "*Shamayim.*"

"*Shamayim*? It's a place where God shines all the time, where there are no troubles."

"Why did she have to die? She took good care of you."

"The doctors said it was her heart. It's called a heart attack."

"My Grandma had a heart attack a few years ago. She died too. I haven't thought about her for a long time, but when you said heart attack I remembered hearing that before."

"Jackie?"

"Yes?"

"Will you miss me when I go back to Greece?"

Would he? Her departure would be yet another loss he would have to endure, the most recent loss being that his dad had been chased away by *Ima* or by the judge or by both of them together. Now, he would not see his dad again. Not soon, not for a long time, maybe not forever. But having a real dad, like most of his friends at *Chabad*, wasn't a particularly urgent issue. He knew his real dad didn't love him, nor did he even like his real dad. He had Uncle Max to take him to Mets games. He had Uncle Max to remind him about bedtime. He had Uncle Max to remind him about brushing his teeth. The departure of his real dad was a minor loss compared to losing Theodora. Theodora's returning to Greece would be much worse.

She had become his close friend. When he was near her, he could see things others couldn't. He felt that, if he stayed at her side, he would see more. Understand more about the world. Understand more about her. Maybe even understand more about *Hashem*. His curiosity about Grandpa's sister knew no bounds. She held secrets in her heart, and he wanted to uncover them. She knew something about *Hashem* that he needed to learn. Of course he would miss her. Terribly. He might never see her again. He squeezed her hands in answer to her question. But then he had to go on with what he most wanted to know. He had to ask.

"Why do you say you're a sinner? All the time. Now, I hear you whispering that in English sometimes."

"Do I?"

"You're praying and you don't realize people can hear you."

"We're all sinners."

"Me too?"

"Well, you're just a child."

"I sinned when I hit Uncle Max. In the privates. You know." He felt himself blush.

It took a long moment for Theodora to fully grasp what Jackie had said. She had never thought of him as capable of violence, but imagined that children might do anything in a weak moment. "Still, you're a child."

"But when did you sin? You're so good. You pray all the time. I know you pray to *Hashem*. And I know people love you. And I ..." He could not say exactly what he wanted to. "What was your sin?"

There was no answer. She released his hands, placed hers on her lap, and looked down. He couldn't tell whether she was praying, but it seemed that her lips weren't moving. If there was prayer, it was all in her head. Minutes passed. Jackie was afraid to move. He was getting very sleepy and longed to lie down with his eyes closed for just a few minutes.

She took his hands again, however, and looked him squarely in the face. She took a deep breath. "I hit my mother, hard. Very hard. Perhaps very much like the way you hit Uncle Max. But I went on doing it for a long time. It seemed I was hitting her forever. I punched her. Again and again. I bit her. I hate to remember this. She fell down like she had died."

"Why?"

A tear rolled down Theodora's cheek. "I didn't want her to send me away. I was scared to be sent away from her." She closed her eyes momentarily and shook her head. "And, may Our Lord forgive me, that was the last time I see her."

"Saw her."

"Saw her."

"How old were you?"

"Six."

"Then you were a child too."

"It was a sin."

"No, Sister Theodora. You just told me I couldn't sin because I was a child."

"I pray to the Lord Jesus Christ to forgive me, a sinner."

Could she not hear him? He had an innate sense of right and wrong. It would be unjust and unfair to take on for herself the role of a sinner for things she did as a child even younger than he was now. And yet, she wouldn't accept his view of justice or fairness. It was a harsh religion, this Christianity, that made children into sinners if you were Christian, but held that Jewish children could not be sinners. Everything started to go bad for him, not when his mother had hurt him, he thought, but when he'd hurt Uncle Max. But he wouldn't even be allowed to pray for forgiveness if what he'd done wasn't a sin.

"Did you do anything else really bad, Sister Theodora? One bad thing can't make you a sinner for the rest of your life."

"Every time I thought about something that wasn't God, that was a sin too."

"I don't understand."

"Maybe you will when you get older, when you try to see God ... *Hashem* ... yourself."

"Did you try to see God? The person Jesus, who is your God?"

"I wanted to see God so very much."

"Did you? Jews know that *Hashem* is not seen, but did you see your God?"

"I feel that I have, Jackie, and yet ... he wasn't the God I thought I would see." She leaned over and kissed him on the top of his head, then put her arms around him and pulled him to her as tightly as she could. As she did so, the desire to cry overwhelmed him. He was ashamed to cry in front of Sister Theodora but couldn't stop the flow of tears even though he didn't know why he was crying. Maybe because she had been crying too. Strangely, he thought he smelled the faint aroma of roses.

"Here, let me fix this." Theodora pulled Jackie's Batman robe tighter around him and redid the knot on the belt. He let her adjust his clothing. It was almost like *Ima* trying to take care of him, almost as if Theodora wanted him, for those few seconds, as a son. He enjoyed being the object of her special care. After a few minutes, he brought his crying under control. She handed him tissues; he blew his nose and wiped his face and handed them back to her.

"Was Fevronia a sinner too?" he asked finally.

"We all are."

"I miss her too."

"She would be alive today if it not for me, if I had not forced her to bring me to America. But I wanted to meet you, to get to know you."

"You came a long way to meet me, Sister Theodora."

"I did." Theodora's candle flickered out; they sat in complete darkness. "And I am very happy I did, to learn so much about you, and God. But also I am very sad, so sad, Fevronia is not to go back alive with me. Only in her box."

"How will they fit the box on the plane with you? With all the seats?"

For the first time that evening, Theodora started to laugh, but then quickly caught herself. "She won't be with me in that way. They will put her box, it's called a coffin, in the big area under. With the ... *pos les? apostkenes?*" She pointed to her open suitcase, not fully packed.

"Suitcases?"

"Suitcases, *nai*. Plenty of room there, I guess."

He hugged her and said, "I'm really tired now, Sister Theodora. Can I stay with you and sleep in your bed?"

A strange, otherworldly orange glow seeped throughout the room, clearly visible to Theodora, but she was sure Jackie didn't notice it. She heard the voice of the Theotokos from within the spectral light say to her, "You may keep him with you always. *Panta tha sai mazi sou.*"

Theodora smoothed out the blanket on her bed, making a place for Jackie to lie down. He did so, in a not quite fetal position, his knees bent slightly up toward his chest. Theodora put an extra blanket over him. He slept almost immediately. She moved to the dresser, where she had temporarily placed the model piano Jackie had given her. She picked it, gently kissed it, and put it back.

The orange glow lingered for a few minutes, then faded to nothing.

MORE HORRIBLE TO FORGET

Nicky and Theodora were in Nicky's car on the way to the airport. He'd asked if Helen wanted to join them. In fact, he'd almost begged her, but Helen had demurred. It would be better for the two of them to be alone together, to be able to talk to each other without a third person present, even a person as important to Nicky as his new wife. He'd reluctantly agreed. Now, with his sister very quiet in the passenger seat, probably praying, he relived his brief conversation with Helen at four in the morning.

"Ask Kal ... Theodora ... if she knows how you can stop seeing Churchill all the time. You're constantly seeing him, wherever we go."

"I don't see ..."

"Don't lie, Nicky. Don't ever to lie to me." She sighed, ready to hug him goodbye at her front door. "I don't know if you'll ever get away from that ghost, and I pray that you do, but if you keep him to yourself, eventually he'll tear you down. If you share him with me, if you admit that he still plagues you, we have a chance to beat him."

"I'm sorry I haven't been honest about ..."

"Just from now on, please tell me, trust me about your ghost, wherever you think you see him. I want to know."

"I will."

"And ask your sister. She's amazing, maybe the most amazing person I've ever met. The two of you, in fact. Quite a pair. So different and yet ... what shall I say?"

"What do you want to say?"

"So linked. Maybe so much two sides of the same coin. And you both love Jackie so much. *Baruch Hashem*. I think our little boy, who's not so little anymore, will miss her terribly."

"You're right."

"So just ask her about Raptis, Churchill, whatever you want to call him."

And now he was trying to figure out how to do just that. What could she do for him? And was this the best thing to talk about right before they'd be saying goodbye again?

She spared him the need to start a conversation. "Nicky, I know you so well and know there's a lot on your mind. Will you share with me, please?"

"Another confession?" He immediately regretted his tone, which to him had sounded confrontational. That had not been his intent.

"No. I wasn't thinking of that, not as I do when I'm in my cell. I shall continue to confess believers when I'm back in Greece. That shall always be my main mission in life. But what is it now that bothers you? Talk to me just as your sister and call me Kal."

"Kal."

"Yes, my beloved brother."

"I still have nightmares about the war. The killings. My killings."

"As do I. It's horrible, I agree, but it would be more horrible to forget, don't you think?"

"I do."

"So you will have to live with these memories."

"But it's also how I always feel I'm being followed, chased by Churchill, the man I fought with, the man who saw much of the innocent blood I spilled. I should have asked you long ago, and now we just have a few minutes."

"Ask me what?"

"How do l get rid of this ghost?"

"If l knew the answer to that, l'd get rid of my own."

"Your own?"

"l still think of Mama, almost every day, and those terrible last moments."

He tried to envision the scene that Kal had described about how she'd been forced against her will to leave their house in Salonika and go with Alex, their family friend, to hide. It was too painful for him to imagine, but yet Kal had to live with the memory of having literally been pushed away by those who loved her. Of having struck Mama down in her frantic but futile effort not to be separated from her family.

"And you can't forgive yourself?"

"We share much guilt, don't we?"

"And the answer?"

"We learn to live with it. And l pray for forgiveness. You should try doing that again." He pulled their car into the short-term parking lot at Newark International. "l think you will, Nicky. l think you will pray and find forgiveness."

"And do you find forgiveness, ever?"

"At the monastery. But only for moments at a time."

"Kal" was the only thing he could say, unable to choke back tears. He reached for her hand.

HOW GOD HAS WRITTEN HIS BOOK

Toward the end of October, the weather in northern Greece is typically pleasant, if cool. It might rain, but periods of rain are generally short. In 1990, however, it had rained much more than usual. The fields were muddy. On the last Saturday of the month, the skies were again a leaden gray and a heavy rain was forecast to start in the late morning. If the rain came too soon, the way to *Microdermis* from the church would be treacherous. How many other problems would crop up before Fevronia achieved the final rest she deserved?

In what was now Mother Abbess Zoe's office, Zoe and Theodora sat facing each other. It was only minutes before the funeral was to begin. The crucified Christ that hung on the wall of the office, seemingly in more agony than usual, stared down at them. Then Theodora stood and looked out the window at the vineyard and, beyond that, the distant purple hills.

Three gravediggers had earlier been led by Theodora to a group of boulders on the edge of the stream. There was no other way to get there but by walking, and they had had to carry their pickaxes and shovels, grumbling to themselves along the way. Once at *Microdermis*, Theodora offered up to the Virgin a brief prayer for guidance, gazed for a minute at the soggy ground, and closed her eyes. She leaned her right ear toward the ground. The sounds of machinegun fire and screams suddenly filled her ears; the smell of what she imagined as cordite and feces mingled in her nostrils; her muscles ached from the guns' recoil. Then the gunfire abruptly stopped, and she heard angels singing in chorus—"Αἰχμαλωσίας ἐπί τοῦ ποταμοῦ"—that she'd heard once before. Captivity by the river indeed.

She kneeled, gritted her teeth, and prayed to the Virgin to block out the sensations. It took at least five minutes of her kneeling and praying for her to regain her composure, the sounds and smells fading to nothing. She stood again unsteadily, took a deep breath, and pointed to where she thought the best place would be, guiding the gravediggers to a spot about thirty meters above the now fast-flowing stream, not far from where she'd been standing. There seemed to be fewer rocks; the ground to which she pointed looked diggable but not too soft.

Now, in the office, she pulled herself out of the memories and turned to Abbess Zoe. "I thank you, Reverend Mother, for the blessing you have granted. I know that what we're doing is most unusual."

Zoe's face formed the smallest of smiles. "It's what Fevronia would have wanted. It was quite clever of you to think of this. Her body will have its eternal rest in this holy ground."

"When Our Lord returns and when those of us who have put away evil are reunited with our earthly bodies, it's where Fevronia would want to find herself. And there she shall find, too, her brother Silenos and be reunited with him. Although she never said as much to me, that she longed to be reunited with him in the world to come, I feel that was Fevronia's urgent wish. To be joined at the end of days with her brother and, of course, in the presence of Our Lord."

"And you, Theodora?"

"What about me?"

"You and your brother. Do you believe that you also will be reunited?"

"We have been."

"I mean after death. After only your souls remain alive. What do you believe?"

"I believed Jesus returned to us. So strongly did I believe that, I would happily have given up this life to be right. And yet, now I know I was wrong. So when you ask me what I believe, I do think Nicky and I and Ada and Mama and Papa will be together again, we should be together again, but ..."

"But you have doubts?"

"I wanted so much to see God."

"Your desire was so strong that you made yourself think you'd seen God."

"That by itself was sinful. I pray to the Lord Jesus Christ to forgive me, a sinner."

"And now you're not sure? About you and your brother?" asked Zoe.

"I want to be right this time, not misled."

"You must choose what you believe, Theodora. There are never guarantees. You must make a choice, just like the choice you made to serve Our Lord for your entire life, the choice you made when you promised to the Holy Virgin Herself that you would devote your life to God. You must create the rest of your life every day by what you choose to believe. Just as God renews His creation on a daily basis."

"Then I will echo to you, if I may, something that a rabbi told me in America, something that fits in so nicely with our own beliefs. I choose to believe that there is a part of God in all of us. I choose to believe that God wants us to make the spaces inside of our souls larger, so more of God can enter. And when Jesus is ready to return, I now know and will never forget that there will be more than one poor sad nun who recognizes His return."

"And being reunited with your brother? With his family, which of course is yours as well? With his daughter? With Jackie?"

Theodora didn't respond for a long minute or two. She heard the bells ring, calling the faithful to the church and to Fevronia's funeral. She tried to imagine what it might be like, at the end of days, to be together with her Jewish family and her Christian family, all at the same time. How could they inhabit the same space and time?

Then, finally, an answer came to her.

"Yes, if that is how God has written His book, He will make that happen. God is the author of all, is He not? Are we not living proof of God's story? I feel that He will bring us together. This is what I fully and freely choose to believe."

ACKNOWLEDGEMENTS

I particularly want to thank four close friends who read earlier drafts of *To See God* and favored me with their thoughts and suggestions: Steven Berger (my cousin as well as my friend), Pierre Dugan, and Joan and Dennis Davan. Their guidance, reactions, and ideas have been immeasurably helpful to me in creating this final version of *To See God*.

Many thanks also go to Black Rose Writing, which has published not only *To See God* but also its prequels, *The Flight of the Veil* (2020) and *The Music Stalker* (2021), as well as to the many people who have read, enjoyed, and—in some cases—reviewed these novels. I love hearing your reactions to these stories. Your encouragement—and the fact that you are still reading my work—keeps me wanting to write.

Finally, I again thank my very patient and loving family, particularly my wife, Laurie, our children Marty and Jean, our children-in-law Drea and Eyal, and our grandchildren, Cole and Neely. Without them, there would be no point.

ABOUT THE AUTHOR

Following a 40-year career as a trial attorney, Bruce J. Berger turned full time to writing, earned an M.F.A. in Creative Writing from American University in Washington, D.C., and now teaches College Writing and Creative Writing there. His two prior novels have been critically recognized: *The Flight of the Veil* won a Bronze Award in General Fiction from Illumination Christian Book Awards, and *The Music Stalker* was a Finalist (Suspense) in the Next Gen Indie Book Award contest. He has also published more than 50 stories and poems in a wide variety of literary journals.

Bruce J. Berger lives in Silver Spring, Maryland, with his wife, Laurie, and their dog, Whiskey, and down the street from grandson Cole and granddaughter Neely, to whom he has dedicated this novel. In time, I hope they will come to read and love it.

NOTE FROM THE AUTHOR

Word-of-mouth is crucial for any author to succeed. If you enjoyed *To See God*, please leave a review online—anywhere you are able. Even if it's just a sentence or two. It would make all the difference and would be very much appreciated.

Thanks!
Bruce J. Berger

We hope you enjoyed reading this title from:

BLACK ROSE
writing™

www.blackrosewriting.com

Subscribe to our mailing list – *The Rosevine* – and receive **FREE** books, daily deals, and stay current with news about upcoming releases and our hottest authors.
Scan the QR code below to sign up.

Already a subscriber? Please accept a sincere thank you for being a fan of Black Rose Writing authors.

View other Black Rose Writing titles at www.blackrosewriting.com/books and use promo code **PRINT** to receive a **20% discount** when purchasing.

CPSIA information can be obtained
at www.ICGtesting.com
Printed in the USA
JSHW050216291122
34007JS00007B/15

9 781685 131579